STAR
OF THE
SHOW

JACQUELINE
WILSON

Illustrated by Rachael Dean

PUFFIN

PUFFIN BOOKS

UK | USA | Canada | Ireland | Australia
India | New Zealand | South Africa

Puffin Books is part of the Penguin Random House group of companies
whose addresses can be found at global.penguinrandomhouse.com.

www.penguin.co.uk
www.puffin.co.uk
www.ladybird.co.uk

First published 2024

001

Text copyright © Jacqueline Wilson, 2024
Illustrations copyright © Rachael Dean, 2024

The moral right of the author and illustrator has been asserted

Set in 12.5/20pt Baskerville MT Pro
Printed in Great Britain by Clays Ltd, Elcograf S.p.A.

The authorized representative in the EEA is Penguin Random House Ireland,
Morrison Chambers, 32 Nassau Street, Dublin D02 YH68

A CIP catalogue record for this book is available from the British Library

HARDBACK
ISBN: 978–0–241–68415–3 ·

INTERNATIONAL PAPERBACK
ISBN: 978–0–241–68416–0

All correspondence to:
Puffin Books
Penguin Random House Children's
One Embassy Gardens, 8 Viaduct Gardens, London SW11 7BW

For Vicky Ireland, with much love

This story is set one hundred and fifty years ago –
when Queen Victoria was on the throne.

Chapter One

It started pouring with rain and Tommy and little Ada began bawling their heads off.

'Shh now. Look, I'll give you my shawl. Huddle under that,' I said, tucking it over them in their baby carriage. It wasn't a proper perambulator. Our big brother, Connor, had fashioned a pram out of an orange box he'd filched from the market and four odd wheels he'd found in a dump. I pulled it along with a fraying piece of rope. It was quite heavy – Ada was only a little scrap but Tommy kept stuffing himself with bread and dripping and was turning into a right lump.

He carried on crying hard and Ada yelled along too.

'Oh, for goodness' sake. *I'm* not crying,' I said, though I

was certainly feeling like it. My frock was clinging to me, my feet were squelching in my old boots, and my hands were red raw with pulling the young ones around.

'Poor little mites,' said a woman scurrying home, holding her apron over her head. She looked at me reproachfully, as if I was deliberately soaking them.

I felt *I* was a poor little mite too. I glared at her resentfully. She tutted her tongue at me.

'What would your ma say if she saw you giving me that look?' she hissed.

I felt as if she'd stabbed me. I stuck my tongue out as far as it would go, and then ran like crazy, lugging the carriage along, scared she might give me a whack for cheek. I didn't stop running until I was safe in Oak Tree Park, my favourite place in all of London.

The sudden run had stunned Tommy and Ada and they'd actually stopped shrieking, though their mouths were still hanging open. I leaned against one of the big oaks, my heart thumping. Each beat was like a word. *Ma, Ma, Ma, Ma!*

Ma died a few weeks after Ada was born. She'd lain in bed after the birth, getting weaker and whiter every day. Maggie

tried to get her to eat but she could only manage a spoonful of broth. She sponged her down and kept her decent but couldn't make her better. I ran for Mrs Marcy, the midwife, and had to pay her the lucky sixpence we kept in our best teapot, but all she did was shake her head.

'She's a goner,' she said, loud enough for Ma to hear.

Ma used up her last drop of energy telling Maggie she must scald the milk and add a teaspoon of sugar to Ada's bottle. Then she closed her eyes and we lined up to kiss her in age order: Maggie, Connor, me, Tommy. Maggie held Ada up so that her pursed lips brushed against Ma's thin cheek.

Pa didn't get a chance to kiss her. He was out drowning his sorrows at the Soldiers' Arms public house. We kept out of his way when he came staggering back, because he had a vile temper when he'd been drinking. I couldn't abide my pa.

I know they taught us at the Ragged School that we must Honour our Father and Mother. It was one of the Ten Commandments in the Bible. A man called Moses got this message straight from God. Perhaps it was wicked to think this, but I thought it depended what sort of father you had.

I loved Ma though. I loved her so much. I could never

decide who I loved most, Ma or my older brother, Connor. Then I loved Ada, because she was so small and helpless, though she had such a piercing scream. I loved my older sister, Maggie, too, but she was always bossing me around and telling me what to do. My younger brother, Tommy, came next to last. We were always fighting. I was very small for my age and he was a huge, hulking boy for *his* age, and he didn't fight fairly either. He sometimes won, which was very humiliating.

Pa came last, last, last.

I sank down to the big roots of the tree and sat down, though I knew I'd be soaking my frock. It was wet through already, so what did it matter? Tommy managed to free himself from his chariot, though I thought I'd tied him in tightly. He came over to me and peered right in my face.

'What's matter, Tess?' he asked. He said it as if he really cared, and I felt guilty for putting him so low down on my love list.

'I'm just missing Ma,' I mumbled.

'Me too,' said Tommy, looking sad. He sighed. 'She gave me raisins. Maggie won't!'

'Oh, Tommy, you're such a greedy-guts,' I said, poking him in his tummy.

'Ma said I'm a growing boy. I'm going to grow and grow and grow, bigger than Pa. And I'll beat him hard!' said Tommy.

He wasn't any good at honouring his father either, but it wasn't his fault. He wasn't old enough for the Ragged School yet.

Ma sent me, Maggie and Connor there because she wanted us to read and write, which she'd never learned to do. She hated it being called a *Ragged* School though.

'I don't let you out the house with a single tear in your clothes,' she'd say indignantly. 'You don't have a hem hanging down anywhere and every button is in its place. We may be poor, but you look like little ladies and gentlemen.'

I didn't think we did, especially not Tommy. He was forever ripping his jacket and wearing out the seat of his trousers, so that he was more patch than material, but Ma tried hard with him even so.

He was trying to scrabble up the tree now, seams bursting all over the place because his jacket was much too small.

'Get down, Tommy! You're getting in a right state. Maggie will give you what for when we go home. You know she's in a really bad mood.'

She'd carried on taking in washing after Ma died. She

wasn't as good at it as Ma, for all she pounded and scrubbed and swore. It had been raining on and off all day so she didn't have anywhere to hang it to dry. It had been dripping off the rack in the kitchen, and those clean sheets and nightshirts and petticoats had been too tempting for Tommy. He'd found a stick in the gutter outside and started whacking them wildly, pretending he was a general and they were enemy soldiers. The stick was dirty – and soon the washing was patterned with mud and grime.

When Maggie saw, she burst into tears. Then she snatched the stick from his fist, gave him a good shaking, and shoved him towards me.

'Take him out before I murder him. I'll have to wash them all over again and my hands hurt so,' she said. They were red raw already and did look very sore. I felt really sorry for her but then she started yelling at me too.

'What were you *doing*, Tess, when I was busy mangling? Why didn't you stop Tommy being so naughty?' she demanded, giving me a shake too.

'I was ... I was ...' I shrugged, pretending not to remember. '*I* don't know!'

'I know what you were blooming well doing! Prancing

around like a Pomeranian and looking twice as daft!' said Maggie.

I felt my face flushing as red as her sore hands. She must have caught a glimpse of me in the living room. I'd pushed the stools out of the way and invented a special rain dance, waving my fingers like drops of rain, and rushing here and there like storm clouds. I felt inspired, as light and nimble as a fairy – not a wretched dog. Her words stung dreadfully.

'Don't you mock my dancing! You're just jealous. Joe loves it when I dance to his music. He says I have a rare talent,' I shouted at Maggie.

'Joe the organ grinder!' Maggie said scornfully. 'And you're the organ grinder's monkey!'

Tommy started sniggering and calling me 'Monkey, Monkey, Monkey', and the noise woke Ada and she started wailing.

'Oh, get out, you little beggars!' Maggie cried. 'Get them *out*, Tess, or I'll put you through the mangle and flatten you!'

She was joking, of course, though she looked as if she'd like to do it.

'It's not fair! Why should *I* have to take charge of them?' I said. '*I'm* a little one too!'

Ma had always babied me because I'd been born too early

and she'd needed to nurse me night and day to keep me going. I'd never quite caught up. I was only four years younger than Maggie and yet I barely came up to her waist. I sometimes used to put on a baby voice too so that Ma or Connor would chuckle and pet me.

'Why should *I* be the one who has to do the washing and the cooking and everything else?' Maggie said, tears spurting down her cheeks.

I should have run to her then and said sorry, even offered to help her scrub the dirty washing over again – but she'd wounded me, mocking my dancing. Was she *right*? Did I really look a fool?

So I sat Tommy in the baby carriage, stuffed Ada in after him, and took them outdoors. I knew Maggie had meant me to take them out of the scullery, not out of the house, but I wanted to make a grand gesture.

I was a little worried now. It had been drizzling sullenly but now it was a steady downpour. It was chilly for late summer, and I was starting to shiver without my shawl. Tommy was as tough as his old boots, so he'd cope with a good soaking, but Ada was only little and very frail. I took her into my arms, wrapping her shawl round both of us. She wailed miserably,

a rasp to her voice now because she'd been crying so long. She kept turning her head, looking desperately for milk.

I'd left her bottle on the dresser at home – though she didn't always take much interest in it when I tried to poke it into her mouth. She badly wanted Ma too.

'Poor little Ada,' I said, rubbing my cheek against the damp fluff of her hair.

There had been other babies that were too weak to thrive. Ma had mourned them all. Sometimes she repeated their names under her breath and had a little weep. I hoped the Ragged School teacher was right and Ma would be up in Heaven now, with her lost babies in her arms.

'But don't you go and join them, Ada,' I said into her tiny ear. 'We need you here with us. I'm going to keep you safe and feed you up. You can have my share of the milk and when you get teeth you can have half my grub too. I'm going to be a good big sister to you, I promise.'

Ada carried on yelling, unimpressed. I tried joggling her up and down but it made no difference. Her eyes were squeezed shut and her mouth wide open, her whole tiny body quivering.

'Don't, Ada! Do stop! Oh, please, please, please!' I said, and I pranced around a bit to see if that made any difference.

She quietened for a couple of seconds out of surprise.

'Oh, you like that, don't you? Let's do a proper dance. Would the little lady be my partner for a polka?' I asked. 'Yes please!' I answered myself, in a little baby voice, though Ada herself didn't look keen.

The polka was the easiest dance ever. Joe the organ grinder taught me. It was just *one, two, three, hop!* then *one, two, three, hop!* with the other leg, again and again, in time to the music. He liked me doing it, because I pointed my feet and held out my skirts prettily, so that folk stopped to watch and put a penny in his cap. He was kind and would give me a penny if his cap was nearly full, but I'd have danced even if he gave me nothing.

Little boys like Tommy jeered at me, but little girls tried to copy me, and grown-ups smiled and called me a 'dainty little darling'. Not a single one said I looked like a performing Pomeranian.

I held Ada under her armpits and started polkaing with her. Her feet kicked in the air as if she was actually trying to join in.

'That's it, lovely!' I said, dancing on.

Ma had always called me 'lovely', as if it was my actual name instead of plain Tess.

'My little Lovely,' she'd murmur.

She couldn't say it now to Ada, but I vowed to say it to her myself from now on. We danced in and out of the trees together, not caring about the pouring rain, though a nosy old nurse in a large cape shook her head at us. She was scurrying along with a large perambulator.

'Get that poor child out of the rain before she catches her death!' she commanded.

I didn't take any notice. She wasn't *my* nurse so I didn't have to do what she said. I felt sorry for rich children, always being bossed around by these cross women flitting about in their dark capes like giant bats.

Another was calling now, rushing around yelling, 'Master Cedric! *Master Cedric Cedar*, it's raining hard! We have to go home! You'll get such a whipping when I find you!'

Master Cedric must've been sensibly hiding from her and I didn't blame him. I could spot a boy hiding in the sodden bushes by the pond. He put his finger to his mouth and I nodded slightly and danced on. That nurse told me off too, but I didn't care and neither did Ada, who at long last seemed happy. Her eyes were open and sparkling. Her mouth was open in a smiley way, and her pale cheeks were faintly pink now.

I'd made her happy! I was a proper little mother to her! I was better than the bat brigade of nurses in the park. I danced about, and Cedric cautiously climbed out of the bush and watched. When I grew breathless at last and stopped, Cedric clapped his hands together.

'You're jolly good at dancing!' he said.

'Am I?' I said. 'Am I really?'

'I'll say!'

'Well, you're jolly good at hiding, Master Cedric,' I said.

'How on earth do you know my name?' he asked, astonished.

'I have magic powers,' I said.

'Really?' He was acting as if he actually believed me.

'No, silly. I heard your nurse yelling for you,' I said. 'You're going to be in big trouble when she finds you.'

'No I'm not,' said Cedric, though he looked worried. 'I'm going to stay here in the park. I'm going to live by myself like Robinson Crusoe.'

'Who's Robinson Crusoe when he's at home?' I asked.

'You haven't read *Robinson Crusoe*?' said Cedric. 'Oh, you must, it's a splendid adventure book about being shipwrecked. Papa reads it to me when he comes to say goodnight.'

I imagined having a father who read me a story. Cedric and I clearly lived in two different worlds.

'My pa don't do stuff like that,' I said shortly.

'Well, you could read it for yourself then,' said Cedric. 'I'll lend you the book when we've finished it, if you like.'

I couldn't read very well myself because there were so many of us at the Ragged School and we mostly just chanted that 'A is for Apple' rhyme that didn't really make sense. I'd had my turn at the class book but it didn't tell any stories. It was just lists of silly names like *cat, fat, hat, mat, sat,* so it wasn't really worth bothering to figure them out.

'That's very kind of you,' I said to Cedric even so. I wasn't going to admit my poor reading. It was highly unlikely Cedric would be allowed to lend a book to a girl like me anyway. And if he did, then maybe Connor might read it to me. He was so clever he could read newspapers.

Ada was fidgeting now, wanting to be joggled about again. My hands were aching from holding her, so I opened the bodice of my frock and tucked her inside. Her head stuck out comically, but she seemed to like it.

'She looks so funny!' said Cedric. 'Like a baby kangaroo.'

'What's that?' I asked.

'Oh, you know. That animal that lives in Australia. It runs about like this.' Cedric dropped to his haunches and leaped about. He wasn't very good at it and keeled over sideways into the sodden grass. Now he had big smears of mud over his cream breeches.

'Oh Lordy!' said Cedric, peering at them. 'Nurse will be so cross!'

'Well, you're going to be living here now, so it won't matter,' I said.

Cedric was biting his lip anxiously. 'I know, but actually I think I need to go home now. Mama and Papa would miss me so if I stayed here. But then, if I do go home, Nurse will punish me.' He sighed heavily.

'Does she beat you?' I asked sympathetically.

'No!' he said. 'But she gives me the slipper and sends me to bed without any supper.'

'She sounds so mean,' I said.

'She sometimes gives me castor oil and that's awful. She holds my nose when she spoons it in so I have to swallow it,' said Cedric. 'I don't like her one bit. And she's especially cross if I get my clothes dirty.' He rubbed at the mud but that only smeared it further.

'Tell you what,' I said. 'Maggie at home is good at washing. We could ask her to wash your breeches for you.'

'But then they'd be wet,' said Cedric.

'They're all wet already!' I said.

'So they are,' said Cedric.

'Come on then,' I said.

'Very well!' he said, smiling.

It was only when we got to the park gates, Cedric and me and little Ada, that I remembered something. Tommy!

Chapter Two

Oh my Lord, Tommy!

I looked all around. Where was the tree we'd been standing under? The tree he was trying to climb. The tall tree that he wasn't big enough to climb. The tree he might now be lying beneath in a crumpled heap.

'*Tommy!*' I screamed.

Cedric jumped. 'My name's Cedric,' he reminded me politely.

'I'm calling for my little brother, Tommy,' I said. 'Where *is* he?'

I tried to remember which way I danced with Ada. I ran

this way and that, clutching the baby to my chest. Cedric followed behind uncertainly.

I found the baby carriage soon enough and peered up the tree, wondering if Tommy was dangling precariously from the upper branches. No, there wasn't a sign of him.

'Tommy!' I screamed again, though my chest was so tight I could hardly breathe and my voice was a little mouse squeak.

Then I heard a chuckle. Familiar spluttering, sniggering laughter. I whirled round and there was Tommy right behind me, hands on his hips, legs wide apart.

'Can't catch me!' he said, and darted off again.

'You little whatsit!' I said, furious. I thrust Ada at Cedric. 'Here, hold her tight.'

Then I charged after Tommy. I was small, but my legs were longer than his and strong from my dancing. I reached him in five paces, threw my hands out, and pushed him to the ground. He landed with a *crump* and started shrieking.

I turned him over and felt his arms and legs but he wasn't really hurt, just indignant. And very, very muddy.

I pulled him up and held him tight by the wrist.

'Come with me at once or I'll thump you,' I said. I turned my head to check on Cedric and Ada. 'You too.'

'You're not going to thump *me*, are you?' Cedric asked.

'Of course not, silly,' I said.

'You're very fierce,' said Cedric, still uncertain.

'Only with Tommy. Because he's so bad,' I said. 'And he doesn't really mind, do you, Tom? You like a fight, don't you?'

'Only if I bash you back,' said Tommy. 'And kick.' He tried, getting me on the shin.

'Don't act so rough!' I said, though I tried to kick him back.

'Are you rough children?' Cedric asked. 'Nurse says I mustn't ever play with rough children.'

'Well, clear off then,' I said, losing patience.

'No, I think I like rough children,' said Cedric, trotting along beside us.

I collected the baby carriage, forced Tommy into the box, and tied him in it with extra knots. Then I laid Ada against his chest and tied her in too, but more gently. I knew Tommy would never dream of hurting her, though he would happily kick me black and blue.

I pulled the carriage along with Cedric trotting by my side. He hesitated when I turned left out of the park.

'Don't we go the other way?' he said.

'No, that's the way to the big houses. Where you maybe live. *We* live in a little house along this way,' I told him.

Cedric peered about him with interest when we went down all the terraces.

'These houses really *are* little,' he said. 'And very dirty!'

'Ours isn't. Ma used to whiten our doorstep every day and now Maggie does it,' I said. 'I do too, though Maggie moans and says I don't do it properly. She's always getting at me.'

'Is she the one who's going to wash my trousers?' Cedric asked.

'Yes, but she won't moan at you, because you're a rich little boy,' I said.

'I don't think I'm really rich. I've only got pennies in my money box,' he said.

I sighed. He might know about people in books and countries I'd never heard of, but he was a bit thick when it came to knowing about real life here.

'*I've* got pennies, heaps and heaps,' said Tommy, still desperately struggling with the knot in the string. 'Let me *out*, Tess!'

'Keep still! You'll tip Ada out if you're not careful! Can't you be a good boy for once, Tommy?' I said.

'Why can that boy walk and I can't? *He* not good. He got mud all over his trousers. He messed them!' Tommy said, sniggering.

Cedric blushed scarlet. 'It doesn't look like I have, does it?' he asked me.

'No, of course not,' I fibbed. 'Take no notice. Anyway, our Tommy's covered in mud too.'

'Will this Maggie be cross?' Cedric wondered.

'Not with you,' I said, hoping it might be true.

'Is she your servant?' he asked.

'If you call her a servant she *will* be cross!' I said. 'No, silly, she's my sister. We don't have servants.'

'Then who does the cooking and the cleaning?' Cedric screwed up his face in puzzlement.

'Well . . . Maggie does. And me.' I knew I wasn't much help. I tried making our dinner when Maggie had a bad stomach but I forgot to keep an eye on it and the stew burned and tasted awful – and I left the milk bottle in full sunshine and it went off enough to give us all bad stomachs. When I tried sweeping the stairs, I forgot to put the brush away and Maggie fell over it and cut her chin when she came down from making the bed. I had a turn at making the bed myself but I couldn't

get the sheets to tuck in properly and I thumped a pillow too hard so that it burst and the feathers turned the room into a snowstorm.

Maggie thought I was doing it on purpose but I swear I wasn't. I just didn't have the knack for housework. And she wasn't that good at it either. We all wondered how Ma had kept everything going so well, even when she was big with babies.

'Poor Maggie having to do all the work,' said Cedric.

'Yes,' I said shortly. 'But my brother Connor works too. He has a proper job. He gets wages.'

Connor worked at the market long before Ma died. He palled up with an old man with a household stall called Bert. He ran errands for him and heaved boxes of pots and pans about. When Bert didn't need him he carried heavy bags and looked after horses when gents in carriages came to get the stall rents. He didn't get a steady wage, but he earned lots of tips because he was bright and cheery and always showed willing. He never spent his money on himself. He always brought it straight home to Ma. She called him her 'diamond boy'.

'Connor's taking me down the market soon,' said Tommy.

'Does your father work down at this market too?' Cedric

asked with interest. 'My papa just works in a bank making money.'

'Our pa is a brickie. You know, builds walls out of bricks. But he's not fit for work sometimes. And he usually spends all his money on Friday nights, after he's got paid. We don't care for our pa much,' I said.

Cedric looked stunned. It was like the time at the Ragged School when a boy was bad and the teacher said sorrowfully that God would be sad. 'I don't care about God,' the boy declared – and got a whipping for it.

'But you must care about your own papa!' Cedric said.

Tommy and I looked at each other and shook our heads, for once in total agreement.

Cedric looked at us, his head tilted on one side as if he was about to ask another question. I tried to think of something to say to divert him but my throat had gone too dry to speak.

'What about your mama?' Cedric continued.

I *knew* he was going to ask that. I swallowed.

'Ma died,' Tommy said bluntly.

'Oh!' said Cedric. 'Oh dear, how sad.'

'She called me Tommy Trouble but she loved me most,' said Tommy.

'She never said that!' I snapped.

'She did so,' said Tommy.

She'd told *me* she loved me the most. Had she whispered it to each of us to make us feel special? Ada was crying again. I wondered if Ma had managed to whisper it in her tiny ear before she died. I resolved to whisper it to her myself, just in case. She needed to feel love like the rest of us. It was no use hoping Pa would be a proper father to her. I don't think he'd even held her once, let alone dandled her on his knee and kissed her little cheeks.

Cedric put his hand out and rested it on mine as I pushed the baby carriage.

'I'm so sorry,' he said quietly.

He was a very sweet boy for all he didn't understand much. I was glad I was helping him. I hoped Maggie might be in a better mood by now.

'Here we are. Home sweet home,' I said. It was a song Ma used to sing sometimes, though she can't really have thought our own home sweet.

'Yes, it's very sweet,' Cedric said valiantly, though our small cramped terraced house was anything but.

I opened the door and the smell of Windsor soap and damp

washing overwhelmed us. I bumped the baby carriage over the doorstep, took baby Ada in my arms and freed Tommy.

He went charging through our living room to the kitchen to find Maggie.

'Come on,' I said encouragingly to Cedric.

He was blinking at our room, with Pa's sagging sofa and our scattered wooden stools and the market boxes Connor had made into a sideboard for our clock and candlesticks.

'I like the paintings,' he said, making a further valiant effort to be polite.

We didn't have any proper paintings, but Ma had stuck pictures from illustrated papers on the wall. They were mostly religious. I liked the one of two children with a guardian angel standing behind them, her wings outspread to protect them. I smiled at Cedric, who was looking anxious.

'Don't worry, Maggie will like you,' I whispered.

'There's a boy and his trousers are ever so muddy!' Tommy yelled in the kitchen under a canopy of dripping sheets.

'Oh, thank the Lord,' said Maggie, throwing her arms round him. She peered round him at me. 'I've been worried sick. Where have you *been*, Tess?'

'You told us to get out and leave you alone,' I said.

'But it's been pouring with rain, you numbskull!' Maggie declared, wiping her sore hands on her skirts. She snatched Ada from me. 'She's soaked right through! She'll catch her death!'

'She's fine. She's had a lovely time. Look at her pink cheeks. It's just like she's been having a bath. I'll rub her dry with a towel in no time,' I said.

Maggie set about stripping Ada and then dried her with a towel, practically pummelling her.

'And you take those wet clothes off too, Tommy!' Maggie commanded. Then she noticed Cedric.

'Who on earth are you?' she gasped, peering at him in astonishment.

'I'm Cedric,' he said nervously, but polite as always added, 'Master Cedric Cedar. How do you do?'

Maggie ignored his outstretched hand and stared at me. 'What's he doing here?' she demanded.

'He's a lovely boy we met in the park and I've brought him back here so you can wash his muddy breeches,' I said.

'As if I haven't got enough to wash!' said Maggie. 'And what was a little lad like that doing in the park by himself?'

'Well, he ran away from his nurse,' I said.

'He ran away from his nurse?' Maggie repeated, as if she could hardly believe her ears. 'And now you've brought him here while this nurse is still out searching for him? Dear Lord, you've *kidnapped* him!'

'No I haven't, have I, Cedric? You wanted to come, didn't you?' I asked him.

Cedric blinked at me. 'Yes, I did,' he declared valiantly. 'But I'll go if you want me to,' he told Maggie.

'Yes, you clear off home before you get us into trouble,' said Maggie.

'But then he'll be in trouble! That nurse of his is horrid,' I said. 'Please, Maggie, just wash his trousers.'

'I've had enough washing for today! And there's no hot water left anyway,' said Maggie.

'Well, *I'll* wash them for you, Cedric,' I said. 'Whip them off!'

Cedric peered round the cramped kitchen. 'In front of everyone?' he whispered. 'Wouldn't that be rude?'

'Oh, for goodness' sake!' said Maggie, and she thrust Ada back to me and pulled his trousers down herself.

We stared with interest at him. The boys didn't wear anything under their trousers in our family, but Cedric was

wearing an elaborate pair of fine cotton drawers with a little drawstring at the end of each leg, all the way down to his woolly socks.

'He's wearing drawers! With ribbons, like a girl!' Tommy snorted.

Poor Cedric blushed painfully.

'You shut your mouth, Tommy! They're special gentlemen's drawers,' I said. 'Cedric is a little gent, not a toerag like you. Here, hold Ada – and don't you dare drop her.'

I took Cedric's trousers and dunked them in the bowl of lukewarm water, whirling them about hopefully.

'Not like that! You've got to give them a good scrub. Here, let me!' said Maggie, as I'd hoped she would.

'It's very kind of you,' said Cedric.

'Not at all,' said Maggie, getting to work with her brush. 'Tess, Ada had better have the last of the milk, but make the rest of us a cup of black tea. And make a slice of bread and dripping and cut it into quarters.'

Cedric looked uncertain when I took the precious small bowl of dripping out of the larder.

'Isn't that . . . fat?' he said.

'It's the meat juices. It's not from *our* meat, we never have

big roasts, but you can buy a bowl from the butcher's for twopence,' said Maggie. 'You've never had bread and dripping?'

'Gimme his!' said Tommy.

'I've had bread and milk,' said Cedric.

'Well, give dripping a try,' Maggie said. She'd obviously fallen for Cedric's charms too.

I gave him his own quarter and after one tentative nibble he relaxed.

'It's delicious!' he declared.

He wasn't so keen on his black tea, perhaps because we'd used the tea leaves several times already so it tasted very stewed, but he drank it up even so. Then he sat patiently on Pa's sofa while Maggie scrubbed and rinsed and wrung and smoothed his trousers. They were still soaking wet of course, but almost as good as new.

'Thank you so much!' Cedric cried.

'Now, you'd better run home quick,' said Maggie. 'Unless you'd like to stay and live with us.'

She was joking, of course – but Cedric took her seriously.

'I should like that very much, but I think I'd miss my mama and papa,' he said.

We laughed at him wistfully, and then I saw him to the front door, squelching a little in his wet trousers, but looking pristine again.

'They're more wet than the rest of me,' Cedric said, plucking at the sodden material.

'It's still raining hard so you'll even up by the time you get home,' I said.

'Yes, I'm sure that's right,' said Cedric. 'Well, goodbye, Tess, and thank you very much for helping me.'

He set off smartly – but in the wrong direction.

'Not that way, silly,' I called after him. 'Here, I'll take you back to the park gates, all right?'

He was very grateful. I went with him further than the park actually, because I wanted to see what sort of house he lived in. It was twice the size of our house. No, three times. It was white too, without a speck of soot on it. I wondered if the maid had to scrub it all over every day, like we scrubbed our one doorstep. They had at least ten steps up to the front door. That was painted deep purple and had a brass knocker in the shape of a lion.

I rather fancied going up the steps and giving the glossy door a good bash with the lion, but Cedric pulled me back.

'No, I'll go in the back way and find Cook. She's my friend,' said Cedric. He paused, looking at me. 'Will you be my friend too, Tess?'

I hesitated. I knew girls like me were never friends with boys like Cedric. If I ever went near any of the posh children in the park, the nurses always flapped their hands and told me to run away. Doubtless Cedric's own nurse would do just that. But Cedric himself seemed to like me.

I didn't really have a friend. I sometimes skipped the

washing line with the girls in our street but they didn't like playing my kind of pretend games, and they mocked me when I danced. Cedric had clapped me enthusiastically.

'Yes, let's be friends,' I said.

'We'll meet in the park!' said Cedric.

'Well, I don't think your nurse will like that,' I said.

'Then I'll give her the slip again,' said Cedric, grinning. 'Goodbye, Tess. I'll see you soon.'

'I hope so,' I said, and then I ran back home. I didn't just run. I jumped on and off the pavement, I stamped in the puddles, I twirled round the lampposts, dancing my heart out in the pouring rain.

Chapter Three

Pa was late getting home. Very late. We waited for supper and then after an hour or so fell upon our scraps of stew.

Maggie looked at the dried-up shreds of meat at the bottom of the pot halfway through the evening.

'We might as well share it,' she said. 'He won't be in any fit state to eat it now.'

So we golloped it down, and Maggie gave Ada several watered-down teaspoons of the gravy.

'You'd better get to bed then, quick,' she said to Tommy and me.

Pa's temper was never reliable, but it was much worse when he'd been drinking.

'You get to bed too, Maggie,' said Connor. 'I'll stay up to help him.'

Dear Connor. He'd been late home himself, after clearing the market gutters and pocketing the bruised fruit and withered vegetables for us. He looked exhausted, because he'd been up since daylight helping set the stalls out, but he didn't snap at us once. He helped Maggie fold the last of the sheets, played a game of soldiers with Tommy, and blew several tunes on his penny whistle so I could have a dance. He even got Ada chuckling, giving her a ride on his knee.

'Don't you stay up, Connor,' I said quickly. Pa was often hardest on him. Connor's cheerful steady ways seemed to annoy him unreasonably. He would punish him unfairly or try to humiliate him. I took a deep breath. 'I'll stay up. We all know he likes me best.'

It was true. I wasn't boasting. I wished I wasn't the chosen one. I didn't want to be Pa's pet in the slightest. It was just because I looked most like him. Not *now*, when he was bloated with bloodshot eyes and an angry face. People in our street said he used to be a fine figure of a man, with his golden curls and his piercing blue eyes, quick with his tongue and light on his feet. He'd danced once too and could get his pick of

any of the girls, though he'd chosen Ma.

He wasn't suited to family life. Not our family anyway –
and he'd got so much worse since Ma died. But he still had
this soft spot for me some of the time. He'd call for me when
he got in the door.

'Where's my little Goldie then?' he'd yell, and I'd have to
go running and smile at him as if I was pleased to see him.

Then he'd ruffle my blonde curly hair, tap me on the nose,
chuck me under the chin, and I'd have to keep the smile firmly
fixed in place or he'd get in a temper. Sometimes I even dared
cheek him a little bit and he'd roar with laughter and call me a
'saucy little baggage', though he'd erupt in fury if any of the
others dared say something similar.

They were all dark with brown eyes like Ma. Even Ada's
baby blue eyes had turned brown, and her tufts of hair had
darkened too.

'I'll stay up with you,' said Connor. 'Just in case.'

'Well, I'm putting Tommy to bed – and I'm going with
him,' said Maggie. 'I'm dead beat.'

She really looked exhausted, her face chalk white, her eyes
ringed with dark circles. She reminded me of Ma.

'Maggie, you are all right, aren't you?' I said.

'No, I'm blooming well not all right,' said Maggie, yawning.

'But I mean . . . you won't die like Ma, will you?' I said anxiously. I didn't always get on with Maggie, but deep down I really loved her.

'Aah!' said Connor, smiling at me.

'She's just scared that if I die she'll have to do the hard work,' said Maggie, but she pinched my cheek fondly.

She took Tommy with her up the stairs, carrying Ada on one hip. The baby didn't sleep in our bed; she had her own little cot. Well, it was actually a drawer, but Ma had got it ready for her, with a tiny feather mattress and the smallest blanket, and Ada loved it.

Connor and I sat together on the sofa, waiting. Waiting and waiting and waiting. I told Connor about Cedric and his visit earlier, and Connor told me stories about the market and some of the other children who worked there, the flower girls who sold posies for a penny, the watercress boy, and his friend Maisie the oranges girl who sometimes gave Connor a perfectly sound orange for nothing.

'She must be sweet on you,' I teased him, and Connor blushed fiercely.

'Could *I* come and work at the market?' I begged.

'You're too little, Tess. They're country nippers, who pick their flowers and watercress before dawn and walk miles to the market,' said Connor. 'While you're still tucked up in bed like a little dormouse.'

'What about the oranges girl?' I asked. 'Your Maisie. Does she go picking her oranges too?'

'She's not *my* Maisie,' said Connor. 'She's just a friend. And you don't get oranges growing here, unless you're very rich and have a huge house and garden with an orangery.'

'Let's be very rich and eat oranges every day too,' I said.

'Chance would be a fine thing,' said Connor. 'Poor Maisie has to get up in the dark and walk to Covent Garden to get her oranges, and then carry them all the way here. It's a really hard life for her, and she's only my age.'

'I'd like a *soft* life,' I said, snuggling up to Connor.

'Wouldn't we all?' he said, putting his arm round me. 'Here, have a little snooze, Dormouse.'

We couldn't relax properly because we were expecting Pa to come stumbling in, shouting and cursing. They preached about the Demon Drink at the Ragged School. For once I listened properly, my ears thrumming. They could have been talking about my pa.

I wished he wouldn't drink so. Ma had once stood up to him when he'd drunk away every penny of his wages and we had nothing to eat in the house, and he knocked her across the room. Now she was gone he was worse, if anything.

I couldn't understand why he liked drink so much. I always had to wrinkle my nose up whenever I passed an ale house because the smell was so bad. It made you act bad too, saying words that would make the Ragged School ladies pass out in a dead faint.

I wished Pa would get shipwrecked like Cedric's Robinson Crusoe and end up on a desert island by himself. I'd sail a ship and rescue him after a long, long time, when he was regretting the error of his ways, and then he'd be a different pa all the time, sweet and soft and never once raising his voice.

I sighed sleepily, knowing it was just a daydream, and then I must have nodded off altogether, because when I opened my eyes again it was pitch dark. There was still no sign of Pa. I listened for the church clock and almost immediately it obliged by chiming the hour. I counted along with it. Twelve strikes.

'Connor!' I whispered, shaking him. 'Pa's still not back, and it's midnight!'

'Oh Lord,' Connor sighed. 'I suppose I'd better go out looking for him. He'll have likely fallen down in a gutter somewhere.'

'Couldn't we just leave him to sleep it off?' I said.

'It's still raining. He could catch his death of cold. Anything could happen to him if he's slumped somewhere, senseless. Thieves might target him,' said Connor, sitting up properly and stretching.

'Well, they'll be out of luck. He won't have any money left, not if he's got this drunk,' I said. 'Don't you just hate him?'

'Tess! Don't talk like that. He's our pa,' said Connor.

'But he's so mean, especially when he's drunk,' I said.

'He can't really help it. He's had a hard life,' said Connor.

That's our Connor. He's such a lovely, kind boy. Pa's nearly always horrid to him, and yet Connor tries his hardest to make allowances for him.

'We've all had hard lives,' I said. I stood up, and gave myself a little slap on each cheek to wake myself up properly. 'I'll help look for him then.'

'Absolutely not. You're much too little to be out late at night,' Connor said firmly.

I lifted my chin and stuck my elbows out, hands on hips.

'I am *so* coming. You'll never get Pa home by yourself. We'll have to coax him, and you know I'm the best at that,' I said.

Connor looked at me helplessly and gave in. 'But if we see anyone rough or threatening, you're to run home like the wind, promise?'

'I promise. And you are too!' I said.

He laughed and chucked me under the chin. 'Deal!' he said.

We crept out of the house as stealthily as we could. If Maggie was still awake she'd try to stop us. She tried to act like Ma now, even though she wasn't very good at it. Poor Maggie. I was very glad I wasn't the big sister. Even so, it didn't make me very fond of her. Perhaps Miss Moaning at the Ragged School was right, and I was a thoroughly bad girl destined to go Down Below. She was really called Miss Morrison, but I tagged her Miss Moaning behind her back.

Everything seemed so different in the pitch dark. They didn't bother with lampposts down our street. The rain clouds hid the moon so we had to hold hands and step carefully, hoping we didn't tread in any rubbish – or worse. It was easier when we turned the corner and walked towards the Soldiers' Arms, the nearest ale house.

When I was very little and heard Pa say he was going to the Soldiers', I thought he meant real army friends. I pictured them strutting around proudly in their bright uniforms, like the toy soldiers at home. But there were no soldiers at the ale house now. They'd closed down the barracks and turned it into a dreaded workhouse. Folk who ended up there never seemed to get out again. It was always Ma's biggest fear that we'd end up there.

The Soldiers' Arms was still brightly lit, but the doors were firmly closed. Connor lifted me up and I peered in the window, but the bar was empty. We looked round the back but there was no sign of Pa.

'Perhaps he went on to the Crown?' Connor said. 'I've heard they let folk drink later there.'

We walked on. There were certainly a few drunk men, reeling home singing loudly or sprawled on doorsteps. Two loutish lads started yelling sweary stuff at us, and Connor put his arm round me protectively.

'Don't you dare use bad language in front of my little sister! Say any more and I'll flatten both of you!' he shouted back so fiercely that they crossed over the road and left us alone.

'Oh, Connor!' I said. 'And they were both bigger than you too!'

'And likely either could knock me over with one blow!' said Connor. 'Still, I frightened them, didn't I?'

'You did! You're my hero!' I said, hugging him.

There was a man slumped in the doorway of the Crown, reaching up as if he was trying to get in, though it was closed now and locked against these desperate men.

'I bet that's Pa,' I said – but when we got up close we saw it was a different, older man, reeking of ale and mumbling senselessly. He belched when I touched him.

'Ugh!' I said, reeling back. 'Why do they *want* to get into this state?'

'Because they're unhappy,' said Connor, settling the man more comfortably. 'Even old Bert drinks half his profits away and then feels like death the next morning. But he's not a bad man – he's just sick of his life. He's long past retiring age and his rheumatics plague him, but he has to keep his stall going to keep out the workhouse.'

'How come you can work all this out, Connor?' I asked.

'Because I'm brilliant!' Connor joked.

'Yes, you're Ma's diamond boy!' I said, and then regretted

it because we both felt the pain of losing her all over again. 'I miss her so,' I mumbled.

'Me too,' said Connor. 'But that weird old woman at the Ragged School insists we'll be reunited in Heaven.'

'Which means I haven't got a hope of seeing Ma, because Miss Moaning says I'm an imp of Satan and destined to go Down Under,' I said.

'Well, if she's right I'll come and join you to keep you company. If Hell's fires are as hot as they say, then at least we'll keep warm in winter,' said Connor. 'But where on earth *is* Pa? He can't just have vanished.'

We hunted further and walked right round the railings of the park in case he'd tried to sleep it off on a park bench. We even went past the park and up where the rich folks lived, where at least the gas lamps were lit so we could see our way easily.

'I think that one's Cedric's house,' I said, pointing. 'No, maybe it's the white one next to it. Or was it the other side of the road?'

'Well, it's hardly likely you're going to be calling on him, is it?' said Connor. 'I reckon that nurse of his would give you a whacking for enticing him away.'

'I didn't! I was trying to help him!' I said indignantly.

'And she doesn't whack anyway, she gives him the slipper if he's naughty.'

'Poor Cedric. He sounds a nice little chap. Pity you can't be friends,' said Connor.

'Why can't we?' I asked.

'Don't be soft. He's not one of us, he's one of them. Rich. Privileged. Talks tremendously la-di-da,' said Connor.

'Ai can talk like thet,' I said.

'Well, you're a little monkey-mimic,' said Connor.

'Imagine living in a great big house like his. So many rooms. We could sleep in a different room whenever we wanted!' I said.

'I could have a room of my own,' Connor muttered wistfully.

'No you couldn't! It would be too lonely,' I said firmly.

We slept in the same bed, Maggie, Connor, Tommy and me, with Ada in her drawer on the chest beside us.

'I wouldn't mind if Tommy had his own room as he fidgets so much,' I added. 'And Maggie's elbows are as sharp as knives – but you and me always have to share, Connor, even if we get as rich as royalty.'

'What about when I get married?' said Connor.

'You're never ever getting married! You're mine!' I said.

'Even after you have your own husband?' Connor asked.

'I'm never ever having a husband,' I said firmly. 'Or babies.'

'So what do you want to do when you're a grown-up?'

'I shall be a real rich lady with beautiful gowns and my own big house and a carriage that takes me anywhere I want,' I said, twirling around as elegantly as I could, pretending to fan myself.

'And how are you going to get the dosh to live this grand life?' Connor asked.

I thought about it seriously as we strolled back past the park. I wasn't really sure how rich ladies earned their money.

'I know! I shall be queen!' I said triumphantly.

'Yes, I can just see you with a gold crown to match your gold curls,' said Connor. 'But hang on, don't we have a queen already? Think again!'

I peered at the houses carefully, noting the cast-iron drainpipes.

'Well, maybe I'll have to steal my money,' I said. 'I'm good at climbing. I could be a burglar and climb up drainpipes, and I'm small enough to squeeze through the littlest windows. And I'll take everyone else's money and then I can be the one who spends it.'

'Tess Andrews! Shame on you! No wonder Miss Morrison says you're going to H-e-l-l!' said Connor.

'I'll share the money with you. And Maggie and Tommy and Ada. But I'm not giving Pa any, because he'll just drink it away,' I said. 'Connor, where *is* he?'

'Lord knows,' said Connor. 'We'll go up and down the street one more time, and then we might as well go home.'

We looked everywhere again, but we couldn't see Pa anywhere.

'You know what, I bet he's gone home while we've been out looking,' said Connor. 'He'll be snoring his head off on the sofa right this minute!'

But when we let ourselves silently into our house, the sofa was empty, and when we crept upstairs Pa's room was empty too, though there was something lying on top of the blanket when I patted it. I gasped, and then clutched it to my chest.

'What is it?' Connor whispered.

'It's Ma's old nightgown,' I said, hugging it hard. 'Oh, Connor, it still smells like her.' I started crying helplessly.

'And it was on top of the bed?' Connor said, putting his arm round me. 'Perhaps Pa puts it there every night?'

'Do you think?' I was stopped in my tracks. Maybe Pa

missed Ma more than I'd realized. Perhaps he'd loved her as much as we did, though he rarely showed it. I struggled with this new feeling inside me. I felt sorry for Pa now. And much more worried about him.

'Do you think we should go out again and have one more look for him?' I asked Connor.

'We could search all night and still not find him, Tess,' Connor said. 'I think he's taken shelter somewhere. Maybe he's passed out in one of the ale houses and they've let him sleep there. We'll look tomorrow if he hasn't come back by then. I think it's best we try to sleep ourselves now.'

We crept to our room. Ada gave a little wail as we came in, and we held our breath, hoping she wouldn't start a proper crying session because we had no milk to soothe her. I patted her gently in her drawer and she gave a small sigh and went back to sleep. I blew her a kiss and then climbed into bed. We didn't bother with nightclothes now because Maggie said she had enough to wash.

She was curled up on the edge of the bed, sucking her thumb as if she was Ada's age. I found myself feeling sorry for her too, though I still wished she wasn't so snappy when she was awake. Perhaps it was just because she was bone-weary

and fed up with having to do a grown woman's work all the time. Maybe she laughed scornfully at my dancing because she longed to dance herself rather than struggle with the chores.

It was exhausting feeling this sudden sympathy for my family. It was a relief to be still exasperated with Tommy, who was sprawled over the rest of the bed, arms and legs stretched right out. I tried edging him towards Maggie and he half woke and kicked at me, catching me right in the stomach.

'You little whatsit!' I whispered. Actually it was a word far worse than *whatsit* this time, and if Ma was still alive she'd have washed my mouth out with soap. I gave Tommy a fierce shove and then jumped in quick, leaving room for Connor beside me.

'Night night, Tess,' he murmured. 'Sleep tight.'

'And hope the bugs don't bite!' I responded. I did hope we wouldn't get bed bugs. Ma had always lived in fear of them, and had changed the sheets regularly, but we'd been a bit lax recently.

I wriggled to get both arms free and then clasped my own thumbs tight. Connor had told me that was what you had to do if you made a wish. I hung on tightly and wished that Ma would still be alive when I woke up in the morning, and Pa

would be safely home and swearing never to touch a drop of drink again, and Maggie would have no more chores and be happy again, and Tommy would have an entire change of personality and become as sweet-natured and sensible as Connor. I didn't need to wish anything for Connor because he was just perfect as he was.

And what about me? I fell asleep still wondering what I would wish for myself.

Chapter Four

Pa didn't come home in the morning. Connor didn't go to the market. We went to the building site where Pa was currently working and asked his mates if they had any idea where he was. He'd worked as usual yesterday, but no one had seen him since they all packed up for the day.

'Likely he'll still be lying in the sawdust in some ale house,' said one man, chuckling.

'Or he's literally drunk himself to death,' said another.

'I'll thank you not to talk like that in front of my little sister, sir,' Connor said with dignity, and we walked away.

We went to every single ale house within five miles that

evening. Many of the landlords knew Pa, but none had a clue where he was now. We were exhausted when we came home, and our clothes reeked of beer and smoke.

'No Pa?' Connor asked, the minute we were through the front door.

'What are we going to do now?' I asked, my voice wavering.

'Well, I'd better put both of you in the wash-tub after supper,' said Maggie, wrinkling her nose as she served us the last of the stew, which was just potato and gristle now.

She was trying to make a silly joke because Tommy was unusually quiet and clingy, and Ada was fretful and had only her sweet tea to suck on. Connor gave me a nudge and we played along, as if it was perfectly normal for your pa to vanish into thin air.

Then Maggie put Tommy to bed, making a fuss of him and singing him to sleep as if he was a baby. Ada cried for a few minutes in her drawer, but then settled too.

'You'd better go to bed too, Tess – you look done in,' said Maggie.

'I'm not one of the little ones,' I said firmly. 'I want to be in on the talk. What *are* we going to do?'

Maggie fetched her purse and opened it for us. It was empty.

'We can manage a day or two more – but Ada can't,' she said. 'She's been crying on and off all day, poor little mite. I went next door to see if Mrs O'Grady would let me have a half pint of milk for her, and she said she'd give it gladly but she didn't have any herself. I even went to that stuck-up Mrs Patterson and she just quoted the blooming Bible at me, going on about borrowers and lenders. Call herself a Christian, when she won't spare a drop of milk for a motherless baby!'

'There's no money left at all?' I asked, jumping up to see if any coins had spilled out of Pa's pockets and fallen down the sides of the sofa.

'None. I've looked everywhere. Pa just leaves me a sixpence or so every morning for the day's food. It's hard enough managing on that. But without it . . .' Maggie's voice tailed away.

'So what are we going to do?' I asked.

'Don't keep asking me! I don't know!' said Maggie, and she burst into tears.

'Oh, Maggie,' said Connor, and he held her sore red hands and stroked them gently. 'You work the hardest of us all, and it's just not fair. We're all going to have to help earn more, especially me. You're the eldest but I'm the man of the house.'

'Connor, you're still a boy! They won't give you a job at the building site, you're simply not old enough. Or big and strong enough either,' said Maggie.

'I will be soon – and meanwhile I'll get some other job, maybe more work down the market. They like me there and they know I'm willing,' said Connor.

'It's not enough just to be willing,' said Maggie, wiping her nose with the back of her hand, though she always tells me off royally if I do that. '*I* was willing to carry on Ma's washing business but it's so *hard*, especially when it rains. What's it going to be like in the winter? I've already had one woman call round moaning, saying her sheets were still damp and smelling musty, and now I've to do them again for nothing or she'll start creating.'

'What a cheek! Why couldn't she hang them up herself?' said Connor. 'Maybe this washing lark is a bit of a waste of time. It doesn't really pay much, for all your hard work. Maybe you could try for a proper job, Maggie?' Connor suggested.

'Not in a laundry!' said Maggie. 'And I'm not going as a maid for some lazy woman too grand to do her own work either.'

'No, I can see that wouldn't work,' said Connor.

'I'm not going to the factory either. Ma made me swear I'd never go there, after that poor girl got her hair caught in the machinery,' said Maggie.

'I know, I know,' said Connor. I marvelled at his patience. I was sorry for Maggie but she did whine so. 'I was thinking more of shopwork. In a gown shop maybe – or a milliner's?'

Maggie's eyes lit up. 'Do you think they'd have me?'

'Well, you could pretty yourself up a bit, act meek and mild – ha! – and I reckon you'd do OK,' said Connor.

'So who's going to do the chores and mind the little ones?' Maggie asked.

They both looked at me.

'No! *I'm* a little one,' I protested, though I'd argued the opposite just ten minutes ago.

'Look, you don't have to do any washing – just our own stuff every now and then,' said Maggie.

'And I could help you with the mangling when I come home from the market,' said Connor. 'I reckon I could do a bit of shopping on my way back too.'

'There's hardly any cooking – I could start a stew off early on a Monday and you'd just need to top it up through the week,' said Maggie.

'So all you'd really have to do is keep an eye on Tommy and Ada,' said Connor.

'And you managed that fine when I was feeling poorly, didn't you?' said Maggie.

'No I didn't!' I said, appalled. I was so determined not to get lumbered that I lost all caution. 'I forgot about Tommy yesterday and got all the way to the park gates without him!'

'What?' said Maggie. 'You left Tommy in the park!'

'No, I went back for him. You see, I met Cedric and he liked the way I danced and—'

'Oh, so you've been prancing about in front of strangers and deliberately abandoning your little brother and sister!' Maggie said furiously.

'No, not deliberately,' I protested. 'And I had Ada with me all the time.'

'Leaving Tommy to fall out of a tree or be abducted by an evil stranger!' Maggie insisted.

'I don't think anyone would *want* to abduct Tommy – and if they did they'd bring him back sharpish,' I retorted.

'Stop bickering, girls!' said Connor. 'Tess, I've seen you playing great games with Tommy, and having wrestling matches. You get on really well most of the time – and you're

fantastic with little Ada. I think you'd be brilliant looking after them. I'm sure it won't be for long. Pa will come back and start earning again and everything will go back to normal.'

'Well, *I* won't,' said Maggie. 'I'm going to get myself a job in a shop, just you wait and see.'

She seemed to have forgotten it was Connor's idea. I glared at him reproachfully.

'How can you side with Maggie against me?' I said bitterly. 'I thought you were my special brother.'

'I am! It's only going to be for a little while. And I can't see what else we can do. You're too little to earn any money, Tessikins,' he said, using my old baby name.

I was determined not to let him get round me.

'I can so make money!' I said. It suddenly came to me. 'I could dance! I could go somewhere busy like the market or the High Street and do my fairy dance, setting Pa's old cap on the ground. I think people would put pennies in, lots and lots.'

'So you're going to be a beggar now and shame us all!' said Maggie. 'If Ma heard you she'd weep!'

'Don't you bring Ma into this. Anyway, she loved my dancing,' I said. 'She called me her special girl.' I started crying, aching for Ma.

Maggie cried again too, and even Connor got watery-eyed.

'Look at us!' he said, blowing his nose on an old rag. 'We're bawling worse than Ada! Let's have a cup of tea and calm down.'

There was so little tea left in the caddy that we decided to give it to Ada for her morning bottle, and made do with hot water instead. Then we went to bed and I curled up and held my thumbs and wished again, so hard I nearly pulled my thumbs right off.

The wishing didn't work. Pa was still missing the next morning. Connor went off to the market really early. Maggie didn't do the washing. She washed herself instead, even her hair, and put on a clean blue frock with a lace collar.

'That's Ma's good frock!' I said, outraged.

'Well, she doesn't need it now, does she?' said Maggie, turning this way and that. 'Does it suit me, Tess?'

It looked surprisingly good on Maggie. It made her look prettier, and quite a bit older too. She didn't have a corset but it still managed to show off her figure. So long as you didn't look at her battered boots, she looked like a little lady.

'You look lovely,' I said grudgingly. 'When I get a bit taller, can I have a turn wearing Ma's dress?'

'Yes, of course,' said Maggie. 'Well, if you're careful. Look at the torn hem of your own frock – and there's a rip under the arm too! You're much too boisterous, running around and fighting with Tommy.'

'I'd be ever so careful – I swear I would. I'd barely move. I'd stay still as a statue, just smoothing the skirt and pretending Ma had her arms wrapped round me,' I said.

'I know. I'm hoping she's here with me, wishing me luck,' Maggie said.

'I'm holding my thumbs and wishing you luck too,' I said,

and I really meant it. 'Don't worry about the little ones. I'll look after them properly. I'll even do a bit of tidying and sweeping if you like. And I'd cook too – but we haven't got any food.'

'Connor's going to do his best scavenging down the market. And I swear I'll get some milk for Ada somehow. There's a boy down at the tea stall who's sweet on me. He always whistles at me when I'm out shopping. I'll have a little chat with him and see if he'll slip me a half pint of milk,' said Maggie.

'You might have to give him a kiss for it!' I said, screwing up my face at the thought.

'Oh well, that mightn't be so bad,' said Maggie, giggling. 'Bye then, Tess. Take care. And, Tommy – hey, Tommy, come here!'

Tommy came leaping down the stairs with only his shirt on – not a pretty sight.

'Put your trousers on at once!' I said.

'Not gonna,' said Tommy, dancing round me.

'Oh Lord, Tommy, don't start playing up now,' said Maggie. 'You be a good boy for Tess and I'll bring you a treat home. Is that a deal?'

'A treat just for me?' said Tommy.

'Yes. Promise. Now put your kecks on and be a good boy,' said Maggie.

He trotted back upstairs.

'He doesn't blooming well deserve a treat!' I said indignantly.

'I know, but it'll make him easier to deal with during the day, won't it?' said Maggie. 'Listen, that's Ada stirring. I've got her bottle ready for you. Now I must fly.'

She gave me a quick kiss on the cheek and then rushed out. I stared after her, wishing with all my heart that *I* was the eldest girl now. Or the youngest, like little Ada, who didn't have to do any chores at all. But it was no use wishing something that couldn't come true. I was Tess, the middle one, and I had to be the dogsbody today.

I changed Ada and fed her, rocking her in my arms afterwards until she fell asleep again, even though her poor tummy must still be rumbling through lack of nourishment. I did my best to wash Tommy's sticky face and grimy hands and supervised his dressing. He insisted he could do it himself, but ended up putting his boots on the wrong feet. He walked about determinedly, knock-kneed.

'My legs, gone wrong,' he said, scratching his head.

'You could try taking your boots off and switching them round,' I said, wrapping Ada in my shawl. She felt so tiny and fragile, like a little china baby. 'Don't you fret, we're going to feed you up, you poor little mite,' I muttered.

'I'm starving,' said Tommy, rubbing his tummy. 'Why take my boots off? I just put boots on!'

'Because they're on the wrong feet, you noodle,' I said.

'Not a noodle!' Tommy said, insulted. 'Not, not, not! I put boots on right.'

'Well, wear them like that then, but don't blame me if your toes turn inwards and you can't walk properly,' I retorted. 'Now, get out of my way while I do a bit of sweeping.'

I was starting to understand why Maggie was so snappy when she was trying to get on with some housework. I tried to make the room look nice, but everything was so makeshift and shabby. Pa's sofa was the only proper piece of furniture. There were dents in the cushions where he generally sprawled. I wasn't sure whether to shake them into shape or not.

'Can I sit on sofa?' Tommy asked.

'Better not,' I said. 'If Pa bursts in the front door and catches you, you'll get whacked.'

'I'll whack him back, bang, bang, bang,' said Tommy

swaggering about, one boot on and one boot off now. He
paused. 'Tess, is Pa dead? Like Ma?'

I nibbled at my lip. 'I don't think so,' I said. 'Someone
would have found him.'

'So where is he?'

I shrugged. 'Who knows. He's maybe just pushed off
by himself.' My voice shook a little. Could he *really* have
simply walked out on us? Walked out on *me*, when I was his
little Goldie? I felt a pang, even though I wasn't sure I loved
Pa. I certainly didn't like him – but I still wanted him to
like me.

'We get a new pa?' Tommy asked.

'No, we'll just be us,' I said. 'Maggie and Connor will look
after us. Now sort your boots out properly and I'll do the laces
for you,' I said, giving up on the sweeping.

I wondered about doing some scrubbing, but after a
minute dabbing at the sink I decided that would be enough.
I visited the privy out the back and wished someone would
have a good scrub in there, but it certainly wasn't going to
be me.

Then I came back indoors and wandered about,
wondering what to do. I almost wished I was at the Ragged

School. Still, there wasn't much point going. They never taught us anything useful, like what to do when you didn't have any money for food.

It was a sunny day, with a bright blue sky.

'Come on, Tommy, we'll go to the park,' I said. 'But no climbing trees, do you hear me?'

'No running away with Cedric boy and leaving me behind!' said Tommy.

'He won't be there. He'll be shut up in his nursery, kept prisoner by that old bat nurse,' I said. 'Poor Cedric.'

However, we saw him almost as soon as I trundled the baby carriage into the park. He was running along bowling a hoop, a sailor hat sitting skew-whiff on his head and one of his long socks round his ankles.

'Hey, Tess, Tommy, Baby!' he called excitedly. He waved, so that he missed whipping his hoop and it careered away from him towards us.

I caught it neatly and had a quick go myself. I'd often seen children bowling hoops and it seemed fun. I was quite good at it actually, and would have loved to go further, but I was determined to look after the little ones better this time. And I wanted to talk to Cedric.

'Thank you so much for catching my hoop!' he said as he ran up to us, supremely polite as always.

'You're not running away again, are you?' I said, peering round. There was no sign of a bat nurse in hot pursuit. 'Where's your horrid nurse?'

'She's gone!' said Cedric, grinning. 'Papa caught her giving me the slipper and dismissed her instantly! She had to pack her bags and go that night. She was so cross! She said it was my fault, and I wondered if she was going to slipper me one more time, but she didn't quite dare. Oh, it was so jolly when she'd gone! Papa even let me stay up for grown-up supper and gave me a sip from his wine glass. And Mama made me promise to tell her at once if my new nurse ever punished me like that.'

'So where is this new nurse?' I said, peering around.

'I haven't got one yet. They're still being interviewed. So meanwhile I have Sarah-Jane, and she's such a sport.' Cedric pointed to a girl chatting to the park keeper, giggling at some story he was telling her.

She had hair even curlier than mine, though she'd crammed a white cap on top, balancing there unsteadily. She had red cheeks and she wore a matching red rose pinned to her apron. It looked very like the red roses still in full bloom in the flower bed.

She saw Cedric pointing and waved back cheerily. She didn't seem put out that he was talking to us.

'Is she a servant girl?' I asked.

'Yes, she's our kitchen maid and she's so jolly,' said Cedric. 'I wish she could be my nurse for ever, but Mama says she's not quite suitable.'

'Why don't your ma look after you?' Tommy asked, having a go at Cedric's hoop too.

'She's too busy to look after me all the time,' said Cedric.

'She's a lady and ladies don't look after their children,' I said to Tommy. 'Mind you don't break that hoop! Don't bash it about like that!'

'It stupid, this hoop,' said Tommy. 'It don't do anything.'

'Yes it does,' said Cedric. 'You bowl it along, do you see?' He demonstrated. He wasn't actually that good at it, and the hoop wobbled this way and that, but I nodded politely. Perhaps I'd caught his good manners. Tommy was immune to any kind of manners and sniggered.

'That look daft,' he said.

'Tommy! You're the one who looks daft, especially when you put your boots on the wrong way round,' I said.

'I never!' Tommy said. 'Shut your mouth, our Tess.'

He took the hoop from Cedric and bowled it at me. He put a spin on it too, so that it hurtled straight into my stomach, which was horribly painful. I yelled. Little Ada in the baby carriage woke with a start and wailed.

'Now look what you've done!' I said, rescuing Ada. I held her close, I patted her back, I danced her up and down, but there was no way of soothing her now.

'Oh dear, why is she crying so?' Cedric asked, distressed.

Sarah-Jane must have wondered too, because she left the park keeper and came dashing over to us.

'Hello, hello,' she said, nodding at Tommy and me. 'Who are you then?'

'They're Tess and Tommy,' said Cedric. 'They're my friends,' he added shyly, going pink.

'How do, Tess and Tommy,' said Sarah-Jane. 'And who's the little mite?'

'It's Ada, our sister,' I said, joggling her about.

'Dearie me, shall I try soothing her?' Sarah-Jane suggested. 'My ma always said I had a way with babies.'

She took Ada and gave her a cuddle, making little cooing noises at her, but Ada couldn't stop now.

'Oh dear,' said Sarah-Jane. 'She's really hungry, isn't she?

Look at her little mouth opening. She wants her bottle. I should take her home at once and feed her, sweetheart,' she said to me.

'We haven't got any milk for her. We haven't even got any tea. We've got nothing at all and I don't know what to do,' I said despairingly.

Tommy stared and then stuck his thumb in his mouth, his eyes watering.

'Oh my, we can't have you starving,' said Sarah-Jane. 'Especially this little one. She's skin and bone. Can't your ma feed her?'

That did it. I started howling as hard as Ada.

'Ain't got no ma no more,' said Tommy.

Ma would have been horrified to hear him. She was always very particular about how we spoke, wanting us to be a cut above the other kids in the street. But I couldn't tell him off because I was crying too much, and feeling a fool in front of Cedric.

He was so kind. He sidled up to me and timidly edged his handkerchief into my fist so that I could mop my face.

'That's a good boy,' said Sarah-Jane. Then she smiled at me. 'Don't fret so, girlie. You come home with us and we'll give the baby a big bottle of milk and daresay find something for you two to eat and all. Off we go!'

She waved cheerily to the park keeper, who looked disappointed she was going so soon.

'Come on then, chop-chop,' she said, as Tommy and I stared at her, blinking.

'You mean, come to *your* home – or Cedric's?' I said.

'Well, we'll have a long trek to *my* home because it's far away on the Sussex coast.' Sarah-Jane laughed. 'No, silly, Cedric's home, only ten minutes away. I'll carry the baby. We don't want her bumping about in that baby carriage when she's so scrawny, poor love.'

'And me too big for it!' said Tommy.

'If you say so, young man. Why don't you put one foot in it and scoot yourself along?' Sarah-Jane suggested. 'And you shut your mouth, little curly-nob, or you'll start catching flies,' she said to me.

I shut my mouth with a gulp. She surely had to be joking, didn't she? Children like us were never allowed in big houses belonging to rich folk. But Sarah-Jane seemed too kind and good-natured to be teasing.

Cedric took hold of my hand. 'You can take a turn bowling my hoop,' he said encouragingly.

I sniffed mightily because my nose was running and I

couldn't give it a good blow on my frock hem because then they'd see I didn't have any underwear. I managed a smile.

'You're on!' I said.

Cedric and I bowled, Tommy scooted, and Sarah-Jane walked along jauntily, murmuring sweet words to Ada. I was pretty sure Ada was soaking wet now but Sarah-Jane cuddled her close without seeming to mind. She was a million times nicer than the bat nurse. I hoped for Cedric's sake that his parents could see that for themselves and say that she could be his nurse for ever. Well, for however long posh children kept their nurses.

I looked about me as we turned right out of the park and saw two smart ladies in feather bonnets, with big bustles under their silken skirts. Maybe their nurses still helped them into their corsets and tied their bonnet ribbons. A gentleman with a moustache walked by, a fancy waistcoat under the jacket of his suit. Perhaps his nurse curled the ends of his moustache for him and did up every button on his waistcoat. I chuckled at the thought.

'Have you cheered up now, Tess?' Cedric said hopefully.

I nodded. 'Cedric, we won't get into trouble, will we? I don't think we're really allowed to go in your house,'

I whispered. 'I know your old nurse wouldn't have let us.'

'Sarah-Jane's different,' said Cedric. 'And Cook won't mind. She often invites the policeman in for a cup of tea, *and* the butcher's boy. He's another of my friends. He knows so many jokes – he always makes me laugh and laugh.'

'But what about your papa and mama?'

'Oh, Papa will be out on business and Mama often stays in bed in the mornings because she needs to rest,' said Cedric.

'She's ill?' I asked.

'I don't think so. She's just got a little stout. Sarah-Jane says Mama's going to bring me a present soon, a special one I can play with. I can't think what it can be,' said Cedric.

'I bet I know,' I said. 'I think she's going to give you a baby brother or sister!'

Cedric stared at me. 'Really?' he asked. 'Oh, that would be lovely. But will it cry all the time like Ada?'

'No. She cries because she's hungry.'

'But she's going to get some milk now, isn't she?'

'I hope so!' I said. And maybe Tommy and I might get a cup of milk too!

Chapter Five

We didn't just get a cup of full-cream milk. We got a slice of ham off the bone, a large slice of buttered bread, and a jam tart hot from the oven. Tommy and I bolted them down, terrified that someone would come charging into the kitchen and push us out the door. Sarah-Jane had mentioned Cook's policeman friend, Alfred, and that made us nervous.

We were a little scared of Cook herself at first, a large shiny-faced woman in a spotless cap and apron, her sleeves rolled up showing great arms almost as pink as the ham. She put her hands on her ample hips and looked fierce when Cedric brought us into her kitchen.

'Oh my Lord, why have you brought a whole bunch of bedraggled little urchins into my kitchen, Sarah-Jane?' she demanded.

'They're my friends, Cook – and they're very hungry,' said Cedric. 'And the baby hasn't had any milk at all for ages!'

'Oh, the little lamb!' said Cook, taking hold of Ada herself and cradling her. 'She's starving!'

'I wondered if we still had one of Master Cedric's bottles tucked away in a cupboard somewhere?' Sarah-Jane asked.

'We have indeed,' said Cook, springing into action. 'Top cupboard, along with the three bears dish and the Goldilocks mug, newly washed, ready for the new arrival.'

'What new arrival, Cook?' Cedric asked with interest.

Cook tapped the side of her nose. 'Just you wait and see, Master Cedric.'

'I think the baby needs changing first, Cook. Can I use one of the new napkins?' Sarah-Jane asked.

'I daresay one won't go amiss. There's a good three dozen ready and waiting in the linen cupboard,' said Cook.

I was taken aback. We only had four makeshift pieces of towel for our Ada, and they were so old and scratchy that her poor little bottom was rubbed raw.

'I'll change her,' I said. It was my least favourite job but she was my sister after all.

'I'll manage, poppet. You're not much more than a baby yourself,' said Sarah-Jane, chucking me under the chin.

She obviously thought me a baby of five or six but I didn't mind at all. I let her carry Ada away while Cook scrubbed my hands, and Tommy's even harder, sat us both on a bench at her table, and served us our wonderful meal. Even Tommy was silenced, and did his level best to eat properly, keeping his mouth shut as he chewed, but he couldn't resist lifting his plate and licking it clean of crumbs when he was finished.

Cedric chuckled and copied him, though Cook tutted.

'Now, now, Master Cedric. There's no need for you to copy these poor little beggar children!' she said.

I didn't mind being called poor, because we were, very, but we weren't beggar children. Ma would have been mortified.

'We don't beg!' I said. 'My sister Maggie's trying to get a job in a shop and my brother Connor helps at the market. I'd get a job too, but I can't think what.' Then it suddenly came to me. 'I can peel potatoes and chop veg and make stew. Could I be your kitchen maid, madam?'

I meant it seriously, because it would be so wonderful to

eat this sort of food every day, but Cook shook with laughter, all of her wobbling merrily.

'Bless you, you funny little mite!' she said. 'And you don't call me "madam", I'm Cook. The only "madam" in this house is her upstairs, and you won't be meeting her, I hope, else Sarah-Jane will find herself in the soup for bringing you kids into the house.'

'Put in the *soup*?' Tommy said, spluttering. 'Cook, can I have jam tart again?'

'It's "please may I have", not "can I" – but I daresay you can,' she said, putting another on his plate.

'You lovely lady,' said Tommy, beaming at her.

He was behaving like a little angel. I felt almost proud of him. And Ada looked stunning when Sarah-Jane brought her back. She didn't just have a clean napkin, she had a long white nightgown trimmed with lace!

'Hey, that's a step too far!' said Cook.

'I know, but her own frock was so wet and dirty I couldn't keep her in it,' said Sarah-Jane. 'Doesn't she look a little angel now?'

'She can't keep it, not one of the new ones. That's Brussels lace!' said Cook, scandalized.

'You'll get put in soup pot!' said Tommy.

'Take it off of her at once. We'll wrap her in one of my kitchen towels,' said Cook. 'I'll warm the milk for her.'

Sarah-Jane sat down on the bench and reluctantly took Ada's new finery off. Ada looked so little in just the napkin. It came right up under her scrawny arms and hung almost to her tiny toes.

'Lord, she's smaller than a skinned rabbit!' said Cook. She filled the bottle carefully and fed Ada herself, cushioning her against her soft chest.

'That's it, little duckie. Suck away at that lovely bottle. Not too fast now, don't want to make yourself sick. That's the ticket,' she said. Then she looked across at me.

'So is your ma poorly?' she said gently.

'Not any more,' I mumbled.

She understood. 'And what about your pa?'

'He gone,' said Tommy.

'My brother Connor and I went looking, but he isn't anywhere,' I said.

'Dear, dear, dear,' said Cook, sitting Ada up gently and rubbing her back. Ada made a sudden surprisingly loud burp, which made us laugh in spite of ourselves.

'My nurse used to get very cross when I did that,' said Cedric. 'I'm so glad she's gone. *Why* can't you stay looking after me, Sarah-Jane? I'll be very, very good.'

'Bless you, sweetheart, I wish I could. But your ma and pa want you to be brought up like a little gentleman and I'm certainly no lady,' said Sarah-Jane. 'You need a proper nurse to look after you.'

Cedric sighed. 'So why can't Tess and Tommy and the others have a nurse to look after them?' he asked.

'Because they haven't got anyone to pay her wages – and she'd earn a lot more than me,' said Sarah-Jane.

'We don't want a nurse telling us what to do. Maggie and Connor do that. We just need some money for food and the rent,' I said.

I saw Sarah-Jane look at Cook, her head on one side as if she was asking a silent question.

'I'm not begging you for the money!' I said, my face burning.

'Just as well, pet, because we ain't got none to spare,' said Cook. She started feeding Ada again but she'd nodded off to sleep, exhausted. 'Bless the baby lamb. Where shall I put her?'

'Back in baby pram, then I go on your lap with bottle?' Tommy asked hopefully.

'Tommy! You're much too big a boy!' I said, embarrassed.

'Oh, he's still young enough to need a bit of loving,' said Cook. 'Come here, pet.'

She handed Ada to me and reached out for Tommy. He clambered onto her big cosy lap and nestled up, opening his mouth like a baby bird.

'Who's my little baby then?' said Cook, playing along, and started feeding him. Tommy's fists clenched in delight.

'Oh, Tommy,' I said, going to lay Ada down in the carriage.

'Let me have one more cuddle with her first,' said Sarah-Jane, scooping her out of my arms.

I was pleased for my brother and sister, but wished someone wanted to cuddle me. Cedric slipped his hand into mine.

'Come and play with me?' he offered.

He spoke quietly but Cook heard.

'You can't take her upstairs, Master Cedric,' she said. 'Your ma might hear.'

'We'll tiptoe,' said Cedric.

'What about Clara? If she catches you, she's the sort to tell tales,' said Cook. 'She calls herself a lady's maid and she doesn't half give herself airs,' she told me.

'When I went up to the linen cupboard I spotted her

trying on the mistress's fancy gown and parading up and down in front of the mirror in her dressing room,' said Sarah-Jane, raising her eyebrows. 'I'm pretty sure she saw my reflection in the mirror. She won't dare get *me* into trouble!'

'There you are then,' said Cedric. 'Come on, Tess.'

He took me up the back stairs right to the second floor. I was astonished that a house could have two staircases. This servants' staircase seemed grand enough to me, so heaven knows what the main stairs were like. Our own staircase at home was falling to bits, and you had to jump over several steps because the wood was so rotten your foot would go right through.

Cedric led me through the green baize door and out into the corridor. There was proper carpet here, and paintings hanging on the wall.

'Oh, there's Gentle Jesus!' I said. They had the same picture at the Ragged School, of a man in a white nightgown holding a lamp up and opening a door. 'We sing about him at school.'

'You go to school?' Cedric said, sounding impressed. 'I'm not going until next year. I'm not sure I want to. You have to live there all term and I shall miss Mama and Papa very much.'

'So how come you can read already?' I asked.

'I had a nursery governess, Miss Tippet. But Mama taught me to read before, when I was very little. And at the weekends Papa and I do lessons – arithmetic and geography and history. They're great fun. When I get the answers right, Papa throws me a little sweet and I catch it in my mouth like the seals at the zoological gardens.'

I knew about arithmetic because Connor had taught me how to calculate pounds, shillings and pence, but I didn't know what geography and history were, and I didn't even know what seals were, but I realized that Cedric's papa was very different from my own pa.

I looked up at Gentle Jesus because Miss Moaning at the Ragged School told me to trust in him, but I didn't really see how he could help.

'Are you praying?' Cedric whispered.

'Not really,' I said.

'Then come and see my nursery,' said Cedric.

I'd thought a nursery was just for babies and expected a cradle and a perambulator – but this was an amazing, huge room for a little boy. It had white walls and blue rugs and curtains with blue rabbits, all startlingly bright and clean.

There was a rocking horse in one corner with a long mane and tail, a fort with many soldiers, several spinning tops, a toy train with its own track, and a white bookcase full of storybooks.

I stood still, hands clasped in wonder. I knew Cedric was a rich little boy and I'd expected him to have a lovely room – but not as splendid as this. He even had a large bed with a bright blue eiderdown all to himself, if you didn't count the fluffy white toy rabbit lounging on his pillow.

'Do you like my room?' Cedric asked.

I liked it so much I could barely speak. I simply nodded. I wanted to wander round the room having a good look at everything, but I was suddenly conscious of my dirty old boots. Perhaps there was mud on the soles? It would show terribly on the beautiful blue rugs.

I sat down and started undoing my shoelaces, though I knew my feet were probably pretty grimy too. Maggie made us have a quick wash in the water left over from her clothes scrubbing, but it was greasy and cold by then, and I generally jumped in and out in seconds.

Cedric stared at my feet when I exposed them, and I went hot with shame – but he was just looking at my blisters.

'They look so sore,' he said. 'I don't think your boots fit you properly.'

That was pretty blooming obvious, but I knew he meant it kindly.

'I haven't got any others,' I said. 'But I like these boots anyway, because they were my brother Connor's. I expect I'll grow into them soon.'

Cedric looked at them gravely. 'But they already look very old.' He ran to a big cupboard and opened it wide. There were lots of little boy outfits: sailor suits and tweed suits and velvet suits and a cream silk suit, hanging neatly in a row. Underneath were all manner of shoes neatly arranged two by two: shiny buckle shoes and leather brogues and kid boots and soft embroidered slippers.

He bent down and took hold of the leather boots.

'See if these ones fit you,' he said.

I stroked the soft bronze kid. 'They're beautiful,' I said. I imagined how daintily I could dance in those beautiful shoes. They were fit for a princess – and I could see they were probably about my size. I wanted those boots almost as much as I wanted Ma to come alive again – but I knew it was an impossible wish.

'You wouldn't be allowed to give them to me, Cedric. And they'd get filthy dirty in days in our mucky streets and likely fall apart the first time I got them wet in the rain. But thank you very much,' I said.

Cedric's face fell, but he could see I was talking sense.

'Then at least borrow *Robinson Crusoe*,' he said, running to his bookcase. He pulled out a big fat book and thrust it at me. I opened it up and squinted at the tiny print. It seemed to dance up and down, mocking me.

'It *is* quite hard to read,' Cedric said, understanding. 'Papa had to read it to me actually.'

'Perhaps I'll just look at the pictures for now,' I said, flipping through the pages. Robinson Crusoe seemed to have a very busy time on his island, making all kinds of things for himself. I hoped he'd have some children, or at least a wife, but he seemed stuck there by himself.

'Doesn't he get lonely?' I asked.

'Yes, but he finds a friend later on – and when Papa and Mama took me to the pantomime last Christmas, he had lots and lots of friends, parrots and bluebirds and seashells and sand fairies, and there were even little furry rabbits too and they all did funny bunny hops!' Cedric said excitedly.

'Really?' I said, thumbing through the book again to see these wonders. I couldn't see them anywhere. 'Are you sure?'

'Oh, they're not in the book,' said Cedric. 'I saw them at the Robinson Crusoe pantomime at Christmas. They were so funny – and there was a wild donkey and he kicked his legs about in such a droll way and then he lifted his tail and it was so *rude*! I shrieked with laughter and Mama got cross, but Papa laughed just as loudly as I did.'

I struggled to understand. 'A real donkey? And rabbits?'

'No, I think the donkey was two men in a donkey suit – and the rabbits were little children. Dancing. You know,' said Cedric.

I didn't know – but I was determined to find out!

'You saw them? Like people clowning in the street?'

'Well, it wasn't in the street – it was at the grand theatre, where they put on the plays,' said Cedric.

'And children dance there? As little as me?' I asked. 'Could *I* dance there?'

'I expect so,' said Cedric, a little uncertainly. 'You're a very good dancer, Tess.'

'I expect I could do a bunny-hop dance,' I said. 'Like this?' I squatted down, put my head on one side like a coy baby rabbit, and sprang up and down.

'Yes, just like that!' said Cedric, clapping his hands.

'Do you think I could perhaps try your kid boots on?' I asked. 'Just to see if they make me dance better?'

'Of course you can,' said Cedric. He handed them to me eagerly. I gave my dusty feet a quick wipe with the drooping hem of my frock and then tried on the boots. They fitted perfectly. Oh, the comfort, the softness, the support!

I tried my bunny-hop dance again and it was so much easier this time. I had extra bounce and managed to spin round and do little twiddles here and there, while twitching my nose bunny-style. Cedric laughed delightedly.

'My boots make you dance brilliantly!' he said.

'Do you think I could possibly borrow them after all? I wouldn't wear them in the street, I'd keep them clean as clean, but I could maybe find this Grand Theatre and dance like a bunny. I'd so love to do that!' I said.

'Then of course you may borrow them,' said Cedric.

'You won't get into trouble?' I asked anxiously.

'Well, Nurse isn't here any more. Sarah-Jane probably doesn't even know I've got kid boots,' said Cedric. 'I don't often wear them anyway, just when I have to go to a party. I don't like parties much – do you?'

'What happens at parties?' I asked.

'You have to make friends with lots of strange children and play games like hunt the thimble and squeak, piggy, squeak, and then you eat a big tea of blancmange and jelly and custard and that rich fruit cake that gives you tummy ache,' said Cedric, sighing.

I stared at him. He was such a peculiar little boy. I had sharp eyes and had often found Ma's thimble for her when she'd dropped it, and I was sure I'd be good at squeaking like a pig. The party tea sounded marvellous and the rare times I'd had cake it had never given me a tummy ache. But I wasn't going to scoff at him, especially as he was so generously lending me his beautiful boots.

I was still worried that Cook and even Sarah-Jane would be horrified if they saw them tucked under my arm, but Cedric solved the problem. When we came downstairs again he beckoned me to the back door where I'd left the baby carriage. He tucked the boots underneath Ada's blanket so that they didn't show. Ada would probably have an uncomfortable ride home, but she'd be so happy to be properly fed that I hoped she wouldn't mind too much.

She was fast asleep in her fluffy towel and they let me keep

it for her. Tommy was fast asleep too, still in Cook's big arms. He woke up, looked around, and smiled.

'I thought I dreaming but I not!' he said. 'This is lovely. And can I – *may I* – have another jam tart, Cook?'

'You've had more than enough, Mr Cheeky Face,' said Cook – but she gave him one even so, and I got one too.

'Now you'd better be off so I can get on with making the lunch, kiddies,' she said. 'Perhaps you'd better walk them home, Sarah-Jane, so they won't get lost.'

'No, I promise we'll find our own way,' I said quickly, because I didn't want her to spot the boots. 'But thank you very much indeed for being so kind.' I even bobbed a curtsy, the way Ma had taught me.

It made them both laugh, and Cook said we could come again another time, as long as we behaved ourselves. We were determined to behave like little angels, even Tommy. Then we hurried home, and Ada slept on soundly on her bed of borrowed boots.

Chapter Six

I was desperate to tell Maggie and Connor about our adventure but Maggie was out job-hunting and Connor was at the market. The house seemed very empty and small and dull. And dirty too. I knew Maggie had done her best since Ma got poorly but now I noticed the grime everywhere, the filthy windows, the dust on every surface, the cracked, unwashed dishes.

I hadn't realized houses could be as sparkling clean as Cedric's and contain such splendid furniture and ornaments, beautifully arranged. I looked around our few rooms and thought how Ma would mind the muck.

Ada was still sleeping peacefully, so I popped her in her

drawer. Tommy was unusually docile. Maybe three jam tarts had helped sweeten him.

'Shall we make the house clean and tidy to give Maggie and Connor a lovely surprise when they come home?' I suggested. 'You could be Mr Duster Man and make everything clean and shiny. And I'll be Mrs Scrub-and-Sweep and work magic.'

I tore up one of Pa's shirts to make four rags. I tied one on each of Tommy's feet and gave him another couple to hold.

'This is the Duster Man song, listen. *I'll dust and dust till I go bust!* Have you got it? And you walk about like this, watch. You have to be very careful,' I said, demonstrating. I rubbed our few knick-knacks clean of dust and then slid up and down the wooden floor.

'This a game?' Tommy asked.

'Yes, it's the best game ever. Go on, give it a try,' I said. 'I bet you can't do it.'

'Yes I can!' said Tommy, and he set to work, shuffling around. He very nearly tipped the clock over on the mantelpiece, Ma's pride and joy, and he dropped the glass flower vase and smashed it, but it was only an old medicine bottle so it didn't really matter. He was actually very good and thorough dusting the floor though, lumbering around the

living room and up the stairs and dusting the two bedrooms too, singing his dust song.

I scrubbed the greasy kitchen flags and used blacking on the stove the way Ma used to. Unfortunately the blacking stayed on my hands and I left fingermarks when I tried to fold the clean washing. I had to scrub my hands raw and then turn the sheets inside out and refold them so the black splodges didn't show.

I tried rearranging the furniture in the living room but there was no way I could make it look more attractive. Pa's sofa was a particular eyesore because there were dark greasy spots wherever he'd laid his head. I tried plumping up the cushions but the whole sofa smelled of him, and it made me feel sick.

If he had been taken ill or died then surely someone would have found him and come to tell us. Everyone knew Big Eddie off the building site in our streets. So *had* he simply walked out on us altogether without even bothering to say goodbye? How could he abandon us? I kicked the leg of the sofa hard – and then backed away from it as if he was actually lying there.

I looked round the living room, hoping I might have made some difference to it, but it looked as grim and depressing as ever. I tried cutting out more pictures from some old newspapers

Ma had taken home from the gutters and stored as kindling. I wished I had some paints to make them more colourful. I was sure Cedric would have a paintbox but I couldn't very well rush round again and ask to borrow them. I knew perfectly well that Cook would think this was taking liberties.

I didn't have any hope of getting picture frames, and I didn't even have any glue. I daubed a few scrapings of dripping from the meat jar on the back of the illustrations and then tried to make them stick on the wall. The dripping smears showed through the newspaper, spoiling the pictures, and they didn't even stick properly. They slid slowly down the damp walls, leaving grease marks.

I sighed, tore them off and scrubbed at the marks. My hands were getting as red as Maggie's. Then I went to check on Ada and Tommy. She needed a napkin change and cried hopefully for more milk, but was reasonably soothed with some boiled water. I played pat-a-cake with her for a while until we both got bored and Ada fell asleep because she couldn't think of anything else to do.

Tommy was so quiet I thought he was napping too, but I found him in Ma and Pa's bedroom. He'd raided Ma's clothes cupboard like Maggie. He had her old worn coat wrapped

round his shoulders, the arms tied round his chest as if she was cuddling him. He was rocking to and fro, muttering under his breath.

I tiptoed away and retrieved Cedric's beautiful boots from the baby carriage downstairs. I put them on my feet, stretching out my toes luxuriously and admiring my flexed calves. Then I crouched and practised bunny hops, as lightly and gracefully as possible. I didn't lose my balance once. I didn't have a looking glass but I felt sure I was doing a perfect bunny dance. Oh, how Maggie would bite her tongue when I danced at this Grand Theatre!

Did they have dogs on desert islands? Maybe I could *actually* prance like a Pomeranian and be clapped for it! I did my best to invent a dog dance. I pretended to be standing on my hind legs, my arms up and my hands down, as if they were paws. Then I twirled around and made little woofing noises to try to make it clear I was a dog. Maybe I needed to go down on all fours, dancing with my arms as well as my legs. I could even add a comical touch and raise my leg as if I was making water!

I heard Tommy clumping down the stairs now and stood up hastily. He still had Ma's coat tied about him.

'You be careful with that coat! Don't you dare tear it,'

I said. 'Take it off now!'

Tommy shook his head.

'Take it *off*!' I repeated.

'Can't,' he said.

'Oh, Tommy, you were being so good for once,' I said.

'I can't, the knots are too hard,' he said, wriggling inside the tied arms.

'Oh, for goodness' sake!' I set about freeing him. A tear rolled down his cheek. 'There's no need to cry!'

'I want Ma!' Tommy said, knuckling his eyes with his freed hands.

'Oh, come here, Toms,' I said, and I tried giving him a cuddle but he pushed me away.

I understood. He didn't want me. He wanted Ma, or a big motherly woman like Cook, not a bony sister not much bigger than him.

'Don't be like that,' I said gently. 'Cheer up. Look, don't you think I've made the living room look nice?'

He peered round, wrinkling his nose. 'No!' he said.

'Well, you've certainly made a difference being Mr Duster Man,' I said valiantly. 'It'll be a lovely surprise for Connor and Maggie when they come home.'

'I want my dinner,' said Tommy.

'We've had ham and bread and jam tarts! You've had three! You can't possibly be hungry now,' I said, though I was feeling empty inside too. There wasn't anything at all to eat or drink in the larder.

'I know what!' I said. 'We'll go down the market and look out for Connor. And maybe we'll find a bruised apple or a squashed tomato on the pavement. Yes?'

Tommy shrugged.

'I'll get Ada,' I said.

'I not going in baby carriage no more!' said Tommy. 'It a squash.'

'That was just because these boots were underneath you,' I said, pointing my toes.

Tommy stared. 'Where you get them?'

'Cedric's house,' I said, trying out a little tap dance. I'd seen beggars dancing little jigs on boards and it seemed easy enough.

'You nicked them!' said Tommy, shocked.

'No, of course I didn't. I wouldn't steal anything off of them. They're lovely folk. Cedric just let me borrow them for a bit. Shall I tell you a wonderful secret? I'm going to a place

called the Grand Theatre and I'm going to be a dancer in a pantomime,' I said.

'Where that?' said Tommy.

'I don't know yet but I'll find out. You wait and see,' I said. 'Still, I'd better change into my old boots just now. I don't want to get these mucky in the street. Hang on a tick.'

I went upstairs and changed my boots, hiding the kid ones right under the bed. If Pa came back he might spot them otherwise, and take them to the pawnshop. He'd even taken Ma's gold wedding ring once, which made her weep. We never had enough money to get it back.

'There, all set!' I said, tapping my way down each stair. I forgot the rotten ones. The wood tipped and I very nearly went tumbling down, head over heels, which would have put an end to my dancing career before I'd even got started.

Tommy and I were out the front door and halfway down the street when he turned to me.

'Take Ada too?' he asked.

'Oh my Lord!' I went flying back home, horrified. What if Ada had choked to death in her drawer while I was marching off to the market! How could I have forgotten my baby sister? It was dreadful enough losing Tommy the other day, but he

was like a bad penny, he would always turn up. But Ada was too little to rescue herself. She could hardly climb out of her drawer and go toddling down the street after us. She could barely sit up by herself, let alone walk.

I ran back upstairs, leaping over the rotten step, and burst into our bedroom. Ada was awake and had kicked off her blanket, but she was just lying contently on her makeshift rag mattress, making soft cooing sounds like a little bird. She waved her toes at me.

'You darling!' I said, picking her up and holding her tiny warm body close to my chest. 'I'm the most dreadful sister in the world. I wouldn't blame you, my little lovely, if you hated me. But please don't, because I love you all the love in the world.'

Ada babbled back to me in her own language. It was heartbreaking to see what a difference a full stomach made. She usually wailed or lay listless, half awake, her eyelids fluttering open and closed.

I changed her napkin yet again – that was the only disadvantage of feeding her properly – and carried her downstairs, ultra watchful of the rotten steps. I'd left Tommy out in the street, and for a moment I couldn't see him and

started to panic over again, but then I saw he'd joined some children up the road who'd tied a rope to a lamppost and were taking turns to whirl round and round.

A boy about my age was telling Tommy he was too young to have a go, and the others were agreeing with him.

'Don't be daft, I bet he can whirl higher than any of you!' I said, running up, the baby carriage rattling. 'You let him have a go or we'll tell our big brother on you!'

Connor was always very gentle with us, but if we got picked on he was quick to lash out in our defence. He wasn't a tall burly lad, but compact and strong and determined, and most of the kids were wary of him.

They let Tommy have a go after that and he clutched the rope hard, kicked his legs, and whirled round like a little trooper. I had a go too, though they protested even more bitterly because I was small and a girl. But I was determined, and when they started calling me names I called them worse ones and pushed them out of the way and had my go, after telling Tommy to keep an eye on Ada.

I pushed upwards and then outwards, and I whirled round too. It was almost like flying. I fancied myself a fairy in this pantomime, whatever it was, and pointed my legs as daintily as

I could, my curls flying. The boys jeered, but I could tell they were impressed. Well, I hoped they were.

I collected Tommy and Ada and we set off for the market, our heads held high. It was right the other side of town, and I wasn't completely sure of the way. I vaguely remembered going there with Ma and Maggie, but for a while Ma had been too poorly to walk all that way, long before Ada was born. She'd been forced to shop from the local grocer's and bought potatoes and carrots from old ladies with their baskets along the main road into town.

I did remember a song Ma had sung on those marketing days: *To market, to market, to buy a fat pig. Home again, home again, jiggety jig!*

I sang it now for Tommy to make him laugh. He was a quick learner and sang it with me the second time.

'We buy a fat pig, Tess?' he said.

'Oh, I've already bought one,' I said, pinching his cheeks. 'He's not very fat, but I'll keep him in a cupboard and feed him jam tarts and he'll soon fatten up enough to make many a roast dinner.'

'Squeak, squeak, squeak,' said Tommy. One of the women up the street had tried rearing a pig in her backyard until the

folk next door started complaining about the stink. We'd crowded round to have a peek at the poor creature. It had squealed a lot, but perhaps Tommy had been too little to remember properly. He sounded more like a mouse than a piglet now.

We played daft games to get us on our way, but we were both tired out by the time we drew near the market. Tommy was whining to get in the baby carriage now, but Ada was asleep and I didn't want him to disturb her.

'It's not far now. Just down this street and I'm sure it's round the corner,' I said hopefully. 'Think of poor Connor, Tommy. He has to walk here every morning while we're still in bed. Have you ever heard him complain?'

'He's big,' said Tommy. 'And his boots don't flap.' He held up his foot to show me that the sole was waggling about like a tongue.

'Well, it's better than going barefoot,' I said. 'Connor had to go for weeks without any boots at all, when they were in the pawnshop.'

'Oh, Connor!' Tommy moaned. 'I bigger than him soon. Then *I* be big brother.'

'I daresay Ada will think you're the bee's knees,' I said.

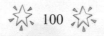

'Will she?' said Tommy hopefully.

'You bet,' I said. 'Come on, race you to the market!'

I started running, trundling Ada along in front of me. Tommy ran too, in spite of his flapping sole, and as we turned the corner I slowed down deliberately to let Tommy beat me.

There it was, right before us, the stalls spread out in the big square like a colourful village, bright with oranges and tomatoes and carrots and cabbages and peppers, all laid out in pretty patterns, and woe betide you if you took anything from the front and spoilt the display. There were bread and cakes to make your mouth water and a tea stall to warm you up and a hokey-pokey ice-cream cart to cool you down. The stalls behind the fruit and veg market sold great rolls of material and jewellery and watches and china and cutlery and pots and pans.

'I bet our Connor's stall is the best,' I said to Tommy.

Little kids ran everywhere, turning cartwheels for a ha'penny and holding horses and running errands – and also stealing an apple or an orange whenever they thought they could get away with it.

'Look, that boy nicked apple!' said Tommy. 'Shall we?'

'No, it's stealing and it's wrong,' I said piously. I wasn't sure we'd get away with it and I didn't want to bring disgrace on Connor. Plus I'd done enough bad things to go Down Under already, according to Miss Moaning.

I hurried Tommy past the fruit stalls because they looked so tempting. Then I saw an old man sitting cross-legged by a big cage of animals, all in together and seemingly good friends.

'Look! It's the Happy Family!' I cried. Connor had told me tales of these unlikely creatures kept together in one big cage. I squatted down and counted them: two cats, five brown rats, a terrier, three rabbits, three monkeys, three magpies and several pigeons (the birds flew about so much I couldn't be sure how many there were). I'd thought Connor was making it up, because any fool knew a terrier would go after the rats, the cats would pounce on the magpies, and goodness knows what the rabbits and monkeys would do to each other. But they were all lounging around serenely, nibbling and pecking at their food, not at each other.

There were little dishes of food beside the old man, neatly set out.

'Do you want to feed one of my animals, dearies?' he said. 'Penny a portion.'

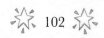

Tommy was eyeing some apple slices.

'Couldn't we eat them ourselves?' he asked.

The old man chuckled. 'If you want, little lad. But it's still penny a portion.'

'We haven't got any pennies,' I said sadly.

'Well, you can have a good look for free, little Goldie,' said the man.

I shivered. 'Do you know my pa?' I asked. 'That's what he always calls me.'

'And no wonder, because you're a pretty little Goldilocks,' said the old man.

I relaxed. 'What are your animals called?'

'They ain't got names as such, but together I calls them my Happy Family. Which one do you like best?' he asked.

'Oh, that funny monkey!' said Tommy. 'Look, he's *cuddling* the rats!'

'That's a lady monkey. I reckon she thinks they're her children,' said the old man.

'Why do they like each other so?' I asked.

'Because I trained them, see. Right from when they was little. It takes time, patience – sometimes it works, sometimes it doesn't. I've given up on birds of prey because unless you keep them fed all the time they look on anything in their cage as dinner. And I had a ferret once who was an angry little devil no matter what. I know gents who keep ratting ferrets down their trousers, but they'd have been screaming blue murder if they'd had charge of my one,' he said, chuckling.

'Can we see it?' Tommy begged.

'No, that one passed away and not before time. He cost me a lot of stock! It's hard enough to make a living out of showing animals. You sure neither of you have a penny in your pockets?'

'I wish we did – but we don't,' I said. 'But thank you very

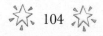

much for showing us your animals. If I ever get to be a famous dancer I'll come back to the market and feed every single one of your animals.'

'Thank you kindly, Goldie. I shall look forward to that,' he said.

I think he was teasing but I didn't really mind.

'Come on, Tommy, let's go and find Connor,' I said.

I manoeuvred the baby carriage in and out the little lanes between the stalls towards the china at the other end. When I turned round to check on Tommy he was busy stuffing half an apple into his mouth.

'Tommy!' I said, shocked.

He ate the rest in two hasty gulps. 'Yeah?' he said, trying to look innocent.

'You stole that apple!' I hissed.

'I was hungry,' said Tommy.

'After three jam tarts, you greedy little pig!' I said, outraged.

'Don't put me in oven and roast me,' he said. 'Where's our Connor then?'

'He works for this old man, Bert,' I said. 'I don't know which stall is his.'

I peered around. There was a huge crowd up at one end,

laughing and jostling and waving their arms in the air. Someone was shouting at them all. It was a very familiar voice. Connor was standing on three boxes, so that I could make out his head above the throng of people.

'Roll up, roll up, ladies and gents, girls and boys, and anyone else who defies polite description!' he shouted. 'Have I got a bargain for you! Who likes a nice cup of tea, eh? Yes, nothing beats it, don't it? So what makes the perfect cup of tea, can you tell me that? Yes, madam, you're so right. The best teapot! And here I have it! Bear with me, my darlings.' He paused, delved down into a great packing case, and brought out a teapot, waving it with a flourish, high above his head.

'That *our* Connor?' Tommy gasped.

'It is, it is! Oh, Tommy, listen to him!' I said, hardly able to believe my ears. Connor always had a quick wit and an easy charm but I'd never dreamed that he could keep a crowd transfixed.

'This isn't just any old teapot. What's it made of? Do you know?' Connor demanded.

'It's china!' someone ventured.

'Too right it's china! Cause it's made in China, where they really know about making tea. It's specially designed to make a

splendid pot of tea: all water, with the merest sprinkle of the magic leaves, to please the tea-totallers, ha ha! Seriously though, folks, this is the finest teapot you can buy. Pop along to Harrods and you'll see the very same teapot, or one extremely like it, for a gold sovereign. Yes, worth a golden coin, or twenty silver shillings, if my figuring is accurate. I could ask you for that twenty bob, and you could pay me, and it would still be a bargain, but I'm not going to ask for that. I daresay I'll end up in the debtors' prison, financially ruined, if I sell this teapot at a loss, but I want to do you a favour. So I'll ask seventeen shillings and six pretty pennies, and even then I'll be making a loss. Who wants to offer me seventeen and six? No? Well, I'll go the whole hog, fifteen bob? Say fourteen, thirteen . . . let's skip this, who wants this beautiful piece of pottery for ten tiny shillings? Nine, eight, seven, six – five bob, there must be a buyer now, because I'll take no less, I'll pack it straight up again.'

Connor barely drew breath throughout this long spiel, and the crowd loved him for it, hanging on his every word. When he stopped there was a sea of hands in the air, some already clasping the correct cash. Someone bought the teapot and waved it in the air triumphantly. I pushed through the crowd and saw old Mr Bert pocketing the cash in his

shoulder bag and giving Connor another teapot, identical.

'Well, blow me, here's another of these beauties. What did that last lucky lady pay? Was it ten bob?' A roar of protest came from the crowd. 'Ha ha, just seeing who's wide awake! Divide by half and what have we got? The bargain of the century, five shillings, who's having it?' Connor said smoothly. 'Sold to the gent in the fine tweed cap. I bet your missus will be thrilled. And if she's not, she can always keep it to hide her savings in if she decides to do a runner.'

'What's he say?' Tommy asked, tugging my arm. 'Why Connor talking so fast?'

'He's getting people to fork out a fortune for a teapot,' I said, dazed.

'He's got a rare patter, hasn't he?' said the woman next to me. 'And he's only a kid too! I've seen him round the market before, but never heard him perform like that. Old Bert must be raking it in.'

'He our brother,' Tommy said proudly.

'Never! Well, you must be proud of him, little 'un,' she replied.

'We are, we are,' I said, glowing. I couldn't get over it.

Tommy got bored after a while and went hunting in the

gutter for more fruit – I threatened to whack him one if he dared steal again. I picked Ada up so no one would trip over her in her carriage and listened for a full half hour as Connor sold four more teapots, and then a whole set of fancy china to a mother for a so-called bargain price of twelve and sixpence for her daughter's wedding present. This spurred several other women to want to buy likewise.

The crowd grew bigger as Connor's fame spread. People came to see this boy wonder with the artful patter, and Tommy and I started swaggering about, telling everybody that he was our brother. I wondered how old Bert might be feeling, and whether he'd resent Connor being such an astonishing success, but he seemed happy enough taking the money, his shoulder bag getting fatter by the minute.

When Connor's voice grew hoarse after all that shouting, he had to take a short break, telling everyone he'd be starting again in fifteen minutes. Some people drifted away, but most didn't budge, wanting to watch more of the show, whether they were tempted to buy any china or not.

I caught hold of Tommy, scared of losing him in the throng, and got him to haul the baby carriage while I held Ada safe in one arm. It was quite a useful way of forging a path in

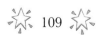

the crowd, because Tommy drove the carriage willy nilly over people's feet if they didn't get out of the way quick enough. Somebody yelled at him angrily and Connor looked up and saw the three of us.

He went bright red, hanging his head and looking terribly embarrassed.

'Oh cripes, were you listening?' he said huskily.

'Of course we were! Connor, you were splendid. How did you manage to keep saying that sort of stuff? It was so funny and it made people fork out so much money!' I said delightedly.

'You brilliant, Connor!' said Tommy, jumping up and down.

Even Ada managed to crow, as if she understood too.

'I think I was making a right fool of myself,' said Connor. 'I'd heard another man selling stuff like that and saw how it worked. I was awake half the night practising in my head, trying to get it to flow. Then this morning I asked Mr Bert if he'd give me a chance. He wasn't that keen at first, but I begged him to let me have just half an hour – and we'd made enough cash by then for him to let me carry on.'

'So will you get all that money?' I asked, wide-eyed.

'Don't be daft!' said Connor. 'But he's giving me a quarter of the profits.'

'That's not fair, when you're doing all the hard work,' I said. 'Can't he give you half?'

'That's not how it works, sis,' said Connor, shaking his head at me. 'But it's still a lot. We're going to have a little feast tonight!' He gave the top of Ada's fluffy head a little kiss. 'And you'll have the finest full-cream milk in your bottle for the next few feeds, little pet,' he added.

'But guess what, Connor – she's already *had* a bottle of milk, and Tommy and I have had ham off the bone, and white bread with butter, and jam tarts,' I said happily.

'I had *three*, yum, yum, yum!' said Tommy.

'So how did you have this fantastic feast?' Connor asked.

'Round at Cedric's!' Tommy said.

Connor tutted.

'And I'm going to do a dance at the Grand Theatre!' I said quickly. 'Once I've found out where it is.'

'Well, hurray for all of us,' said Connor. I could tell he wasn't taking my boast seriously, but I was determined to show him. 'And what about Maggie?' he continued. 'I wonder if she's had good luck too.'

Chapter Seven

'Maggie!' we shouted, as soon as we were in our front door.

There was no answer. The kitchen and living room were empty.

'Maybe she got a job and they let her start straight away,' said Connor.

'Wait till she hears about you being King of the Market!' I said proudly. 'She'll be so pleased. And maybe she'll be just a little bit pleased that I've tidied up the house and made it look nice. Well, sort of.'

Connor looked round. 'Yes – well done, Tess,' he said, sounding a little bewildered.

I suppose the house didn't look that different, apart from

the walls with the greasy stains where I'd tried to stick pictures.

'I've swept everywhere,' I said quickly.

'And I been Mr Dust Man, haven't I, Tess?' said Tommy, leaping about.

'Next you're going to tell me little Ada has polished the floor scooting around on her napkin!' said Connor. He stretched and yawned. 'I feel really done in now, yelling my head off all day.'

He walked over to Pa's sofa and sat down on it, leaning back and spreading his legs out. Tommy and I instinctively looked at the door, as if Pa might burst in any moment.

'I don't think Pa's ever coming back,' said Connor. 'So I'm the man of the house now.'

'Yes you are!' I said.

'Can I be man too?' Tommy asked, and leaped up on the sofa beside Connor.

'You're the big boy,' said Connor, tickling his tummy.

'And I'm the big girl,' I said, doing a happy dance over the clean floorboards, though my feet hurt, rubbed sore by the long walk to the market and back.

I went upstairs to check that no one had crept into the house and stolen the beautiful kid boots – and discovered

Maggie lying face down on the bed in her petticoat, crying.

'Oh, Maggie, what's the matter?' I said, running to her. I sat down on the bed beside her, patting her back. 'Don't sob like that, everything's all right. Our Connor's started doing this amazing patter at the market and he sold a great crate of china for old Bert. And I've done the housework – did you notice?'

Maggie went on crying.

'Please don't take on so. Has someone been horrid to you?'

She howled harder. I lay right down beside her, trying to see her face. 'What's happened, Mags? And where's Ma's frock? Don't say someone's stolen it right off your back!'

'Don't be silly,' Maggie sobbed. 'I've hung it back in the wardrobe. I'm not going to get it creased. It's *Ma's*.'

'And you look really lovely in it,' I said, trying to cheer her up.

'Not lovely enough. No one would give me a job!' Maggie wailed. 'One woman laughed at me and told me to run home to my mammy.'

'How rude!' I said indignantly. 'I thought you looked very grown up in Ma's frock.'

'And another said she wouldn't want a kid with such rough

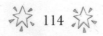

red hands touching her fine silks and snagging them.' Maggie wept, clenching her fists.

'Your hands are smooth as smooth,' I said, which was such a silly thing to say, though it stopped Maggie sobbing for a moment to snort at me.

'They *are* rough – I know they are, but what can I do about it?' she said despairingly. 'I tried a milliner's too, because I can sew neatly. I mightn't have any hats myself but I love to look at ladies wearing them, and I know they take on young girls. When I knocked on the door and asked, the woman there said she might consider taking me on as an apprentice in a year or two.'

'Well, that's something at least,' I said.

'No it's not. Because it turns out she wants to be paid a fortune for it. You don't earn anything for the first two blooming years – so what's the point of that? We need money now! There's poor Ada literally starving to death for want of a bottle of milk and there's nothing in the house for our supper.'

'No, no, it's all right, Maggie. Ada had a full bottle of milk at Cedric's house, and the cook there gave Tommy and me ham and jam tarts. Our Tommy was dreadful, begging for more, and—'

'You went begging? Oh, how could you, Tess! Don't you have any pride? What will they think?' Maggie interrupted.

'We weren't begging! Cedric and his maid *invited* us, truly, cross my heart, *and* they said we could come back. But anyway, we've got food for supper too, as Connor spent some of the money old Bert gave him and we went to this general food store and bought a whole basket full of stuff, and a quart of milk for Ada, and some porridge oats too, to help fill her up. So it doesn't matter if you can't find work, Maggie. Connor can provide for us now,' I declared.

I hoped this would comfort her, but she started a fresh burst of sobbing.

'I'm the oldest. I should be providing, not having to rely on my younger brother!' she wept.

'Well, you could carry on with taking in washing?' I suggested timidly.

'I'm not even any good at that! I went to start the ironing and somehow I've got black marks over the sheets and I'll have to wash them over again, and I'm not sure they'll come clean, and then none of the customers will pay me!' Maggie wailed. 'I'm useless at everything!'

My heart thumped. I knew I should own up. It wasn't fair

to let poor Maggie berate herself like this. Yet she'd be so furious. Perhaps it might be better to wait till she'd calmed down a little.

To my great relief Connor came bounding up the stairs.

'I couldn't work out who you were talking to, Tess. It's you, Maggie, home already! How did you get on?' he asked, though I shook my head and put a finger to my lips to try to warn him.

'I couldn't get any job at all,' said Maggie dully.

'That must have been horrible for you,' said Connor. 'Still, you don't have to worry, sis. I know it sounds mad, but I got old Bert to give me a go at getting more customers and it worked a treat.' He started to tell her about it, coming out with some of his patter. I'd heard the jokes already, but they still made me laugh.

Maggie stayed stony-faced. 'Good for you,' she murmured. She didn't sound as if she meant it.

'No, Maggie – I'm not showing off, honestly. I'm saying you don't need to worry about getting a job. I can provide for us now,' Connor said.

'And I'm going to be a dancer at the Grand Theatre,' I said. 'Do you want to see my bunny dance?'

'Oh, for pity's sake, stop that drivel about being a

dancer!' Maggie screamed. 'Who would ever want to watch
you bouncing about being a blooming bunny? You wait till you
try to get a proper job, Tess. You're even more useless than me!
Please, go away, both of you, and leave me alone.'

I flounced off, horribly wounded. I'd tried to be so sweet
and sympathetic – how could Maggie be so cruel? I was jolly
well glad I hadn't confessed to dirtying the sheets.

'Don't take it to heart, Tess,' said Connor when we were
downstairs. 'She didn't mean it. She's very upset, that's all.'

'Well, why does she have to turn on me? She always does,'
I said.

'Perhaps she's a bit jealous of you,' said Connor, unpacking
our big bag of shopping. The big poke of sugar had already
been untwisted and Tommy had white sprinkles round his
face. 'You greedy boy, Tom!' said Connor, but he just gently
pinched Tom's nose.

'*Jealous?*' I said. 'Because I can dance?'

'Maybe because you're little and cute and you've got
golden curls and can get away with murder,' said Connor,
giving my nose a pinch too. 'Come on, you two, give us a hand.
Bacon and egg and fried tomatoes and then a slab of lardy
cake – how does that sound?'

'It sounds marvellous,' I said, immensely cheered. 'But you do think I'm good at dancing too, don't you, Connor?'

'Yes, of course I do,' said Connor, getting the frying pan out of the cupboard. 'Shall we make porridge too and try giving Ada her first proper food?'

I picked Ada up and said in a baby voice, 'Yes please, Connor, yum, yum, yum,' as if she was saying it herself.

'Can I have porridge too, with lots of sugar?' said Tommy.

'We'll all have it. We'll eat until we're bursting!' said Connor, as the bacon started to sizzle in the pan.

'And tomorrow will you help me find the Grand Theatre?' I asked him.

'Find the what?' Connor asked.

'It's where the panto-thingy is! *Robinson Crusoe.* Cedric went to see it at the theatre and told me about it,' I said.

'I haven't got a clue what you're on about, Tess, but I'll do my best,' said Connor. 'Now lay the table like a good girl and see if you can make us a pot of tea.'

'In the teapot that definitely didn't even cost five bob!' I said.

'Cheeky girl!' said Connor, laughing.

He cooked our meal and I made the tea.

'Shall I call Maggie?' Tommy asked.

'Maybe you take hers up to her, Tess,' said Connor.

I pulled a face but did as I was told. Maggie was curled up now. She'd stopped crying but was sucking her thumb like a baby. I stopped being angry with her, set her meal down on the floor, and patted her shoulder.

'Love you, Maggie,' I mumbled, and then left her alone.

She didn't come back downstairs – but when we eventually went up to bed I saw her cup and plate were empty, so at least she didn't miss out on our feast.

Connor kissed us goodnight the way Ma used to. Pa never had kisses for anyone, not even me. I hung onto Connor, wrapping my arms round his neck.

'Will you take me to the Grand Theatre tomorrow?' I begged.

'I don't know where it is, Tess. And I have to go to the market to help Bert with the china crates and do some more selling. I can't let him down. We need the money,' said Connor.

'Yes, I know – but I *have* to go,' I said urgently. 'Please, Connor. *Please!*'

'I'll see if I can work out a way,' he said. 'Now go to sleep like a good girl.'

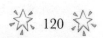

'Thank you, oh, thank you!' I said.

'I haven't said I'll take you,' said Connor.

But I knew he wouldn't let me down. I went to sleep and had dancing dreams all night long. I woke when it was still pitch dark. Someone was shaking me.

'What?' I mumbled, trying to wriggle away.

'Shh! It's me, Tess,' Connor whispered. 'Don't wake anyone else. Jump up and put your frock and boots on. We'll ask folk down the market and see how far it is. Maggie will have to look after Tommy and Ada. I know how much this means to you.'

I shot out of bed, wide awake now.

'I love you for ever, Connor!' I whispered, and then rushed to get ready. I was so quick and quiet no one else stirred, not even Ada in her drawer. Connor and I shared a slice of leftover lardy cake for our breakfast as we walked on our way. It was great to be outdoors unhampered by the baby carriage. I danced along in my broken boots, clutching Cedric's kid boots in the food paper bag.

'What's that you've got in there?' Connor asked.

I hesitated. 'It's something secret to help me dance better,' I said, sensing Connor might not approve.

He shook his head at me. 'You're a funny little kid, Tess,' he

said. 'Don't get your hopes up too high, will you? You're sure there really is a Grand Theatre? It's not just make-believe?'

'I'm certain,' I said with dignity.

We were so early hardly anyone had started setting up at the market, though old Bert was there already, feebly trying to lift one of the heavy crates.

'Here, Mr Bert, let me do it,' Connor said. 'Tell me, have you ever heard of the Grand Theatre?'

'I'm not a theatregoer myself, son. Apart from the Gaiety Music Hall with those saucy lasses. Is that the one you mean?' Old Bert gave him a horrible wink.

'No it's not,' said Connor shortly.

The woman setting out her cutlery on the next stall called over to us. 'I've been to a grand theatre,' she said. 'My hubbie took me to a show there on my birthday.'

'A panto-thing?' I asked.

'Dunno about that. It was just a lot of words and posturing. To tell the truth I fell asleep, but then I had been up since five at the market,' she said.

'So which street is it in?' Connor asked.

'It's not here, it's Kingtown,' she said. 'We took a cab there. We was really living it up.'

'Can we take a cab too, Connor?' I asked.

'We'll walk it,' said Connor. 'It's only a mile or so.'

'More like a couple,' said the woman. 'Still, you've got young legs.'

'And those legs are staying right here, standing on them boxes, so you can do your fancy patter again, sonny Jim,' said old Bert. 'Else you don't get paid.'

'I've got to take my sister there. She'd never find it on her own,' said Connor. 'I'll be back before the crowds start. We came specially early. Please, Mr Bert.'

'Who's going to help me set up? I can't haul those crates around,' old Bert grumbled.

'I'll do them for you now, quick as quick. Then I bet we'll be back again before you've got everything unpacked,' said Connor.

'Do you want this job or not?' said old Bert. 'I've given you this chance and now you're dictating to me when you'll start work. I've never heard the like! You're not going nowhere.'

I could see *I* wasn't going nowhere too! I was desperate. So I did what sometimes worked when Pa came home in a rage. I burst into tears. Not angry, noisy, snotty crying. Pathetic weeping, as if I was heartbroken.

I don't think it had any effect on hateful old Bert, but the knives and forks lady was genuinely moved.

'Oh, the poor little mite. Have a heart, Bert. Young Connor earned you a fortune yesterday. You can at least let him look after his sister,' she said.

'She's faking it, the little brat,' said old Bert.

I could have kicked him, but I managed to keep crying pathetically.

'Tell you what – you don't need to work for Bert no more, Connor,' said the woman. 'I'll gladly have you. You'll be shifting all the silver I've got in stock by noon! And if you don't want to work for a woman then there's any number of stallholders would want you pattering for them. You've got a gift for it, lad. Work for someone who appreciates you.'

'You leave off! He's my apprentice, like. We have a deal. Right, Connor, clear off, but be back in an hour or there'll be trouble,' Bert said, sniffing.

'Thank you, Mr Bert. Thank you so much,' said Connor, quickly hauling crates out of the lock-up shed at the back of the stall.

I made myself thank old Bert too – and I went to the knives and forks lady, reached up and kissed her on the cheek.

'Thank you!' I whispered.

'Bless you, dear. Tell me, why are you so keen to see the grand theatre? Do you want to go to a performance?'

'I want to *be* the performance!' I said. 'I'm a dancer.'

'Well, I can see that now. You're such a lovely, graceful little girl,' she said.

I kissed her again, thrilled that she should say such a special thing.

'Hey, Tess, calm down,' Connor said, opening up the last of the crates. 'There you are, Mr Bert. I won't let you down, I promise.'

He took my hand and we hurried off.

'Do you know the way to go, Connor?' I asked. I didn't think I'd ever been to Kingtown, though I'd vaguely heard of it.

'I've been there for another of the market fellows, fetching stuff from a warehouse. It's a huge place, mind you. But I'm sure we'll find it,' said Connor – though he didn't look sure.

We set off at a smart pace, so fast that I had to skip along to keep up with Connor.

'Am I going too fast for you, Tess? I forget your little legs aren't as strong as mine,' he said, slowing down a little.

'No, no, we need to go fast so that that cross old Bert man doesn't make a fuss if you're late back,' I said. 'In fact, let's run!'

'Mr Bert grumbles a lot, but he's actually quite a softie underneath,' said Connor. 'And he really needs my help now, so he's not going to get rid of me – I hope! Come on then, little 'un.'

We ran for ten or fifteen minutes when we got to the main road out of town, until I was utterly breathless, but I was determined not to hold us up. Connor himself started wheezing, so we walked for a while, and then alternated running and walking every five minutes or so. I was so happy to be having this special time with Connor, and thrilled that he was doing his best to make my wishes come true. When I wasn't chatting breathlessly to my brother, I was planning further moves for my bunny dance, even varying the way I held my head and twitched my nose.

'Why are you making funny faces at me?' Connor asked, grinning.

'I'm just being a bunny, that's all,' I said, managing a series of bunny hops to show him.

'I can do that too!' said Connor, showing me.

So we ran, we walked, we hopped all the way to Kingtown. When we were on the outskirts, we asked a labourer if he knew where the Grand Theatre was, but he shook his head and said he'd never heard of it. Then we asked a washerwoman collecting up sheets and pillowcases in her huge wicker basket. She was twice Maggie's height and size and it made me realize how much harder it must be for Maggie to scrub bedding for people. No wonder she was always so tired. I thought of those black marks on the last lot of sheets and felt guiltier than ever.

The washerwoman yawned, shook her head wearily, and said, 'Search me!'

I was beginning to lose heart. Maybe the knives and forks lady had been wrong and the Grand Theatre wasn't in Kingtown at all. Cedric seemed such a grown-up little boy, but maybe he'd got muddled.

Connor squeezed my hand. 'Don't worry. We'll find someone else to ask. Maybe they're the wrong sort of folk. Hey, we'll ask that gent over there!'

He ran after a tall gent in a top hat walking briskly and carrying a briefcase.

'Excuse me, sir, but would you happen to know where the Grand Theatre is?' Connor asked in his politest voice.

'I'm sorry, I don't think we have a Grand Theatre,' he said.

'Do you know any other towns where it might be, sir?' I asked desperately.

'I'm afraid I can't stop – I must catch the early train,' he said, walking on – but after a few paces he turned round.

'We do have a theatre here. It's the Mountbank. It's not especially grand, like the theatres in the West End, but they put on a very good show,' he said. 'Last year's pantomime was very jolly.'

Of course! Cedric had simply described the theatre as grand – and that was what the knives and forks lady had meant too.

'So where exactly is it, sir?' I begged.

He consulted his pocket watch and broke into a run, but pointed to the right. We called very grateful thank-yous after him and then set off down the road he'd indicated. I thought we'd probably have to ask again and again, but the road led us steadily into town and there, looming in the distance, was a very big red brick building with a fancy roof and big white steps leading up to gleaming golden doors. There was a large sign in elaborate writing. I couldn't quite get the hang of reading it, but it began with M.

'Is it the Mountbank Theatre?' I asked Connor.

'It is!' he said. 'Thank the Lord!'

'It *is* grand,' I breathed. 'Connor, do you think the doors are made out of real gold?'

'Maybe gilt,' said Connor. 'But don't they shine?'

A woman in a pinafore came out of one of the doors as we spoke, with a duster and a tin of Brasso in her hands. She started giving the doors a determined rub.

'Oh my!' I said, and leaped forward, up the white steps. 'Excuse me!'

She jumped and dropped her duster. 'You gave me such a fright, you silly little girl!' she said, clutching her chest. 'What are you up to, eh?'

'I'm sorry. I didn't mean to startle you. Is this the grand theatre where they have the pantomime?' I knew the proper name now!

'It is indeed,' she said, picking up her duster and starting rubbing the door handles.

'The Robinson Crusoe one with the bunny dance?' I asked, to make sure.

'The very one. I took my grandchildren to see it on opening night, seeing as I get free tickets for working here.

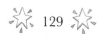

They had a whale of a time,' she said, shaking her head fondly.

'Did they like the bunny dance?' I asked.

'With the little kiddies hippety-hopping about the stage? They loved it!' she said.

'I'm going to be a bunny dancer!' I told her proudly.

'Are you, dear? Where's that?' she asked. She was nodding at Connor now, as if she was humouring me, which was worrying.

'I shall be dancing here. Every day if they like,' I said.

'Bless her,' she said to Connor. 'They're really sweet when they have an idea in their head,' she remarked.

'I think our Tess is serious,' said Connor awkwardly. 'And she really is a good dancer. I don't know where she gets it from. None of us can dance. Maybe Ma did, long ago.'

We both sniffed. 'Our mother died a little while ago,' Connor mumbled.

'So sorry, dears. Still, you've still got your pa, I hope,' she said, so concerned she stopped polishing.

'Well . . . he's not actually around,' said Connor.

'So how are you managing?' she asked.

'I'm selling china down the market,' Connor said. 'I actually made a killing yesterday. In fact, we have to get back

now, so I can start my patter. I fetched a good crowd yesterday, didn't I, Tess?'

I was fidgeting restlessly.

'But what about me? I have to be in the pantomime!' I said urgently.

'I don't think that's very likely, pet,' said the cleaning lady. 'Seeing as there ain't no pantomime on at the moment – it's too early in the season.'

'Yes there is! It's *Robinson Crusoe*. I know all about it. I've even read the book,' I said, exaggerating wildly so she'd take me seriously.

'I daresay you have, but you can't read what the current show is, even though it's right in front of you,' she said, tapping at a big poster in a glass cage beside the golden door.

I squinted at it. There were more curly letters that were difficult to decipher. I thought the first letter was an H. And then was the second an A. And the third an M.

'"Ham" and a squiggle,' I said. 'Is that "bread"? Or "roll"?'

'I think it's "Hamlet",' Connor murmured. 'He's a man in a famous play.'

'Is he one of Robinson Crusoe's friends?' I asked.

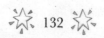

'The panto's been and gone. It was just for the Christmas season,' said the cleaner.

'Can't I do a bunny dance in *Hamlet* then?' I persisted.

The cleaning lady pressed her duster to her face as if she was trying to stop herself laughing.

'I don't think there's any dancing in *Hamlet*, especially not by fluffy bunnies. It's what they call a tragedy, dear.'

It felt like my own personal tragedy. I had genuine tears pricking my eyes this time.

'Come on, Tess,' Connor said gently, putting his arm round me.

I shook him off, so furious I was even cross with my dear brother.

'Ooh, little bit of a temper here!' said the cleaning lady, laughing openly now. 'But don't get too het up. They'll be casting for a brand-new pantomime next week. Not *Robinson Crusoe* again. It's *Cinderella!*'

'*Cinderella?*' I echoed. I didn't have a clue what that was about, but I wouldn't admit it. 'Is there dancing in that?'

'Oh yes. Lots. Especially at the beginning and the grand transformation scene at the end,' she said.

'Dancing for children?' Connor asked.

'Hordes of little kiddies fight to have a part.' She smiled at me properly. 'So come back on Saturday about this time. The auditions don't start till eleven, but there's always a queue.'

'I shall come,' I said. 'And I will get a part.'

'That's the spirit,' she said. 'Never give up.'

'That's our Tess,' said Connor – and he sighed.

Chapter Eight

It seemed an even longer walk home, but I didn't care. My head was full of dances I could show them. When I'd waved goodbye to Connor at the market I started practising. I went to the park and whirled round the duck pond and weaved my way between the trees. My old boots were rubbing my feet sore now, but I didn't want to risk changing into Cedric's kid boots. I needed to keep them pristine for the audition.

I wasn't quite sure what would happen there. Connor didn't have much idea either. He said it was probably like an interview and then I'd do a bit of dancing. He was more worried about getting me there on Saturday, anxious about upsetting old Bert. I told him I didn't need to go with him next

time. I was sure I could remember the way. Connor wasn't sure at all and kept worrying.

He was also fussed about whether it was respectable or not.

'I wish Ma was here to tell us,' he said. 'Or even Pa.'

'Pa wouldn't care. And don't let's talk about Ma,' I said quickly. 'It will make us sad and I want us to be happy, happy, happy. We don't need anyone else looking after us. You're King of the Market and I'm going to be Queen of the Theatre!'

'What about Maggie?' said Connor.

I didn't want to talk about Maggie either. I didn't want to go home to see her. I stayed in the park for hours, lolling about between dances. I very much hoped Cedric and Sarah-Jane might come along. I thought Cedric might know about *Cinderella*. Perhaps they'd invite me to their home again, and Cook might give me another splendid meal.

I thought about wandering along to their big white house and knocking on the back door. It seemed a little bit cheeky to go rushing round the very next day. It might be different if I had Ada and Tommy with me, because they were little and Ada certainly needed feeding up. I was small for my age, and skinny as a matchstick, but I wasn't sure that would count.

I hung about the park instead, not sure whether I dared

try. There were some posh children sailing boats on the pond while their nurses perched on the park bench, nattering to each other and knitting. I wandered over and watched the boats bobbing up and down. The ducks were quacking irritably, not liking their home being invaded.

'Watch you don't get pecked,' I said to one boy about Cedric's age.

'Go away, girl,' he said haughtily. He clearly didn't have Cedric's sweet personality.

'It's not your pond. *You* go away,' I retorted.

'Nurse says we're not allowed to talk to ragged children,' he said.

'I'm *not* ragged!' I said crossly.

The boy was looking pointedly at my boots.

'They're just my old boots,' I said quickly. 'These are my new ones, see?' I held out the paper bag containing Cedric's bronze beauties.

'Did you steal them?' he said.

'No I didn't, you hateful little toad,' I said. I felt like pushing him into the pond alongside his boat, but he was already opening his mouth to yell for his nurse so I scarpered hurriedly.

I trudged round the other side of the park where the flower

beds were, and the hokey-pokey ice cream cart. I looked at the man selling them, my mouth watering.

'If I did you a special dance, would you give me the smallest little serving of ice cream?' I asked.

He was hateful too, telling me to get lost in a very rude way.

I stomped about, clutching Cedric's boots as if they were my precious babies. Life would be so different if I'd been born in a big white house, and had my own room and toys and beautiful clothes and magical boots, and a pa who read me stories and took me to the Christmas pantomime. Still, then I wouldn't have had my own dear Ma, and Connor, and sweet little baby Ada. I could manage without Maggie. And it would be a joy to be rid of Tommy at times.

I wondered how they were managing without me. I knew Connor had expected me to go straight back home and help Maggie. I didn't quite want to. I wandered on and came across two girls about my age arguing about whose turn it was to push their doll's perambulator. It was so big and splendid our Ada could have comfortably fitted inside it. They were posh little girls in immaculate pinafores but they looked friendly enough.

'I like your pram,' I said.

They smiled at me in a friendly way. In fact the older one even offered me a turn at pushing it.

'I'd better not. Your nurse might not like it,' I said. She was strolling along behind them, but she looked plump and comfortable, not the fierce bat sort at all.

'Nurse says we must be nice to poor children,' said the younger one.

I wasn't really thrilled at that response, but I was a child and I was so poor I couldn't have an ice cream, so I couldn't really take offence.

'Have either of you heard of *Cinder . . . Cinderfella?*' I asked.

'*Cinderella!* That's our favourite fairy story,' said the older one, and the younger one waved her arm in the air and said, 'You *shall* go to the ball, Cinderella!'

'It's a story then?' I said delightedly. 'Can you tell me what happens?'

'It's about a poor girl and she's got mean sisters who order her about,' said the older one.

I was starting to love this story already!

'And her sisters get to go to this ball to meet a prince,' said the younger one.

'A ball? Like that sort of ball?' I said, pointing to some children throwing a little India rubber ball about.

'No, silly! It's a splendid dance and everyone wears beautiful long ball gowns, and Cinderella's fairy godmother works magic and gives her the prettiest ball gown of all,' said the older one, her face glowing.

'So there's a proper dance in the story!' I said, overjoyed.

This was so much better than *Robinson Crusoe* and the bunny dances. I could be a fairy in the pantomime and dance at the ball!

'Thank you so, so, so much!' I said, and I danced off. I was wearing my broken boots, but I put a kid boot on either hand too, and waved my arms around, doing a double celebratory dance all the way round the park.

I made my way home now, so thrilled I was even ready to face Maggie. I simply had to tell someone or burst! But to my surprise the house was empty. No Maggie, no Tommy, no Ada. I checked everywhere to make sure, and then sat down at the table, my heart thumping.

If Maggie had taken them to the park then surely I'd have bumped into them. She couldn't be delivering the clean washing because it was still piled in the basket, rumpled and stained with

black marks. A crazy thought was in my mind and I couldn't shake it away. What if Maggie was so miserable she'd run away like Pa? Would she have taken Tommy and Ada with her? Maybe she'd gone soon after Connor and I crept out. Maybe she'd left them behind and they were scared when they woke up to find us gone. Maybe Tommy had bundled Ada into the baby carriage and gone looking for Maggie. Perhaps they were lost now . . . Or had some wicked person stolen them away?

I smacked the top of my head, trying to stop thinking such wild thoughts. If someone had stolen Tommy then surely they'd pop him back within ten minutes because he was such a pest. But then I remembered Cook rocking him and feeding him more jam tarts. Was that where he'd gone? Would he remember the way? And could he push Ada that far by himself? I was pretty sure he could.

I hid the kid boots right under the bed again and then set out determinedly. My feet were hurting badly now, but I did my best to ignore them. I limped along as fast as I could, past the park and then along the streets of beautiful tall houses until I came to the white house. I ducked round the back quickly in case someone was looking out of the grand windows and I knocked on the trade door.

I waited, chewing at my lip and clasping my hands, praying to Gentle Jesus. Miss Moaning would have been impressed. I had to wait a very long time. Sarah-Jane came to the door at last, looking worried, her hair half hanging down from under her cap.

'Oh, it's you, Tess,' she said, not really sounding pleased to see me.

'Please, Sarah-Jane, I promise I'm not taking liberties, like Cook said, but I had to see if Tommy and Ada are here,' I said.

'What?' Sarah-Jane shook her head distractedly. 'No, no, dear – and I'd sooner they didn't come round anyway because we're at sixes and sevens at the moment. The mistress has been taken poorly and the doctor's come and it's all very worrying. Come back another time.'

'So they're really not with you? So where else can they be?' I begged her.

'I don't know, pet. Don't worry, you'll find them. That Tommy's likely just hiding from you. Now I must go to help the mistress,' she said, and closed the door in my face.

I didn't know what to do next. I'd convinced myself that they'd be here. I went back into the park and had a quick run round to see if they might somehow be there now, but there

was no sign of them. I walked past the grocery store to see if Maggie was doing more shopping, I went round the places where the women sent their dirty washing to Maggie, I went to the neighbours on either side of our house – but no one had seen my siblings.

I went indoors again and paced round the rooms, telling myself that Maggie might simply have cheered up and taken Tommy and Ada out somewhere for a surprise, but it seemed so unlikely I couldn't make myself believe it.

In the end I heated the copper boiler and plunged the dirty sheets into a pool of soapsuds. I took my frock off because my sleeves wouldn't stay rolled up, and set about the washing in nothing but my shift. I pummelled and scrubbed and rubbed frantically, my arms aching, but every spot of blacking needed individual attention, and even though I tried my very best the marks all remained stubbornly present.

I started crying in frustration, and eventually gave up, giving the sheets several laborious rinses. By the time I had hauled them out again, squeezed them as hard as I could and then fed them through the mangle, I was utterly exhausted. I managed to hoist them up onto the washing line, cursing them for staying stained after all that hard work, and then fell on Pa's sofa and lay flat out.

I was fast asleep in less than a minute.

I woke to the sound of the front door slamming. I was still so drowsy I leaped off the sofa, terrified that Pa had come back and would wallop me – but it was Connor.

'Hey, Tess,' he said. 'So glad you got home all right. I was so worried about you.'

'Oh, Connor!' I cried, and ran to him. 'Maggie didn't bring Tommy and Ada to the market to see you, did she, Connor?'

'What? No! Where is she then?' Connor asked, sniffing. 'She's been busy washing those sheets, bless her!'

'*I* did them. And it was a blooming waste of time because they're still dirty!' I said, stamping my foot in frustration. It made my boot press hard on my blister and I winced with pain.

'*You* did the sheets?' Connor said. 'Oh, you champion! I bet Maggie was pleased with you.'

'She isn't here! She hasn't been back all day – and Tommy and Ada must be with her. I've looked and looked everywhere, I even went to Cedric's house, but no one's seen her. Oh, Connor, what's *happened* to them? You don't think . . . you don't think it's something really bad?' I said, clutching him.

'Of course not,' Connor said firmly, but he looked worried

just the same. 'Perhaps they've gone visiting someone. Or –
or – well, I don't know. But there'll be some simple explanation.
They'll turn up any minute, you'll see.'

And at that exact moment the front door opened and in
came Maggie, pushing Ada in the baby carriage, while
Tommy sauntered in, eating a big pie.

'Oh, Maggie, where have you *been*?' I said. 'I thought you'd
run away!'

'Poor Tess has been so worried,' said Connor.

'Well, you two can talk. You went off together at the crack
of dawn and left us without even saying goodbye,' said Maggie.
She lifted Ada out and handed her to me, with a half-full bottle
that had been tucked in beside her. 'Here, give her a feed while
I get supper started. I suppose it didn't occur to you that you
could chop up some bacon and tomatoes and get them ready
for the pan?'

'Don't nag at Tess,' said Connor. 'Look, she's even washed
those dirty sheets for you and hung them up by herself.'

Maggie glanced at them. 'Well, she's wasted her time,
hasn't she, because they've still got those black marks all over
them! For goodness' *sake*. Didn't you try adding some baking
soda to the water and soaking them first?' Maggie moaned.

'How was I supposed to know that's what you do?' I said. 'Tommy, what's that you're eating?'

'It's mine. Because I was a good boy,' said Tommy smugly. He held it to his chest and dipped his head to take little bites, as if he was scared I'd snatch it from him.

'Have you been begging food?' Connor asked. 'You don't have to do that. I've earned really good money today.'

'Well, so have I!' said Maggie, tossing her hair back. Her cheeks were flushed and her eyes sparkling. She fumbled in her pocket and brought out a handful of silver.

'That's heaps of money!' I said.

'Yes – I bet it's more than you made, Connor,' said Maggie, looking triumphant.

'So what job have you got?' I asked, in awe.

'Never you mind,' said Maggie. 'But I'm wanted back tomorrow. And for weeks after that. So *I'll* be the number one breadwinner, won't I?'

She started cracking eggs into a jug and whisking hard, preparing to make a pancake.

'Who's taken you on then?' Connor asked. He looked Maggie up and down. She wasn't in Ma's frock; she was in her own tattered dress and her boots weren't in much

better condition than mine. She hadn't even brushed her hair properly.

'I told you, mind your own business,' said Maggie, putting a little butter in the pan.

'That's the good butter I bought us yesterday! Don't waste it for frying!' said Connor.

'Pancakes taste better with butter – and I can buy as much as I want now,' said Maggie, patting the shillings back in her pocket.

'We rich now,' said Tommy, still chomping on his pie. 'Maggie's being painted!'

I thought he meant someone was literally painting her all over, and stared. Connor was quicker off the mark.

'You're being painted by some artist?' he asked, looking horrified.

'Yes I am,' said Maggie, tossing her hair and smiling.

'Who would want to paint you, so dirty and tousled?' Connor said. 'What's he really after? Does he want to paint you without any clothes on? You're not going back there, do you hear me?'

'I hear you – and I don't give a stuff. You can't order me about – you're younger than me! And as if I'd agree to

taking my clothes off! How dare you insult me!' Maggie said furiously.

'I'm trying to protect you! Tell me where this filthy old artist geezer lives and I'll go and give him a piece of my mind!' said Connor.

'Oh, you will, will you?' said Maggie. 'Well, my artist isn't a geezer for a start. She's a lady.'

'What?' said Connor.

'She a lovely lady,' Tommy said. 'She gave me heaps to eat and then I played in her garden. I digged up earth with a spade and she laugh and say it giant moles!'

'What are you talking about?' said Connor, shaking his head. 'Artists aren't ladies.'

'Well, that's all you know, stupid. She's a famous artist. She showed us some portraits she'd done of children. And they all had clothes on – party frocks and sailor suits and the like – so there!' said Maggie.

'You haven't got a party frock,' I said. I wished *I* had one to dance in. It would make me look so much more fairy-like. 'Maggie, listen: I'm going to be in the new pantomime at the Mountbank Theatre!'

'What are you going to play – the back end of a horse?'

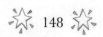

said Maggie. 'Stop making up silly stories, Tess – you're getting too old for that malarkey.'

'Well, you're making up stuff too, aren't you?' Connor asked. 'This lady is painting *you*? How come? Did she drag you in off the street or what?'

Maggie sighed theatrically. 'I took Tommy and Ada out because they were driving me mad at home. I was wondering about trying for a job over at the candle factory, but it smelled so bad there I couldn't face it. We stopped outside the baker's, peering in at the window at the buns and cakes and pies, and Tommy was nagging me to buy him a Bath bun, and I was arguing because we've got to save up for when the rent man comes, and he was saying I was mean and he was hungry, you know how he creates.'

'I scream!' said Tommy proudly.

'And this lady came out of the shop. She doesn't dress like a proper lady, she was wearing this ugly smock thing and her hair was tied up with a bootlace – but she spoke posh,' said Maggie.

'She asked if I hungry and I say starving!' Tommy said.

'After eating three jam tarts yesterday and a lovely supper too!' I pointed out sternly.

'She took us inside the shop and let Tommy and me choose whatever we wanted. I couldn't believe it. Ada started grizzling then, and I dared ask if we could have some milk for her, and Miss Rosa, that's her name, said we could come home with her and she'd make sure the baby could drink her fill,' said Maggie.

'So you went off with this complete stranger?' Connor asked. 'A weird-looking woman dressed like a scarecrow?'

'She nice. She give us buns,' said Tommy.

'It's the oldest trick in the book, luring children away with treats,' said Connor.

'I'm not a child,' said Maggie.

'Well, you've certainly acted like one! She could have been luring you away to start a wicked life of sin,' said Connor.

'What's that?' I asked with interest.

'Never you mind!' said Connor firmly.

'Well, if a wicked life entails sitting in a splendid studio, posing for a picture while eating sugar plums, then I certainly think that beats washing other people's dirty sheets,' said Maggie. She fried the bacon and tomatoes in a separate pan and then added them to the giant pancake. My mouth started watering. Even if Maggie divided it into four quarters it would still make a sizeable meal.

'So what sort of picture is it?' Connor asked, still very suspicious. 'Why didn't you tidy yourself up a bit for it?'

'Because she wanted me as ragged as could be. She even messed up my hair. And she wrapped Ada in some sort of rag rather than her fluffy new towel,' said Maggie. 'Don't stand there gawping at me, you two. Set the table and make the tea.'

'What on earth would Ma think of you, having your picture painted looking like a street urchin?' said Connor, which was a low blow.

'I think Ma would be proud of me for earning money for the family,' said Maggie. 'And it looks like it's going to be a lovely picture of me and Ada. She's calling it *The Little Mother.*'

'Ugh!' said Connor. 'I'm not listening to any more of this! You're not to go back there, do you hear me?' He stood up and slammed out the door.

For an awful moment Connor reminded me horribly of Pa.

'Do you think he's going to the ale house?' I asked Maggie anxiously.

'I don't know and I don't care. How dare he lecture me when I'm the eldest and I haven't done anything wrong! I don't care what he thinks anyway,' said Maggie, though I saw her hands were trembling as she flipped the pancake again.

'I eat his pancake?' Tommy asked eagerly.

'For pity's sake, you've only just finished eating that oyster pie Miss Rosa gave you! You must have hollow legs,' said Maggie, shaking her head at him.

I went to the door and looked out into the street, wanting to call Connor back, but there was no sign of him. Now someone else was missing. I couldn't seem to keep all my family together at once. I clenched my fingers over my thumbs and wished Connor to come back instantly, but it didn't work.

'Come and sit down and eat your pancake, Tess,' said Maggie, serving it up.

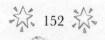

'I don't think I'm hungry any more,' I mumbled.

'I have yours?' Tommy asked.

'You sit and eat your own share, Master Greedy-Guts,' said Maggie.

I was relieved to see she left the largest share in the pan, taking it off the stove and covering it with a plate.

'There now. You eat up, Tess,' Maggie said, putting another quarter on my plate. 'Don't worry about Connor. He's annoyed because I've earned twice as much as he did. His pride's hurt.'

I hated it when she criticized Connor, but I couldn't help wondering if she was right. I ate my pancake slowly, tiny forkfuls at first, but then I gulped it down. Tommy was watching me, and stuck his bottom lip out when I ate every morsel.

'You greedy-guts, Tess,' he said.

'You button your lip,' said Maggie, swotting at him but deliberately missing. 'That's the ticket, Tess.' She patted my back and then exclaimed at the sharp wings of my shoulder blades. 'You really need feeding up – you're skinnier than any of us. Maybe it's all your prancing about!'

'I dance – I don't prance,' I said.

'All right, all right. Sorry.' Maggie put her head on one side. 'Did Connor really take you to a theatre this morning?'

'Yes, but it was closed up and the old pantomime isn't on any more. But I'm going to be in the new pantomime, *Cinderella*. I'm going to be a fairy,' I said.

'Don't you have to get picked specially? You can't go and get a part just like that,' said Maggie.

'Well, they'll pick me, won't they?' I said. 'I've watched heaps of girls round here dancing and they jiggle about and trip over their own feet. None of them dance like me.'

'Well, that's true enough,' said Maggie. 'We'll just have to wait and see then, won't we?'

Chapter Nine

Connor stayed out till eight o'clock, when Tommy and Ada were fast asleep. It was a huge relief to hear his footsteps outside the door, but my tummy clenched in case he came reeling in like Pa, in a foul mood and stinking of drink. But it was clear immediately that he hadn't had so much as a drop, though he looked exhausted.

Maggie served him up his share of the pancake, though it had dried up rather, but she fried the last two rashers for him, and gave him a chunk of bread too. She didn't say a word to him and he didn't say anything to her either, but they nodded at each other, and I could tell they were both sorry for their quarrel. When Maggie was rinsing the sheets

yet again after their soak in baking soda, Connor put his arm round me and I relaxed against him.

'I was scared when you went out, Connor,' I whispered.

'I'm sorry. I won't ever do that to you again, little Tess,' he said, giving me his crust to chew.

'Where did you go?' I wondered.

'I walked round and round, trying to calm myself down – which was daft of me, because I'm so tired I'm ready to drop. I don't know what to do. Maybe this lady artist means well and I was getting steamed up over nothing,' said Connor.

'I could go with Maggie tomorrow, if she'll let me. Then I'll be able to tell you about her,' I said. I paused. 'So long as you say I can go to the theatre early on Saturday.'

'You artful baggage,' said Connor. 'I don't know about this pantomime lark either. I'm not sure it's suitable for you to take part. I don't think Ma would have approved.'

'Ma always said I was a good little dancer,' I insisted.

'Well, yes, I suppose she did,' said Connor. He rubbed the frown lines above his nose. 'It's so difficult being the man of the house now. I can't work out what's right and what's wrong.'

'That's simple,' I said. 'Everything that I want is right, right, right.'

'You're a bad girl,' said Connor, though he hugged me tight. 'Heaven help your future husband. You'll run circles round him.'

'I don't want a husband!' I said, thinking of Pa. 'I'm going to be a famous dancer and then I won't need a husband to keep me. I'll keep myself. But maybe I'll have a little baby like Ada because she's so sweet.'

'You'll do no such thing!' said Connor. 'Come on, up to bed with you, you little baggage.'

I did as I was told. Before I went to sleep, I heard Connor and Maggie talking at last, and it sounded as if they'd made friends. I was fast asleep by the time they came upstairs too.

Connor left for the market before I woke up. Maggie wasn't in bed, but when I went downstairs I found her in the kitchen, the irons heated, labouring away at the sheets.

'Have the stains come out?' I asked.

'More or less,' said Maggie. 'I still don't know how they got there though.'

She was standing right next to the stove as she spoke. I struggled to keep my eyes staring straight back at her. Luckily the stove was splashed with pancake batter and bacon grease so it didn't look as if anyone had been near it with the blacking for weeks.

'Shall I make breakfast then?' I wanted to get into Maggie's good books so she'd take me to see this Miss Rosa. I rather hoped Miss Rosa would paint me too.

There wasn't much bread left in the crock. 'Never mind, we could have Ada's porridge,' I suggested.

'I'll do it,' said Maggie. 'You have to keep stirring it. *You'll* go into a daydream and forget, and nothing tastes worse than burnt porridge. Just set the table.'

'Well, I could iron the sheets,' I said. It looked more fun than washing them, and much less effort.

'You, iron sheets!' said Maggie. 'They'd be patterned with scorch marks in no time!'

'Look, I'm only trying to be *helpful*,' I said.

'You can be helpful by looking after Tommy and keeping him out of mischief,' said Maggie. 'I can't take him to Miss Rosa's again, Gawd knows what he'd get up to.'

'No fear! I'm not getting lumbered with him. I have to

practise my dancing,' I said. 'Anyway, I'm going to be coming to Miss Rosa's too. Connor said I had to.'

'Don't start! I'm the eldest. You'll do as I say. I'm not having you showing off to Miss Rosa like a performing monkey, thank you very much,' Maggie snapped.

I rather liked the idea of inventing a monkey dance. I always loved it when the barrel organ man came down our street, and begged for a chance to stroke the weird little creature. Perhaps there was a monkey in the Cinderella pantomime? I could be a fairy *and* a monkey. I would look cute in a furry suit with a little red cap on my head. I could be a mischief monkey, darting here and there, snatching someone else's cap and trying to wear it myself. It would come right down over my head and everyone would laugh because I looked so comical . . .

There was a sudden smash! One of our plates had slipped from my hand and was now shattered on the stone floor.

'There! What did I say about daydreaming?' Maggie said crossly.

'Connor will get us a new one from his market stall,' I said. 'That one was cracked already. *And* chipped.'

I squatted down and started gathering the bits up hastily and a sharp edge of china scratched my finger.

'Ow!' I said, straightening up. 'Look, Maggie, I'm bleeding!'

'Well, don't come anywhere near the sheets!' said Maggie. 'You're so useless, Tess!'

'No, I'm not. Ma always said I was her special girl,' I said.

'Ma always said I was her eldest and best born,' said Maggie, holding my finger under the tap.

'Oh, Ma!' we both said simultaneously, and we suddenly stopped bickering and hugged each other.

'I do miss her so,' said Maggie.

'Me too, me too, me too,' I agreed. I paused. 'Pa's gone too, but I don't really miss him. Do you?'

'It's bad to say it, but if we can manage moneywise I don't care if he never comes back,' said Maggie. 'It was all right for you, Tess, you were always his favourite. He'd give me a clout as soon as look at me. And no matter what I cooked for him he always moaned and said it was either burnt or underdone.'

'Well, I think you're a great cook,' I said loyally. 'That porridge is looking good. I think Ada's wailing upstairs now. Shall I change her and bring her down and feed her some?'

'That would be good of you. I didn't really mean it when I said you were useless. You can be really helpful at times,' said Maggie. 'I'm not a very good big sister to you, am I?'

'I'm glad you're my sister,' I said. It was as if we were suddenly tamed and could get on together like the creatures in the Happy Family cage.

I felt fond of little Ada too when I gently picked her up from her drawer, changed her napkin and found a clean baby frock for her. It was still too big for her because she was such a pale scrawny little thing, but she had pinkish cheeks now and looked a lot better.

I kissed her tiny toes and she gurgled happily.

'I'll always be a good big sister to you, Ada,' I promised her fondly.

I couldn't honestly say I felt the same about Tommy, who was wide awake now and bouncing on the bed fit to bust the springs.

'Get off of there!' I said, but my arms were full of Ada so it was impossible to catch him and stop him. 'If you break that bed we'll have nowhere to sleep, you silly boy!' I said.

'Yes we will. We can sleep in Ma and Pa's bed next door!' said Tommy.

'No we can't!' I said. I suppose it made sense, but I felt it was too soon. Ma hadn't died that long ago. It was a special place, to be treated with respect. And fear too! If Pa came

back and caught anyone sleeping in his bed, he'd be so angry. He could be such a scary father – and yet there were times when he'd take me on his knee and sing me a silly song and call me his "little sweetheart". Perhaps I did miss him too.

'Do you miss Ma and Pa, Tommy?' I asked him.

'No, no, no!' he said, bouncing even higher – but then he sat down abruptly. He banged his head on the bedpost and burst into tears.

'Oh, Tommy! Did you hurt yourself?' I asked.

'I want Ma kiss it better,' he said. He looked so little and pathetic that I felt a pang inside. Maybe I did love him dearly after all – though I still wasn't sure I *liked* him.

'Tell you what, Tommy. Ma's an angel in Heaven now, but you're her special boy. If you close your eyes tight and promise not to peep, I think she might fly down from Heaven just this instant and give you a quick kiss better. So sit up nicely, close your eyes, and see what happens,' I said.

Tommy did exactly as he was told. I held Ada tight, bobbed forward on tiptoe, kissed the top of his head, and leaped back.

'Ma!' Tommy whispered, and his whole face lit up. 'Can I open eyes to see Ma, Tess?'

'You can open your eyes but she's gone now, Tommy. She

only gets a split second to whizz here and back. But did you feel her kissing you?' I said.

'I did, I did! It was Ma, I felt her!' said Tommy.

'That's lovely,' I said. He really did have a red bump high up on his forehead but his tears were drying now.

'Ma kiss it better!' he said in awe.

I had a sudden artful thought. 'So if you're a very good boy today, Ma *might* come back and kiss you goodnight,' I said.

'I always good boy,' said Tommy. 'But I be even gooder!'

Why hadn't I ever thought of this trick before? Poor little Tommy. He was still so easy to fool.

'Let's go downstairs and tell Maggie you're going to be a good boy at Miss Rosa's,' I said. 'And I'll say I'll be a good girl and look after you while she's having her picture painted, is that a deal?'

We shook hands on it – but it was a waste of time.

'You're not coming, either of you. You'll muck around and make a mess, Tommy. And *you*'ll pick things up and break them and start pestering Miss Rosa to watch you dance,' said Maggie.

She was possibly right, but we both argued fiercely. It was no use. When Ada was fed and given a quick wipe, Maggie took her in her arms, scorning the baby carriage.

'Now, you two, try to keep out of trouble,' said Maggie.
'The sheets are up on the rack, airing. Take them down
carefully mid-morning, Tess, and get them folded up. Then
wrap them in brown paper and string, neatly mind, and deliver
them. Here's the list of house numbers and the bedding they've
sent. The sheets are much the same, so it don't really matter
who gets what. Take them round and make sure they pay you.
Put the money in your pocket, take it home, and hide it in the
old teapot with the spout missing. Every single penny, mind!
Bye then.'

She was off before we could protest. We played around for
a while. I tried to teach Tommy the bunny dance but he kept
tipping over when he attempted a bunny hop and added
another couple of bumps to his head. Ma had to make another
couple of quick trips from Heaven to make it better.

Then I worked hard on my fairy dance and tried to teach
Tommy that too, but he even managed to fall over in that,
tripping over his own feet. He was the most galumphing fairy
in the whole world, though I think he was really trying.

Then I washed my hands extra thoroughly, using the
carbolic soap that stung and left a horrid smell on my fingers,
to make sure I didn't leave any more prints on the sheets.

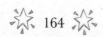

I folded them as neatly as I could and parcelled each up in brown paper. I was silly enough to let Tommy play with the string and he got it into knots, but at long last I managed to unravel them all and tie up every parcel.

It was the most exhausting, boring, fiddly work, but it was done! I'd show Maggie I wasn't useless. I'd done as good a job as she did. Well, I hoped I had.

I piled the parcels up in the baby carriage and then Tommy and I started the boring trek around the houses, delivering the sheets. A few folk weren't at home, which was a great nuisance. I couldn't simply open their doors and leave them in the kitchen because then I wouldn't get any money. These ones had to be trundled home again.

There were often problems even when the women were at home. Several argued that the sheets were two days late and so they weren't paying. Others came out with all kinds of reasons why they couldn't pay me this time but swore they'd pay the next. A few well-off women in the nicer streets had more than one lot of bedding and wanted me to collect their dirty sheets at the same time, which mixed things up a bit.

Even so, by the time we'd finished our round my pocket was jingling, full to the brim.

'We earned heaps!' said Tommy, sticking his hand in my pocket, about to help himself to a handful.

'No you don't! Get out of there!' I said, giving him a shove.

'Not taking all! Just little bit. You have some. We eat little pies?' he suggested, licking his lips.

'No, we mustn't! There's some leftover bits at home. Maggie says we've got to give her every penny so she can pay the rent man,' I said sternly – though my mouth was watering too.

It was long past dinner time and there was pitifully little at home now. Some people had refused to pay. Maggie couldn't possibly know we were fibbing if we added another couple to the list of non-payers.

But I would know. And probably Gentle Jesus. I wished I'd never gone to the Ragged School. Miss Moaning had had a horrible impact on me.

'We're not spending a single penny,' I said virtuously.

'Meanie!' said Tommy, looking as if he might be ready to start stamping and yelling.

'Careful now. Remember Ma could be looking down on us,' I said.

He looked up at the clouds above as if he could see Ma peering down at him. He decided to change tack.

'We go Cedric's house for jam tarts?' he suggested, brightening.

'We can't go there. Not now. Cedric's mother's ill and Sarah-Jane sent me away yesterday,' I said.

'Not Sarah-Jane, we see Cook!' Tommy protested.

'Well, I want to see Cedric, very much as a matter of fact,' I said, thinking wistfully of his crammed bookcase where there might be a copy of *Cinderella*. 'But we're not going there, and that's that.'

'We go park then? Cedric there?' Tommy asked.

It would be wonderful if we could bump into Cedric and Sarah-Jane by accident. We scurried home with the baby carriage and the new lot of dirty washing because it was too cumbersome to drag round the park, and then we set out again immediately.

'No baby carriage,' Tommy said firmly. 'I big boy.'

'Yes, you are. You only have to go in it when Ada's here too. You have to hang onto her so she doesn't fall out. That's what big brothers do,' I said.

Tommy nodded solemnly. I was so pleased with myself. I'd somehow learned how to handle him. Maybe Ma was looking over me too. I don't know why this Miss Rosa lady wanted to

call Maggie's portrait *The Little Mother*. *I* seemed to be acting like a little mother now.

It was a disappointment when yet again there was no sign of Cedric in the park, though I saw the same girls I'd spoken to about Cinderella. I wanted to find out more, but when I approached, one looked nervously over her shoulder and I saw her nurse shaking her head this time.

I flushed and changed direction rapidly, grabbing Tommy's hand. *Just wait till I'm a famous dancer*, I told myself. *Then families like that will flock to come and see me. They will talk about me with awe.* It was a very soothing thought.

I was still hot and bothered though, so weakened in my resolve about the rent money. I treated Tommy and me to a penny hokey-pokey ice cream each, and we enjoyed them enormously.

The afternoon still seemed very long. Tommy went upstairs to bounce on the bed again. I knew he was doing it but I couldn't summon the energy to go up and stop him. After a while the thudding stopped, and when I dragged myself up the stairs to make sure he hadn't banged his head so hard he'd knocked himself out, I found him sprawled on the bed, sucking his thumb, nodding off to sleep. I lay down

with him – and we were still there when Maggie came back with Ada.

She'd bought lamb's liver and more bacon and milk and a loaf *and* penny buns with today's earnings and still had plenty of change.

'I can't believe it!' she said. 'Who knew I could ever earn so much simply by sitting still! Miss Rosa says I'm a marvellous little model. She's been commissioned to illustrate a children's book and she says she wants me to pose for that too. And she's going to introduce me to some of her artist friends and thinks *they*'ll want to paint me too. She says I have a haunting face.'

'What "haunting" mean?' Tommy asked sleepily.

'Like a ghost!' I said, but I didn't really want to tease Maggie. I was happy for her.

She was pleased with me too. I told her that several people wouldn't pay for their washing and she just shrugged.

'Never mind. I don't need to wash their dirty old sheets any more. I'll do those ones you collected today and then we'll tell them to go hang. We're practically rich! If we can find someone to mind Tommy, you can go back to school, Tess,' she said.

'Not blooming likely!' I said. 'I'd sooner wash a hundred

sheets myself than go back to Miss Moaning! I'm going to be
a fairy in a pantomime, you wait and see!'

Connor came home from the market with more money
in his pocket. Apparently he'd been even more of a success,
and even old Bert had a grin on his face by the end of the day.

'He was in such a good mood I told him I wanted to take
the morning off on Saturday but he isn't happy about it at all,'
said Connor later, when we three older ones were lounging in
the living room in the dim evening light. 'I'm so sorry to let you
down, Tess, but I don't see how I can take you.'

'You won't need the whole morning off! If we get up really,
really early, you'll be able to start at the market the usual time,'
I said.

'But I'll have to wait with you while this audition takes
place. We don't know how long that's going to be. There might
be lots of kiddies taking part,' said Connor. 'I was wondering,
Maggie, could you tell your Miss Rosa that you can only sit for
her in the afternoon on Saturday?'

'I can't take Tess! I'm not messing Miss Rosa about. I bet
I've earned more than you today. My job's more important
than yours!' said Maggie. 'We've got to stop pandering to
Tess about this dancing nonsense. It's just make-believe. As

if she could ever be a dancer in a million years, a kid from round here!'

'How dare you say that!' I shouted, hating her all over again. 'Who would have thought *you* would have your picture painted, when Pa always said it was a pity you were the plain one when you were the eldest?'

There was a shocked silence. Even Connor looked horrified. It was true, Pa *had* said it, right to Maggie's face – but I knew it was terrible of me to repeat it. I was so hurt that they weren't taking me seriously. I *knew* I was a good dancer. I simply had to go to the audition on Saturday. I didn't need Maggie to take me. I didn't even need Connor. I could go by myself. I would show them!

There was a terrible argument, but I didn't let it get me down. I looked after Tommy and waited. On Friday night, Connor and Maggie tried to talk to me. Maggie was mean to me and Connor was gentle but adamant that he couldn't take me to Kingtown and the Mountbank Theatre.

'I shall go by myself,' I declared.

'But you're much too little to find the way there and all the way back,' said Connor.

'Wait and see,' I said fiercely. 'But I can't drag Tommy

along with me. One of you will have to take care of him or he'll have to stay at home by himself. Because for once I'm putting myself first. So there!'

They stared at me, astonished.

'For goodness' sake, Tess, stop acting like that,' said Connor. 'Can't you see reason? I can't lose my job! Not now, when it's going so well.'

'And I can't let Miss Rosa down, you nasty little minx,' said Maggie, still smarting after I'd insulted her.

'Well, I can't let *me* down!' I said. 'And I'm going!'

I felt that Ma might be looking down on me, shaking her head sorrowfully, but I couldn't help it. I had to show them. I think they still thought I wouldn't go through with it.

I didn't sleep properly that night, and when I heard the distant church clock chime six I slipped out of bed, fished for Cedric's boots underneath it, grabbed my clothes and scampered downstairs. I took two minutes dashing out to the privy, another two washing my face and brushing my hair, and one more minute dressing in Ma's frock.

It trailed on the ground, but it was pretty and clean, and I hoped I didn't look too much like a clown in it. I could always hold up my skirts daintily. Then I stuffed a slice of bread in my mouth, drank from the tap, and set off while Maggie and Connor and Tommy and Ada still slept.

I danced down the road triumphantly. I had done it! I was going to get a part in the *Cinderella* pantomime or bust!

Chapter Ten

I set out confidently enough, but I wavered when I got to the edge of town, not quite sure which direction to take for Kingtown. I hoped it was simply straight on. And then on and on and on. My old boots had started rubbing by now but I didn't like to change into the beautiful kid boots. The soles were so soft. I was scared they'd be worn threadbare by the time I got to the theatre.

Every now and then I stopped a fellow traveller on the road and asked if I was going the right way. Sometimes they shrugged. Sometimes they nodded. A couple of silly lads insisted I was going in the wrong direction entirely and I should turn round – but they were smirking and nudging

each other and I knew they were simply having a lark.

It was starting to be a very tedious journey, with no shops or houses to look at, and no dear Connor to chat to. Once I heard running footsteps behind me and I whipped round hopefully, wondering if it could be Connor himself, desperate to catch up and say sorry. Perhaps he'd felt so bad when he woke and found me missing that he'd decided to let old Bert go hang and follow me. Only it wasn't Connor at all, it was some man dashing along in an ill-fitting suit, his battered bowler hat askew.

'You gave me a fright!' I said, as he barged past.

'So sorry, petal! I overslept and I'm late for my new job,' he gasped, and carried on, his arms pumping with effort.

In two minutes he was out of sight. Silly man! But I liked it that he'd called me "Petal". I started doing a petal dance, pretending to fall this way and that, but I tripped on Ma's frock and tore the hem. It was only a little rip but I was mortified. I resolved to sew it up as carefully as I could the moment I got home.

I started to worry whether I would trip again when I was doing my dance at the theatre. Ma's frock was much, much too big for me. Perhaps I'd have been better off wearing my own

frock. But it was too small, and patched and shabby too – a sad old rag. I could never look a proper fairy in *that* dress.

I marched on, and at long last I was on the edge of the town. I'd made it! I couldn't quite remember which street to turn into for the theatre, but as soon as I asked a woman if she knew where the Mountbank Theatre was, she nodded and gave me exact directions. Before long I saw the domed roof and the bold sign and I ran, in spite of my sore feet.

The white marble steps were empty. There was no queue. I was first! I sat down triumphantly and changed my old boots for Cedric's kid splendours. My toes wiggled joyfully as I slipped them on. I stuck my legs out, turning my ankles this way and that, admiring them.

'My, they're a fine pair of boots!'

I thought at first it was a child as small as me. We were certainly the same height, and her own boots were about the same size as mine, but she was dressed like a lady in a fancy pink silk frock and she wore a bonnet trimmed with pink roses. Her face was a pretty pink too but it seemed unnaturally bright, as if she had maybe painted it on. She didn't have the look or expression of a little girl. She looked like an older woman, though her eyes were as blue and bright as any child's.

She stroked one of the boots with a chubby little hand.

'My my!' she said. 'Fancy swapping?' She seemed ready to unbutton her own stout black boots.

'No thank you,' I said quickly.

She gave a merry little peal of laughter. 'Only joking!' she said. 'So what are you doing sitting here on the steps? The theatre won't open for hours yet.'

'I have come to be a fairy in the *Cinderella* pantomime,' I said grandly.

'Oh, I say, have you indeed! Well, that's grand. I'm going to be in the pantomime too,' she said.

I stared at her. Was she still teasing me?

'Truly. My name's Goody Godber. Have you heard of me?' She looked as if she expected me to say yes.

'I don't think so,' I said, hoping I wasn't being impolite.

She stood up straight and struck an attitude, her arms akimbo, her rouged mouth one big grin.

'Ain't you seen my picture?' she asked. She took my hand and pulled me up the rest of the steps. There were new posters either side of the golden doors. I saw portraits of a majestic gentleman with a moustache, a very buxom fair lady, a darker, slimmer lady – and there she was, a tiny woman standing in

exactly that pose. There was writing underneath. I could make out two big Gs. Goody Godber!

'It's you!' I said.

'It is indeed, as I live and breathe,' she said, doing a little rat-a-tat-tat with her feet and striking another attitude. 'Little Goody Godber, the Pocket Ballerina, from when I was five, though I danced right through my twenties under that moniker. And now here before your very eyes, Goody Godber, character actress extraordinaire, miniature star of the Mountbank Theatre. Not *the* star – you have to be born a Mountbank to gain that honour – but I holds my own. I even have my own

gentlemen admirers hanging round the stage door, I'll have you know!'

'I'm honoured to meet you,' I said, and I held out my skirts and bobbed a curtsy.

'Ah, bless you, dearie!' Goody said, chuckling.

'Do you have a part in the play that's on at the moment?' I asked.

'I do indeed. We're giving old Will Shakespeare a run for his money. Six weeks from today of *Romeo and Juliet*.'

It meant nothing to me, but I assumed she must have a main part.

'Are you Juliet?' I asked.

She cackled at that. 'Hardly, my dear. Although Mrs Regina Mountbank what plays her is equally unlikely, seeing as she's well into her thirties and growing a tad stout. But then Mr Hercules Mountbank is a very odd Romeo, even though they are man and wife in reality. He's not even like old man Montague, Romeo's papa. More like his grandpapa. But there you go. He who owns the company, and indeed the entire theatre, gets to play the juiciest parts.'

'So what do you play?' I asked.

'I'm the nurse,' she said.

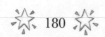

'Oh! Is there a baby in the play?' I asked.

'Nah, I'm Juliet's nurse. She's meant to be two weeks shy of her fourteenth birthday, so she's . . . how old?'

'Thirteen,' I said. I didn't need Miss Moaning to teach me simple numbers. Connor had taught me my pounds, shillings and pence sums when I was Tommy's age, so I could never be short-changed.

'Bright girl! I think you might make an excellent fairy. What dancing school do you attend?' she asked.

I stared at her.

'Dancing school?' I queried. 'I've been to the Ragged School but they don't teach dancing there.'

'No, I wouldn't think they would. So who taught you, dearie?'

'I've taught myself,' I said proudly. 'I'm very good at it.'

She stifled another chuckle, which was disconcerting.

'I'm sure you are, my pet,' she said quickly. 'And we can't fault you for eagerness. The auditions don't start till eleven.'

'I know – but I wanted to be here first,' I said.

'That's what I like to hear. Eagerness and determination. When you're short of stature like me, you have to be ultra eager and determined or you don't get any chances at all.

But I don't believe you're waiting in the right place. You need to go round the back, to the stage door. Here, I'll show you.'

She held out her hand in a friendly fashion and led me right round the grand building to the back. It was far shabbier. The stage door was simple, painted wood, not gold, and the paint was peeling at that. There weren't any steps to sit on.

'Perhaps you'd like to run off to the tea stall down the road to take a little refreshment before your long wait?' Goody suggested.

'No, I'd like to be first, so I definitely get a part as a fairy,' I said.

'I see,' said Goody. 'Mm. Well, I wouldn't want to deter you. And there's the old saying, you know: "First come, first served". I like your spirit. What's your name?'

'Tess, Miss Godber.'

'Sweet and simple. But you seem a smart little thing. How old are you, Tess?'

'Only six!' I said, hoping to impress her.

'Six? My my,' said Goody, but she narrowed her eyes. 'We small girls like to knock a bit off our ages, don't we?'

I was surprised. No one else had ever questioned me.

They just took it for granted I was telling the truth. But somehow I didn't mind her knowing.

'Well, I'm actually nine.' I thought quickly. 'In fact, several weeks shy of ten.'

'You *are* smart,' she said, looking tickled. 'Don't worry, I won't tell. Good luck, Tess.'

Then she curled her fingers and held her thumbs!

'I do that too!' I said, astonished.

'Of course. It's what we theatre folk do,' said Goody.

So I was already theatre folk, even though I hadn't got started yet!

She waved goodbye, waggling her fingers, and then disappeared through the stage door. I waggled mine back and then did a little happy dance and waved my old boots in the air, their tongues flapping.

Then I settled down to a long, long wait. I was too keyed up and excited to get bored. I kept planning my dance in my head, tapping out the rhythm. Should I stick with one dance, or should I offer them a whole variety: a fairy dance, a bunny dance, perhaps even the happy dance I'd just invented?

I was trying it out again, experimenting with some new fancy steps and twirls, when the stage door opened. It was

Goody. She'd taken her bonnet off and let loose a great mass of shiny ringlets. They were startlingly red. I'd never seen hair that amazing colour before and stared in awe.

'Don't tell me, you're struck silent by my crowning glory,' she said, laughing. 'Compliments of Dr Filament's Discreet Hair Colouring for Ladies – though there's nothing discreet about this shade, is there, my duck?' She was holding a cup of milky tea and a slice of shortbread sprinkled with sugar. 'A little snack to keep you going,' she said, offering them to me, and then she bobbed back inside the stage door.

I drank my tea and nibbled my shortbread. I hadn't realized how hungry and thirsty I was. I slurped the tea to the last drop and licked every speck of sugar from my lips and fingers. Goody popped back outside again a quarter of an hour later.

'I was thinking, ducks. You've probably come a long way, and you've still got a very long wait. You're probably needing to answer a call of nature. Nip inside with me and I'll show you the facilities. But keep shtum or you'll get me into no end of trouble with the management.'

I nodded gratefully and crept inside after her, tiptoeing in my kid boots. I had to hold the cup and saucer in one hand as I was clutching my old boots in the other. I was so excited to be

inside a theatre at last that my hands shook and the cup started rattling on the saucer.

Goody steadied it for me. She tiptoed elaborately towards the glass window of a little office, her finger to her lips.

'We have to watch out for old Harry! He's a stickler for following the rules. He likes nothing better than to rush to Mr Mountbank and tell tales,' she whispered. She bobbed down, so I did too, and we crept past, making sure our heads didn't poke up so they could be seen through the window.

Someone tapped on the glass from the inside. Goody pulled an anguished face – but she relaxed when she saw a young man peering out at us. A man in a blue suit, with a strange ridge in his oiled hair, left by a tight-fitting hat. I suddenly recognized him.

'It's you! You're the man with the bowler who was running like mad!' I said. 'It's your first day, isn't it?'

'It is indeed,' he said, nodding at me and bowing from the waist to Goody. 'A pleasure to meet you, madam! I've seen you in so many productions and admired you from afar ever since I was a young boy.'

'You're still a young boy, my dear! So where's grouchy old Harry?'

'He's retired. And I'm his replacement. I'm Frank,' he said.

'Well, welcome to the theatre, young Frank. And thank you for the adulation. Never get enough of it! I'm just taking this little lady to use the facilities before her audition. I take it you have no objections?'

'None whatsoever,' said young Frank. 'So long as you duck round a corner if you spot Mr Mountbank approaching. He's given me strict instructions not to let anyone in before eleven on the dot, as it's audition day.'

'I daresay,' said Goody. 'Come along then, Tess, quick sharp.'

She led me down a corridor, turning left and right, and right and left, going up and down stairs until I was dizzy – and then we stopped outside a door marked WC. I wasn't sure what these letters stood for, but when Goody opened the door it was obvious. I scuttled in and relieved myself gratefully. When I came out, she led me down yet more corridors until we arrived at another door marked *Miss Goody Godber*. I recognized the double Gs and smiled.

'This must be your room!' I said.

'It is indeed. My own dressing room at last, after years

and years of being crammed in with the chorus and who knows who. I've even shared with the back and front end of a pantomime horse (spry gents with a reputation, but they were sweet to me and treated me like a little lady – which I am). There, dearie, come and have a gander at my room!'

It was very small but then so was she. There was a large mirror, cracked in places but still showing our reflections, with a slim counter in front of it, and a chair with two cushions on it. Goody half lifted me onto the cushions so I could see my own face.

'You look a little pale, ducks. Let me put a blush on your cheeks.' She opened up an elaborate make-up box and started applying rose carmine to my face. I was a little worried that it was too bright and might make me look much older than I wanted. But she rubbed most of it off, applied a little blue to my lids, and fluffed up my curls with her own hairbrush.

'There now!' she said.

I blinked at myself in the mirror. I looked like one of the beautiful china dolls I'd seen in the arcade!

'Thank you!' I breathed.

'My pleasure, dearie,' she said. 'Well, I'd better take you back outside. You've still got a while to wait – but you're all

prepared. I'll be watching you and wishing you the very best of luck, little pretty-boots Tess.'

She led me to the stage door. Young Frank waved to me from behind the glass. It was as if I was part of the theatre already! I was still first in the queue, thank goodness, though another girl and her mother joined me soon afterwards. She was a pretty girl – prettier than me, with big brown eyes and naturally pink cheeks with dimples and fair curly hair. Her curls were very even, as if her mother put them in rag papers at night, but they looked as good as mine, if not better. She was wearing a beautiful ice-blue silk dress with a white lace trim, snow-white stockings and blue satin slippers without a single scuff.

Oh dear. If I was choosing fairies, I was sure I'd pick her over me! She looked as if she was having the same thought as she looked me over. She had a smug little smile on her face. Her mother did too.

But maybe she couldn't dance as well as me? And she didn't have Goody Godber wishing her luck.

'Good morning,' I said politely, the way we'd been taught at the Ragged School. 'Do you happen to know Little Goody Godber, the Pocket Ballerina? She's a friend of mine.'

The girl and her mother stared at me. I hoped they were impressed.

'She's playing a nurse in *Romeo and Juliet*,' I said. 'And she's going to be in the pantomime.'

'Really?' said the mother. 'We love panto. Little Larissa here was in *Robinson Crusoe* last Christmas, weren't you, darling? She always got an extra round of applause at the end, when she took her curtsy, bless her.'

That shut me up! She'd been in a pantomime already! *She*'d performed a bunny dance! I could just imagine her in a brown bunny suit with big floppy ears. She'd blink her big brown eyes and twitch her small snub nose and look adorable.

Then another mother arrived with two little girls absolutely identical, with long glossy hair down to their waists and wearing cream frilled dresses with cream slippers to match. They knew Larissa and her mother. The mothers made polite conversation though they didn't seem to like each other much. Larissa and the twins chattered together and kept pointing their toes and twirling about.

Well, I could point and twirl. And I had natural golden curls. And I was wearing Ma's best frock and Cedric's kid boots – but somehow my frock looked crumpled and bigger

than ever now, and Cedric's boots seemed clumpy beside the other girls' satin slippers.

Then more girls arrived with their mothers, and thank goodness a few were dressed in a makeshift way like me. There were even several tiny girls in true rags, their hair matted, their faces dirty, their mothers with pale pinched faces. But at least they had mothers with them. A few of the children had obvious grandmothers, and there were little bunches of girls with one mother looking after the lot of them – but they all had someone.

I scowled at them all, terrified that I might break down and cry in front of them. I wanted Ma so much. I couldn't see any clouds from where I was standing, pressed right up against the stage door by the gathering crowd, but I listened hard and thought I heard Ma's voice in my ear wishing me luck. I bent my head and nestled down into the neck of her frock, breathing in deeply just in case there was still a little of her lovely Ma smell in the folds of the material.

'Why is that weird girl hunching up like that? What does she look like!' Larissa remarked to her mother.

For two pins I'd have punched her – but I didn't want to be caught brawling when they opened the stage door, and the

time was getting near at last. I straightened up, glared at her, and then turned my back.

Then the door opened up a crack and young Frank eased himself out.

'Right, girls!' he mumbled nervously.

No one paid any attention.

'Shout?' I suggested to him.

He took a deep breath. 'RIGHT, GIRLS!' he bellowed, and they subsided and started pushing forward wildly, so I was very nearly flattened.

'STAND STILL! NOW LINE UP SLOWLY AND CAREFULLY, WITH NO PUSHING!' he shouted. 'THEN WHEN I SAY – *AND NOT BEFORE* – MOVE FORWARD SLOWLY AND FOLLOW ME! ANYONE TRYING TO CHARGE FORWARD OR PUSH IN FRONT OF ANYONE WILL BE IMMEDIATELY EJECTED FROM THE BUILDING!'

He had everyone's attention now. The crowd started doing its best to start a long, unwieldy line.

'Brilliant!' I whispered.

Frank gave me a happy wink and then opened the door to let me in.

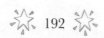

In spite of his command not to push and shove, Larissa and the twins and goodness knows who were running flat out, and I had to spread my arms and push back a bit to keep my place, but I did it.

I expected we would enter the corridor rabbit warren, but he took us a different way, through another door to what seemed like an entirely different world. There was red carpet on the floor, row after row of velvet seats with gilt arms, huge chandeliers twinkling above us, balconies in tiers at the sides, and a massive stage with scarlet curtains. I stood still in awe, and Larissa and the twins bumped straight into me.

They did their best to push past then, but I wasn't having it. I pushed back and managed to make my way to the front, where a lady was waiting with a notebook and pen. She waved one hand in the air for silence. She had such a steely presence that everyone quietened immediately and stood stock still.

'Thank you very much,' she said. She didn't raise her voice, but it was clearly audible to everyone even so.

'My name is Madame Bountiful,' she said. It seemed a weird name to me but I didn't dare snigger. 'Many of you will know me already. I am the trainer for all junior performers. Those chosen for our next pantomime will be reporting to me

daily and working extremely hard. If there are any slackers here, kindly leave the auditorium immediately!'

Everyone turned round, just to see if someone was mad enough to declare herself a slacker, but no one moved.

'Now, I want you to seat yourselves on the left-hand side of the auditorium – NOT YET! When I say. Keep strictly to your place in the queue. Then when I beckon you, proceed up the steps at the side onto the stage. I will give you a card with your number on it. You will give your music to Mr Higgs at the piano here.' She indicated a thin man with thinning hair and very large teeth, almost as big as his piano keys. He waved to us. I lifted my hand tentatively, not sure whether we were supposed to wave back.

What had she meant when she said we should give him our music? How could I do that? I made up tunes in my head when I danced, but how was I supposed to 'give' them to him?

'Then you will sing your song, dance your routine and act your prepared piece,' Madame Bountiful continued.

My heart started banging against the bodice of Ma's frock. Sing a song? I wasn't any good at singing! Act a prepared piece? I didn't have anything prepared! Oh, why hadn't I known that you had to do this? I thought all I had to do was dance.

'Then you must march across the stage, go down the right-hand steps, and sit yourself quietly in the right-hand seats. When everyone has performed I will confer with the judges and we will call the numbers of the girls we've chosen.' She gestured to two people in the front row, though we could only see the back of their heads. I'd thought judges were frightening people in wigs and gowns who sent people to prison, but this didn't seem likely.

I was busy contemplating this and trying hard to see if I was right when I scurried to sit down on the left-hand side, as commanded. I saw a grand old man with strangely flowing brown hair almost to his shoulders. A beautiful lady sat beside him in a purple gown with a lilac lace trim. And someone sat on the other side of her, scarcely visible because only the tips of her red curls were visible. It was Goody!

I felt a little bit better. She was my friend. I had at least one of these judges on my side already. But I was still panicking, not knowing what to do about the music, the song or the prepared piece. I held my thumbs to try to calm myself and found my palms were wet with fear.

Madame Bountiful was looking straight at me. She lifted her hand and beckoned imperiously. But girls were still filing

into their places, the mothers sitting at the back. Did she mean me to go up on the stage now before everyone was seated? I didn't want her to shout at me!

Larissa gave me a sharp shove. 'Go on, you stupid girl!'

Madame Bountiful was frowning. I stood up, suddenly dizzy, so that the whole theatre seemed to slant sideways. But I managed to struggle out of my seat, make my way unsteadily to the steps, climb them somehow and walk on stage for the first time.

Chapter Eleven

I took the card from Madame Bountiful and then dithered, not knowing what to do.

She sighed. 'Weren't you listening? Go and give your music to Mr Higgs.'

She pushed me in his direction. His piano-key teeth gleamed at me encouragingly. I went right up to him and whispered in his ear.

'I'm so sorry, I don't know how to give you any music, sir.'

'Oh dear, did you forget to bring it with you?' he asked. 'Your sheet music,' he prompted, when I looked dazed.

I was even more bewildered. How on earth could you create music with a sheet?

'Never mind. Tell me the name of the piece and I'll probably know it and can play along as you sing,' he said obligingly.

'Yes, but I didn't know I had to sing a song. Couldn't I do a dance?' I asked.

'If you like,' said Mr Higgs, though he sounded uncertain.

I went to the middle of the stage, held out my arms as if I was spreading my wings, and started drifting slowly on tiptoe. There were smothered sniggers from my audience. Madame Bountiful clapped her hands for silence and glared at me.

'You must perform your song first!' she said.

'But I don't really know any songs,' I admitted. 'Can't I just dance?'

'No, you cannot,' she snapped. I saw she was starting to hold up the number two card, ready to dismiss me before I'd even got started.

'I'm sorry. Of course I will sing a song first,' I gabbled, thinking wildly. *Did* I know any songs? Miss Moaning had taught me several hymns, but they were very slow and droney and I didn't think they'd go down well. I suddenly remembered a song Pa sang when he reeled home from the ale house. That would have to do.

'*I might have had a few, and now I want to spew, because I'm telling you – I'm in a pickle; I'm such a naughty boy, but I give the ladies joy, but now I'm telling you –'twas just a tickle!*'

'STOP!' Madame Bountiful shouted, as shocked exclamations and screams of laughter came from the auditorium. 'Get off this stage at once, you little guttersnipe. How dare you make a mockery of these auditions!'

I didn't know what I'd done wrong, but I knew I'd blown it. I slunk off the stage, trying very hard not to cry. I wanted to run straight out of the theatre, but I'd left my old boots under my seat and had to go back to collect them. Larissa and the twins were openly laughing at me now, which made my humiliation so much worse.

'Hang on now, Madame B!' a voice rang out.

I looked round. Goody had risen from her seat and had rushed up the steps. She only came up to Madame Bountiful's waist, but she had her chin up and spoke commandingly.

'Give the kid a chance! She hasn't a clue what she's singing, bless her. Six years old if she's a day, and as innocent as the daisies in the fields. She might not even hold a tune very well, but she could be trained up, and I doubt she's got a prepared piece to act out, but let her dance on the stage at the very least

before you turn her down! She's been waiting here since crack of dawn.' Goody was a very small woman but she had a very loud voice, and she clearly had a lot of clout in this theatre. 'Don't you agree, Mr Mountbank?' she said, her head on one side.

The impressive velvet-coated gentleman with the long hair stood up. He'd been roaring with laughter, but now he did his best to compose himself.

'Very well, little girl. Do as Miss Godber suggests and dance, my dear, to entertain us even more,' he said, mopping his brow with a silk handkerchief.

I wasn't a fool. I knew he was hoping I'd make a further laughing stock of myself. But I'd show him! I'd show them all! Oh, dearest Goody, thank you for sticking up for me.

I raised my arms again, pointed a toe, and then started my fairy dance. I wasn't scruffy Tess in borrowed boots and a frock that trailed on the floor. I was a fairy, light and delicate. I took a few steps, then leaped in the air, head back, one leg bent, the other gloriously straight, and then I left the stage and flew up in the air, right over their heads. Well, I did in my mind's eye. I flew out of the theatre, into the sunlight, across the meadows, skimming the wild flowers, then higher

than the skylarks, up and up to the clouds. I twirled round
and round, arms out, one leg down, the other whipping me
on my way, my dress whirling up to my knees, and then at
last I flew back, into the theatre, down onto the stage, and
landed with a deep bow.

There was a silence. Everyone was staring at me. Then
Goody jumped up on her seat and started cheering and
clapping. A few of the other children clapped too, but most sat
stunned. I dared looked at Madame Bountiful. She didn't look
impressed.

'What sort of airy-fairy dancing is that?' she said.

'That's what it *is*. Airy and fairy,' I said, a little out of breath.

'Well, it's not ballet. I didn't recognize a single step,' she
snapped. 'Who on earth trained you to dance like that?'

'No one trained me,' I said.

'So it's to her credit, ain't it, Mr Mountbank?' Goody said.
'She's a true original. Like me. She'll go far.'

'I don't want a child that does her own steps. I want a
properly trained fairy who dances like the others,' said Mr
Mountbank, getting out of his seat and walking to the stage.

'I'll be trained, sir. I'll dance like all the others. I just want
to be in your pantomime,' I said.

'Well, go and sit down on the right, like a good girl. I have to see the others first before I decide on my twelve fairies,' he said, and he waved the back of his hand at me.

I grabbed my boots and scampered over to the other side, right at the front. I sat there, my heart thudding so hard I could hear it in my ears. Thank goodness they'd forgotten about my prepared piece, as I didn't have one. I was still totally bewildered and my fingers were holding my thumbs so hard it was a wonder they didn't snap right off. Maybe, just maybe, I'd won them over. I decided I loved Goody more than anyone in the whole world, even Connor.

Larissa was now beckoned up onto the stage. She handed some sort of thin booklet to Mr Higgs, who looked relieved and set it on the piano ledge in front of him. He played light prancy music, and Larissa started singing. She had a high clear voice though she sang the words in a funny trill, which sounded far too fancy for me. Still, I could tell it was a suitable song from Madame Bountiful's pleased expression. When Larissa finished she was then told to dance. I leaned forward eagerly.

It was very odd dancing. She kept doing the same steps in a little pattern. Then she twirled round and round, but in a very jerky way, not free and flowing like me. But she was very

light on her feet – perhaps her little satin slippers helped. Her
head poked one way, then the other, so that her own golden
curls flew out prettily, like the golden halo on Gentle Jesus's
head. She finished her dance with a beautifully executed curtsy.
I'd thought myself so clever with my bow, but of course fairies
were feminine and curtsied.

Then she started on her prepared piece. She was talking
in a silly voice, emphasizing every word: '*Over hill, over dale,
through bush, through briar* . . .' I didn't know what she was on
about. It seemed a silly piece to have chosen. But then she
said, '*But I do serve the Fairy Queen,*' and my spirits sank. It was
a fairy piece of prose. *She* was a fairy. It was perfectly chosen.

When she finished, she curtsied again and Madame
Bountiful clasped her hands and actually said, 'Well done,
my dear.' My spirits sank even lower. All I'd managed to do
was offend her with a silly song and irritate her because my
dance didn't seem to be the right sort of dance.

Larissa sat down beside me, smirking. She was careful to sit
leaning away from me, as if I smelled bad. She didn't say
anything. She didn't need to. We both knew there was no doubt
she'd be picked.

It was the twins' turn next. They went together and held

hands as they sang a duet about sisters. I thought it was pretty sickening. They even blew each other a kiss at the end. However, it seemed to go down well, and it was a novelty to see two identical girls singing along together, with the same mannerisms and expressions on their round faces.

Their dancing was a different sort to Larissa's. They were more like the acrobats at Connor's market, the ones who cartwheeled and somersaulted for pennies. The twins hurtled around, not really in a dainty fashion, but when they both leaped high in the air and turned a double somersault they looked as if they were actually flying like fairies. I felt they'd both get through.

So that was three places already, and Mr Mountbank wanted twelve. I didn't need Connor to tell me that meant there were only nine places left – and yet there were still at least fifty children to come.

I lost heart very quickly. Most of the girls were so slick and polished. I was painfully aware why Madame Bountiful complained that I hadn't had any training. There were a few girls who clearly hadn't been trained either, mostly the ones in ragged frocks. They tried, and sang a bit and kicked their legs about, though their boots were as broken as my own and made

it almost impossible for them to dance daintily. Some didn't look as if they wanted to be on the stage at all, and kept peering anxiously at the pinch-faced mothers who had brought them along. I hoped they wouldn't get whacked if they didn't get a part.

Sometimes some of the immaculately dressed girls made a mess of things out of sheer nerves and sang off-key or so hurriedly that Mr Higgs couldn't keep up. Several wobbled while dancing, and one poor tall girl on stork legs attempted a twirl and fell sideways, landing with her legs splayed. There was an unkind titter – but I could understand. This was no time for kind, sisterly feeling. We were pitted against each other and all we could do was wish the others failed.

I tried to keep track of the girls who were clearly going to be picked. I counted up to eleven quite quickly. I hoped that I would somehow be number twelve – but then another girl sang so beautifully that Mr and Mrs Mountbank actually clapped, and there were dancers who seemed even better than Larissa.

I stopped counting after I got to twenty-four clear winners. It was too heartbreaking. I wanted to creep out of the theatre and run away, but when the poor stork girl who had fallen

tried that, Madame Bountiful shouted at her imperiously.

'YOU, GIRL! DID YOU NOT HEAR ME? ALL CANDIDATES MUST BE SEATED THROUGHOUT THE AUDITIONS AND WAIT FOR THE RESULTS! SIT DOWN, THIS INSTANT!'

She collapsed in a heap, covering her face, as if she thought we wouldn't be able to see her just because she couldn't see us.

Larissa tutted scornfully. She was really the most unpleasant girl I had ever come across. I was glad there was a big gap between us. I didn't want to brush against her accidentally. If she tutted like that if I didn't get chosen, I'd kick her with all four of my boots. Oh Lord, it was so obvious now that I *wasn't* going to be picked for a part. If I was one of the judges, *I* wouldn't choose me. I hoped Goody would vote for me even so, but there wasn't any chance Mr Mountbank and his wife would do likewise.

Finally the very last girl sang and danced and spoke and scampered off stage. Madame Bountiful shouted another command.

'I WANT ABSOLUTE SILENCE, PLEASE, WHILE THE JUDGES CONFER!'

My throat was so dry now I couldn't have talked even if I'd

wanted to. The three judges in the front row were comparing notes, sometimes nodding, sometimes disputing. I could only see the top of Goody's head. I was number one so I must have been discussed first. Had they nodded or shaken their heads? I couldn't be sure.

They seemed to be taking such an age to pick twelve numbers. But at last Mr Mountbank signalled to Madame Bountiful. She went up to them, they all conferred, and then she bustled back onto the stage, a piece of paper in her hand.

'LISTEN VERY CAREFULLY TO SEE IF YOUR NUMBER IS CALLED!' she cried.

As if we would do otherwise!

She opened her mouth. 'Number two.'

Number *two*! Had I misheard? She'd left out number one! She said numbers three and four too. Larissa and the twins were all silently whooping, jiggling around in their seats. Then she said numbers 7, 13, 16, 19, 22, 27, 35, 39 and 45. Twelve numbers. Twelve chosen girls. But not me, not me, not me!

I felt tears stinging my eyes. Larissa saw my face and shook her head at me, as if she was asking what else I expected. And she was right. Why would anyone pick me? I was just a street

urchin in my ma's frock, who sang the wrong song, didn't have a prepared piece, and maybe couldn't even dance. I felt myself shrinking inside.

Other rejected girls were openly sobbing now, and several of the mothers were calling out indignantly.

'SILENCE!' said Madame Bountiful. 'I HAVEN'T FINISHED YET! I STILL HAVE TO ANNOUNCE THE UNDERSTUDY.' She paused. Every unpicked girl in the theatre leaned forward.

Madame Bountiful took her time. She was staring at this last number on her paper as if she couldn't quite believe it. She actually sighed before she spoke.

'The understudy is . . . number one.'

Me! I'd been picked after all! Oh glory, oh joy, oh hurrah! I didn't know what an understudy was, but I was so glad it was me. At least I had a part in the pantomime – didn't I?

Madame Bountiful had one last bellow. 'WILL THE THIRTEEN CHOSEN YOUNG LADIES KINDLY STAY BEHIND FOR FURTHER INSTRUCTION, WHILE THE OTHERS DEPART FROM THE BUILDING.'

I turned round and watched as they straggled out. Some of the mothers were in tears too. They mostly consoled their

poor rejected daughters, though several seemed to be telling them off, and one horrid ma was actually giving her girl a good shaking. I thought of my dear ma above the clouds, sure she was smiling down proudly at me.

The delighted mothers of the twelve chosen ones came rushing to congratulate their daughters. Larissa's mother was first.

'You did wonderfully, darling child!' she said. 'How amazing to be picked first of all!'

Larissa wriggled happily. She couldn't fail to be picked first as the fairies were chosen in numerical order but it seemed petty to point it out. I didn't want to be spiteful.

Larissa had no such reservations. 'Poor you,' she said to me, though she was grinning broadly.

'Why am I poor? I've been picked too, didn't you hear Madame Bountiface?' I retorted.

'It's Madame Bountiful, you ignoramus,' said Larissa, drawling the long word. 'You're not going to be a fairy, you silly.'

'No, I'm going to be an understudy, and I bet that's even better than a fairy,' I said stoutly.

Larissa and her mother went into peals of mocking laughter.

'Bless the child!' said the mother. 'An understudy isn't a part, dear. You just sit in the dressing room and try to make yourself useful helping all the others. You're simply there in case one of the special fairy girls is taken ill.'

'But that never happens,' said Larissa, preening herself. 'At least, not to me. I've never missed a single performance, have I, Mama? I've been in *Little Boy Blue*, *Red Riding Hood* and, of course, *Robinson Crusoe*. Wait till Mr Mountbank does *Babes in the Wood*! He's practically promised I shall be the Girl Babe, hasn't he?'

'Yes, my love, and I daresay you will be Chief Fairy in this production. I have yet to see the script, but I wouldn't be surprised if you have a named part,' said her mother.

I couldn't bear to listen to them any longer. I braved Madame Bountiful's wrath and ran towards Goody. She saw me coming, and came to meet me.

'There now! Are you happy, ducks?' she asked.

'Yes, I am – you were wonderful to speak up for me. But I'm not a fairy, am I?' I said. 'Is an understudy a sort of servant?'

'No, absolutely not!' said Goody. 'You study like the other fairies and learn the songs and dances and exclamations. It will be marvellous training for you.'

'Who will be doing the training?' I asked. 'Not old Missus Bountiface?'

'The very one,' said Goody, cackling. 'But she's good at her job, I'll say that for her, and to be frank, you need a bit of whipping into shape.'

'I won't be whipped!' I said.

'No actual whipping allowed, you noodle. Just a few lashings from her tongue. But the panto always has a long run – from Boxing Day right through to March. Those little fairies will come down with coughs and colds and agues galore. There's your chance! You go on in the poorly girl's place. It'll be your time to star.' She came closer and whispered, 'And if they all stay hale and hearty I'll creep up behind one and knock her over!'

I burst out laughing, cheered at last.

'Why are you being so lovely to me, dear Goody?' I asked.

'Well, us odd little girls have got to stick together, haven't we? Now, Madame's clapping her hands. She'll want you up on the stage with the others. Better move sharpish. I'm off now I've done my judging duties, so as I can have a little break before the afternoon matinee. But I'll be seeing

a lot of you over the next few months,' she said, giving my cheek a fond pinch.

'I do hope so!' I said, and I gave her a big kiss on her very rosy face.

Chapter Twelve

I stood on the stage with the twelve fairies. Madame Bountiful made me stand a little apart from the others, to make it absolutely clear I hadn't actually been given a part. I didn't protest. I had to try and keep in her good books somehow. I wasn't going to let the old trout spoil my chances.

Mr Mountbank came on stage too and delivered a long lecture about our being lucky little girls to be taken on by his illustrious company. He told us that his father, and indeed his grandfather, had been well-known theatrical names, honoured throughout England. He felt we were a talented little bunch, but we had to work extremely hard from now on. It was an accolade to take part in a Mountbank pantomime

and we mustn't ever forget it.

Mrs Mountbank fanned herself during this speech – but I rather think she was using her big feathery fan to hide her yawns. I fidgeted rather, as my legs ached after my long walk and dancing display. I was conscious of a Bountiful glare, and hurriedly composed myself. I noticed that the other girls were standing upright, knees together and their toes turned out. It looked a little comical but I arranged my own legs in that position too.

We were told that we had to report back to the theatre every morning (apart from Sundays) for rehearsals as each and every one of us had to be a polished performer by opening night.

'That includes you, little number one at the end of the line,' said Mr Mountbank.

'Yes, sir. Certainly, sir,' I said, and even managed a little curtsy.

'You'll need extra help with your singing and your acting,' said Mr Mountbank, lighting a cigar and taking a puff. He wiggled his eyebrows and there was a lot of subdued tittering.

'However, you're a fine little dancer, though you need to be trained up to perform the right steps,' Mr Mountbank said,

with another puff. 'With my years of experience, I can spot a natural talent. We might make a Lola Montez of you yet!' He gave me a wink.

I didn't have a clue who he meant. I didn't care. He said I was a 'fine little dancer'! Oh glory! Put that in your pipe and smoke it, Miss Snooty Larissa!

He sauntered off, Mrs Mountbank following behind, swishing her silken skirts. Then we had more orders from Madame Bountiful. We must turn up at the theatre at nine sharp on Monday, suitably dressed in white practice outfits with white satin slippers. She glanced at me as she said it. I was biting my lip, wondering how on earth I could conjure up these items by the day after tomorrow – but I covered my teeth and smiled as if it was no problem at all. We had to bring our own small refreshments and be out of the theatre by two in the afternoon.

We nodded and chorused, 'Yes, Madame Bountiful.'

'We are still making adjustments to the script so I cannot share it with you right now. However, I expect each and every one of you to consult your fairy stories and know the entire plot of *Cinderella* when you arrive on Monday morning,' she said, with yet another glance in my direction, the hateful pig.

I nodded and joined in the chorus of 'Yes, Madame Bountiful' even though this seemed another impossible task.

Then she clapped her hands and said we could go at long last. I charged out of the theatre, clutching my old boots and changing into them down an alleyway ten minutes away. Then I started the long trudge towards home. My feet were sore but I skipped and jumped and leaped about, not caring who saw me. I might only be an understudy, but I was part of the theatre now!

Some folk stared at me. Some laughed, some clapped, some patted their heads as if I was soft in the head. I danced higher and harder, just to show them. A couple came round the corner – a big burly man and a buxom woman quite a bit younger. She wore the sort of clothes Ma would have called 'fast'. He wore a cap and a shabby suit with a yellow spotted scarf knotted round his neck like a tie. Pa used to wear a scarf exactly the same. And a suit like that, with the trousers bunched up. And a cap grey with grime . . . It *was* Pa!

I stopped still, blinking fast, wondering if I was simply imagining some random man was Pa. But he was looking straight at me, his eyes narrowed, taking in my ruffled curls and Ma's frock.

'Pa! Oh, Pa! It's me, your little Goldie!' I called. 'Where have you been? We've looked everywhere for you. The rent hasn't been paid. And guess what, I'm going to be in a pantomime!'

But he'd already retreated back round the corner, pulling the woman with him. I ran after him, but the sole suddenly flapped right off one of my boots. I tripped and went flying, and by the time I'd picked myself up, gathered up Cedric's boots and charged round the corner myself, the couple had disappeared.

I wandered up and down the road for a full ten minutes, going down dark alleyways, even knocking at several lodging houses and asking if Pa lived there. But he'd vanished. He'd run away from me, his own daughter. He didn't want to come back. He didn't want his family. He didn't want me.

'Well, I don't want you either!' I shouted, just in case he was hiding somewhere. 'Stay away from us for ever with your horrible new woman! As if we'd ever want *her* for our ma! How could you take up with her when our own dear ma's not long gone?'

I shook with rage, crying in anger rather than sorrow. Then I marched off, hobbling now, though I had the sense to

look for my cast-off sole to see if Connor could hammer it back into place. It was so unfair! I'd been so happy and now Pa had spoilt it all.

No, I wasn't going to let him do that! I'd been a fool to rush after him. He didn't deserve to be part of our family any more. We were our own family now, Maggie and Connor and Tommy and Ada and me.

I recited our names over and over again, and gradually calmed down. When I got home at last, I scattered Epsom salts in a big bowl of water and soaked my poor feet. Then I put my broken boot upside down on the cobbling last and tried tapping in little nails myself with the hammer. It was quite heavy for me to control and I was scared of hitting my own thumb, so several nails got knocked in sideways, but after bashing away I managed a makeshift repair. There! I didn't need a pa. I didn't even need Connor. I could mend my own boots. I could walk all the way to the theatre and back. I could get a part in a pantomime.

I'd been hours and hours at the theatre but I didn't expect anyone to come home till half five or even six. It was a delight when Maggie came home at three, with Ada in her arms and a big bag over her shoulder. I greeted her warily, scared she might

be very angry with me for slipping out of the house so early and not looking after the children. She just smiled at me joyfully and gave me the biggest hug ever.

'I've been so worried about you, Tess, you bad little baggage! Connor kept telling me you'd manage by yourself but I could tell he was worried sick too. He was going to try to leave the market at midday to see if he could find you. Did you get terribly lost?' Maggie asked. 'And what on earth are you doing wearing Ma's frock? It's far too big for you. Look, you've got the hem dirty from it trailing on the ground!'

'I'm sorry, Mags. I did try to hold it up all the time.'

Ada had got a little squashed in our big hug and started whimpering.

'Hush now, darling. I'll give you a feed in a second. Look, Tess, more goodies! Miss Rosa got worried because I came over all faint as I was in such a bother about you. She insisted we go shopping and I've got all manner of treats in the bag, even jam tarts for Tommy, plus two whole pints of milk for Ada!' Maggie said.

I looked round. 'Where *is* Tommy? Is he playing with those big lads again?'

'Connor took him to the market because I made such a

fuss about lumping him along to Miss Rosa's,' Maggie said guiltily. 'I know, I shouldn't have. But then *you* shouldn't have sneaked off like that, Tess.'

She gave me a little shake, back to being fierce Maggie again and blaming me. We started to argue but then the door opened and Connor came in, with Tommy riding him piggy-back.

'Gee up, horsey, we're home!' Tommy shouted happily. 'Can we gallop round the house now to show the girls how nicely we do it?'

'No, we cannot!' said Connor, sliding him off and shifting him onto Pa's sofa. *Our* sofa. 'Horsey's blooming exhausted!'

He came rushing over and seized hold of me. 'Are you all right, Tess?' he asked hoarsely. 'How could you worry us so? I've been all the way to the wretched theatre but they wouldn't let me in, though I begged and pleaded.'

'Oh, Connor, I'm so sorry! I didn't mean you to come after me! Will old Bert give you the sack?' I said anxiously.

'Well, he'd be stupid if he did – we sold most of the stock in the first three hours. I nearly lost my voice. Folk went berserk, practically fighting each other to get a bargain. I couldn't believe my eyes. It's cheap tat, same as ever, but I suppose they

get taken in by my patter,' he said. 'We've made a small fortune.' He jingled his pockets.

'Well, *I* might make our fortunes too,' I said, standing up straight. 'I'm going to be in the *Cinderella* pantomime, see!'

They stared at me. Even Tommy stopped bouncing on the sofa. Ada sucked her fist, puzzled by the sudden silence.

'Truly?' said Connor.

'Absolutely truly,' I said. 'Well, almost.'

'Aha!' said Maggie. 'You're making it up again, aren't you?'

'No I'm not! I'm going to be a fairy and Goody says I'm sure to get a chance to perform with the others, but I have to bide my time because I'm the understudy and need extra training,' I gabbled.

I had to go through the whole adventure in detail while we all sat on the sofa. It was most satisfying. Connor and Maggie and even Tommy sat spellbound as I recited the whole story. Connor was most taken by my account of Goody, and thought she sounded wonderfully strange and kind. Maggie was incensed by Larissa and said I should stamp on both her feet to serve her right for being so hateful. Tommy laughed at my

imitation of Madame Bountiful. I drew myself up, stuffed a
pillow down Ma's bodice, and stuck my nose in the air with
pinched nostrils, as if there was a bad smell. I even got her
voice right, so harsh, genteel and grating.

'And this creature is going to train you?' said Connor. 'I
don't see why. You can dance beautifully already. *You* should be
a proper fairy!'

'Yes, like I said, stamp on Larissa and take her place!' said
Maggie.

'I stamp on her like that silly lady at market!' said Tommy,
grinning.

'Don't you dare do that again!' said Connor, trying to
sound stern, but he couldn't help grinning too. 'Tommy was

mostly as good as gold,' he told us. 'And it wasn't really his fault that he had to stamp on that woman. There was such a rush to buy, and she surged forward and knocked him right off his perch on the edge of my stand. He couldn't get away because I'd tied him to the post for safety – I couldn't risk him wandering off. The woman gave him a cuff on the head for it too, though it was her fault not his – so I don't blame our Tom for retaliating.'

'Might you want to take him to the market again?' Maggie asked hopefully.

'Well, it might not be a bad idea. He's a game little chap and most of the punters thought him a right little card. He'd pick up a teapot and copy my patter and they'd roar with laughter,' said Connor.

'Then that's much more fun for you than being dragged along with me to Miss Rosa's,' Maggie said quickly.

'And he can't come with me because little brothers aren't allowed,' I said. I hadn't been told this, but I was pretty sure it was true. 'We start rehearsals on Monday and I have to be there at nine sharp. Is that all right?'

Connor and Maggie looked at each other.

'I suppose – if you promise to keep to the main streets,' said Connor.

'And never talk to anyone,' Maggie added.

'Oh, thank you, thank you!' I said fervently, though I think we knew I'd have gone whether they gave me permission or not. 'There's only just one thing . . . well, two things really.'

'Oh-oh!' said Maggie. 'Spit it out then!'

'I have to wear a white practice dress,' I said. 'Short, with a sticking-out skirt.'

'Well, how on earth does she expect us to provide you with some daft fancy outfit?' said Maggie, but she was looking through to the kitchen. She was staring at the sheets still piled in a corner. 'I suppose I could cut one up to make a frock and give it a good wash and iron by Monday morning,' she said thoughtfully.

'Oh, Maggie, would you? But won't the owners be furious if one of their sheets goes missing?'

'Who cares? I'm not going to be a washerwoman any more. I'm a model now. I shall sit for Miss Rosa while she finishes my portrait, then she needs me for the illustrations in this storybook, and *then* she's going to introduce me to some of her lady artist friends and she's sure they'll want to draw me too. She says I have a very striking face and beautiful dark eyes,' said Maggie, fluttering her eyelashes.

'And so you do,' I said, feeling I should butter her up. 'And then the other thing . . .'

'Yes?' said Connor.

'I'm supposed to wear white slippers,' I mumbled. 'Do you think you could make me some out of the sheet, Maggie?'

'It wouldn't work,' she said, shaking her head.

'I'll buy you some slippers tomorrow,' said Connor, jingling his earnings again.

'But it's Sunday tomorrow,' I said. 'The shops will be shut.'

'Not up at Spitalfields,' said Connor. 'I'll see if one of my pals from the market might give me a lift there in their cart.'

'You're the dearest brother and sister in the world!' I declared.

'And what about me and Ada?' Tommy asked.

'You are too. We're the best family ever,' I declared. 'Thank goodness Pa's not coming back.'

'What do you mean? He could still turn up any time,' said Maggie.

'I don't think he wants to,' I said. I took a deep breath. 'I saw him today.'

'*What?*'

'And he saw me, I know he did, and I called to him, but

he ran away from me!' I said, my voice going croaky.

'Are you sure you weren't mistaking some other man for him?' Maggie asked.

'No, it was him, clear as day,' I insisted.

'And he ran away from you?' Connor said, sounding anguished. 'How could he do that?'

'He's got a new lady friend. She was with him,' I said.

'*Pa?*' said Maggie. 'Who'd want a man like our pa?'

'Well, she didn't look very nice,' I said. 'Ma would have hated her. And we wouldn't want her for a new ma, would we?'

'You're so right!' said Maggie, and she clapped her hands together. 'Good riddance to him. We'll manage on our own.'

We had a gloriously large supper in celebration of our changes of fortune and went to bed early. I fell asleep as soon as I snuggled up between Maggie and Tommy – but woke when I heard the church clock down the road strike midnight. There was one more task to be achieved.

I had to find someone who knew the story of Cinderella.

Chapter Thirteen

Connor drew round my feet on a piece of cardboard the next morning and then took it off to Spitalfields with him on a quest for my silk slippers. Maggie measured me from neck to knees to ankles and spent hours cutting out and stitching a white practice outfit. I made myself useful stuffing a chicken and peeling vegetables for a slap-up Sunday dinner. We even had a rice pudding for afters, with jam on top. Ada had her own little portion of chopped chicken and carrot and potato, with rice pudding to follow.

Connor was back home in time to have his. He presented me with a pair of white slippers in their own white satin drawstring bag. I'd never owned anything as beautiful. Even

Cedric's kid boots looked dull and ordinary beside my special dancing shoes!

Cedric! He was my only hope now. If he was an expert on Robinson Crusoe then surely he'd be well acquainted with Cinderella too. I still didn't want to go round to his house, especially on a Sunday, but I thought I'd have one more try searching for him in the park. I knew many posh folk spent most of the morning in church, but I hoped Cedric might have a little park outing in the afternoon.

'You two have a rest this afternoon,' I said to Connor and Maggie. 'I'll take the little ones out to the park.'

'*You're* a little one too,' said Connor. 'I'll come too and then you can dance around to your heart's content. I'll just have five minutes to let my meal go down and then we'll be off.'

He lay down on the sofa, stretching luxuriously. It was already losing Pa's shape and it no longer smelled of him. Connor's eyes closed and he was sound asleep in seconds. I waited hopefully but he didn't stir.

I changed Ada, settled her on Tommy's lap in the baby carriage and set out for the park with them. Maggie was still stitching away, humming to herself the way Ma did when she

was mending our clothes. I blew her a grateful kiss and then we were off.

I went directly to the duck pond. I saw Sarah-Jane first, chatting to the park keeper as he raked leaves from the path. She was wearing a black shawl over her maid's uniform. Perhaps it was her Sunday best? And there was Cedric with a bag of bread, feeding the ducks.

'Cedric, Cedric, I do that too!' Tommy yelled, practically tipping Ada on her head in his haste to get out.

'Wait, Tom! I'll push the carriage nearer!' I said. 'Stop mauling poor Ada!'

'Don't want Cedric see me,' Tommy shrieked. 'He'll think I baby too.'

'He'll think you're a banshee if you yell like that,' I said, picking Ada up so Tommy could scramble out.

Tommy went haring off to Cedric, slapping him between the shoulder blades and nearly pushing him into the pond. Cedric was wearing a crisp blue-and-white sailor suit, with a little naval cap on top of his head. He had a broad black band round one of his sleeves. Black shawl, black band. I suddenly realized their significance.

'Oh, poor Cedric!' I said, trundling the carriage up to him.

He smiled at me, but he looked a little wan and sad. Tommy had commandeered his bag of bread and was feeding the ducks himself.

'Would you like to feed the ducks too, Tess?' Cedric offered politely.

'No thank you. Tommy, give that bag back to Cedric this second!' I said.

'It's perfectly all right. I'm a bit tired of feeding them myself,' said Cedric.

I reached out and fingered the black band on his arm.

'I'm so sorry, Cedric,' I whispered. 'Is it – is it your ma?'

'No, Mama is very sad and ill, but the doctor says she will get better. It's my little sister who died,' said Cedric mournfully.

'I not know you had sister!' said Tommy, nibbling a crust of bread.

'I didn't know I had one either,' said Cedric. 'I think the doctor brought her in his black bag. But she was too little and she died. I never even got to hold her in my arms.' He looked as if he might start crying.

'You can hold Ada if you like,' I offered.

I didn't think he'd take me up on the offer. Tommy always fought hard *not* to hold her. But Cedric seemed keen. I showed

him how to hold her so she was comfortable, relieved that Ada still had a clean napkin and was in a happy mood. Her cheeks were even pinker today, probably from her Sunday lunch, and her wispy hair was getting thicker so her scalp didn't show through so much. Maybe she was going to have golden curls like me!

Cedric held her reverently, like Mother Mary holding the baby Gentle Jesus in the cattle shed. Miss Moaning would be amazed to see I remembered the story so well, even though I couldn't read most of the words written in her Bible.

'She's so sweet,' Cedric breathed. 'Oh, how I wish my own baby sister hadn't died.'

'You have ours,' Tommy offered.

I tutted at him, hoping he was joking. 'You can certainly play with Ada any time you want to,' I said. 'Look, she likes peek-a-boo.' I hid my face and then peeked out. Ada chuckled appreciatively. I did it again. She laughed as if she'd never seen such a funny thing. I did it yet again. She positively chortled.

Her delight made Cedric and me laugh – even Tommy.

'I'd like to play with her lots and lots,' said Cedric. 'But only in the park. If we went to my house Mama might see and cry.'

'You're such a thoughtful boy,' I said. 'Unlike some.' I gave Tommy a frown. He ignored me totally and helped himself to more bread.

'Cedric, I wonder if you could do me a very big favour,' I said, edging nearer to him.

'We want jam tarts with Cook!' said Tommy.

'No we don't! Well, we do, obviously, but I can see it's a bad time to come calling when everyone's sad about the baby. I was wondering, do you know the story of Cinderella?'

'Yes I do!' said Cedric. 'I love that story. I have it in my big book of fairy stories. Would you like to borrow it?'

Miss Moaning's Bible was a big book with very tiny print. I wasn't sure I'd be able to read Cedric's book either.

'Perhaps you could just tell me what happens. I know it's about this poor girl, Cinderella, and she has two nasty sisters and she has a fairy godmother but I don't really know what else. Could you tell it to me please?'

'Of course,' said Cedric.

We sat on a bench together, Cedric carefully holding Ada, while Tommy fed himself and the ducks and then careered round and round the pond until he got dizzy and fell over. Cedric was an excellent storyteller. He told me how horrible

Cinderella's stepmother and sisters were to her, and how they got invited to a splendid ball – a very special dance, given by a king and queen for their only son. Cinderella wanted to go to the ball too, so her fairy godmother turned a pumpkin into a golden coach (I wasn't quite sure how this worked, but it didn't really matter). The fairy godmother gave Cinderella a beautiful frock to wear and glass slippers.

'I have white satin slippers!' I said. 'Though I hope you don't mind if I borrow your kid boots a bit longer, Cedric. Are you sure Cinderella has *glass* slippers? Mightn't they cut her feet?'

'Well, it's magic, you see,' said Cedric. 'And Cinderella has to leave the ball by midnight, even though she's having a lovely time with the handsome prince. She runs away as the clock strikes but trips and leaves one slipper behind. Then the prince tries to find Cinderella because he's fallen in love with her, and says he will only marry the girl whose foot fits this glass slipper. Every lady in the land tries to squeeze her foot into the slipper – the mean ugly sisters even try cutting their toes off! – but of course Cinderella is the only one who fits the slipper and she gets married to the handsome prince.'

I *loved* this story.

'So guess what, Cedric!' I said. 'I'm going to be in the pantomime, in *Cinderella*! Well, probably. I'm the understudy.'

'So you'll be Cinderella?' Cedric asked, his eyes wide.

'No, because she's a lady and I'm only a girl,' I said. 'I shall be a fairy and I shall dance and dance.'

'I shall ask Papa if I can come and watch you and I shall clap and clap!' said Cedric, and he very gently held Ada's little hands and helped her clap too.

Chapter Fourteen

We settled into a routine over the next week. Connor and Tommy set off for the market every day. They became a special little double act. Tommy was unbelievably well behaved, throwing himself into his role as a mini market trader. He handled all those sets of china and never dropped so much as a teacup. He was generally tired out by the afternoon and had a nap on a pile of rags under the stall. He sometimes even climbed on old Bert's lap and nodded off there.

Maggie and Ada went to Miss Rosa's every day. Maggie didn't seem to mind assuming one pose and sticking to it. She said she didn't care how long she sat still – it was so lovely not to do any washing and have time to sit and daydream. Ada was

content to be held and rocked and fed regularly. Her hair grew even curlier, her cheeks were always rosy, and her scrawny little body became much plumper.

'Ada's definitely going to be the beauty of the family,' Maggie said, as proud as any mother.

I'd been considered the prettiest up till now, but I didn't mind. Well, not too much. *I* was practically a pantomime star, going to rehearsals every day. It wasn't quite how I imagined it would be. It was very tiring getting up early and walking all the way to the theatre each morning – and then trailing all the way back at the end of the afternoon, when my whole body was aching.

I'd never thought dancing would be such hard work. It wasn't even *proper* dancing, not yet, and we weren't on the stage. We had to go to the practice room, a large dull room at the back of the building with barely any furniture, just a piano for Mr Higgs and a rail round three of the walls. They called this 'the barre', but I've no idea why.

We had to start the day doing our warm-up exercises. I liked the first one best, prancing. As Maggie had often pointed out, I was good at this. I loved leaping about in my white practice outfit and white satin slippers while funny Mr Higgs played jolly

music. I was just as good at it as any of us, better in fact. Madame Bountiful even said 'Well done!' to me, though it practically killed her. I was good at jumping jacks too. I liked jerking about like one of those funny toys in the market, though I found myself getting out of puff, my heart thumping.

The barre raises were a bit harder, though I couldn't understand why it was so hard to raise myself up and down. I was glad we had to face the wall so that the other girls couldn't see me wobbling about. The hip rolls were worse. I could manage shoulder rolls, any old fool can wiggle shoulders, but the butterfly stretches were a real killer. It seemed utterly stupid to try to make our legs into butterfly wings, when flapping our arms would be so much easier.

I hurt from the very tops of my legs to the tips of my toes. I couldn't even attempt the splits. My legs utterly refused, though most of the other girls could manage them. Larissa was the star of the class when it came to splits. We were told to watch her. She did it so effortlessly, with a smug little smile on her face. I wished she would carry on until she tore herself into two separate girls, like the twins.

The last warm-up exercise was breathing. I did that, heavily. I was tired out before we could get started on our

proper dancing for the day. Only that wasn't really *dancing*. We had to stick to rigid rules. There were five positions for our feet, which always had to point out, the way Madame Bountiful showed us. Sometimes she lifted her skirts up to her plump knees and looked so comical I had to bite the inside of my cheeks to stop myself giggling. We even had special positions for our arms – we weren't allowed to wave them about however we wanted. Then when we were allowed to do a twirl-around, Madame Bountiful called it something fancy and yelled at us to keep our heads up and our backs straight, giving so many orders for our arms, our legs, even our necks, that I felt every part of my body was going to fly straight off me in protest.

The more I tried, the clumsier I got, and I ended up falling over several times.

'It's just as well she's only the understudy,' Larissa muttered to the twins, loud enough to make sure I heard too.

The twins themselves weren't actually too nasty. Their names were Jennifer and Penelope, but they were always called Jenny and Penny. They were so alike, with their long hair tied up in topknots and their beady little eyes and bendy bodies. No one could tell which was which, even Madame

Bountiful. They didn't seem to mind. They often answered together. They were both very good at the dance exercises but not as graceful as Larissa.

The only other complete beginner apart from me was a very pretty little girl who was only five, by far the youngest of us. She was called Elsie. She didn't say much but she smiled at everybody and sucked her thumb whenever she had the chance. She didn't have a proper practice frock and danced barefoot in her skimpy shift and a pair of long drawers, but Madame Bountiful didn't have the heart to tell her off.

Her mother was allowed to stay and watch. She was a gaunt woman with an old faded frock, holes in her stockings and boots in as bad condition as mine, and she was very humble, always bobbing everyone a curtsy. There were no chairs so she had to stand all the time and looked very tired, but whenever Elsie did a little hop and skip and twirl she clapped her hands and called out, 'Well done, our Else!' Elsie always beamed at her ma and giggled shyly.

I loved watching them but it was painful too because they made me miss my ma so much. I pretended I could hear her saying, 'Well done, our Tess!' inside my head, but it wasn't the same.

We got on to the proper dances eventually, but Madame Bountiful didn't explain what we were supposed to be doing, so it was hard to think myself into the part. I tried to be as light and fairy-like as possible in one dance, only to discover we were now learning these little scuttling moves because we were supposed to be mice! I wanted to stay being a fairy, not mess around being a mouse, though it was apparently part of the pantomime and I could become a fairy again later on.

'Only you won't ever get to be a fairy or even a mouse, because you're just the understudy,' said Larissa.

We had singing lessons too with Mrs Mountbank herself. She told us repeatedly that she had been a trained opera singer, but she had a very trilly warble that I didn't really like. I thought it much too fancy. I certainly couldn't sing like that in a million years, but luckily we had quite simple songs to learn for the pantomime. We had to do a lot of dull exercises before we got started, singing 'do-re-mi' and other silly words going up and going down. At first I got muddled and sang them in the wrong order. I learned not to sing above a whisper so that nobody noticed if I went wrong.

I memorized the songs quite quickly though because the words in those made sense. We had an opening number about being fairies singing our song, and please forgive us if we ever went wrong – and then we had to strike an attitude, hanging our heads and looking coy.

'The audience will have their work cut out forgiving Tess because she goes wrong so often,' said Larissa.

Then we had to do a skipping song about being little mice, singing in silly squeaky voices which I found quite fun, though Mrs Mountbank kept nagging that we still had to 'e-nun-ci-ate' so that the audience could understand the words. Then we had another song about going to the

ball, and isn't it *fine*, and we're having a good *time*, and lots of other silly lines like that. The last song was a wedding one, and we had to sing like chiming bells. It was incredibly complicated and everyone went wrong, not just Elsie and me.

We also had drama lessons with Mr Mountbank. He seemed very scary at first, with his bushy eyebrows and bristling moustache, and he kept tapping the floor with his fancy cane for silence. I wondered if he might poke someone with it, or even give them a whack, but I soon learned to relax around him. I found I thoroughly enjoyed his first lesson. He sat us down cross-legged and told us about the history of pantomimes and the productions his own father had been involved with at Drury Lane, wherever that was. When Mr Mountbank Senior was producing *Cinderella* he had *fifty* children performing as fairies, and four *real* fine white ponies drawing a golden coach across the stage.

I clapped my hands in excitement. Madame Bountiful was sitting in with us, and shook her finger at me furiously, but Mr Mountbank didn't mind a bit.

'Ah, it's little number one!' he said. 'I like your enthusiasm, child. How are you getting along?'

'I'm getting along splendidly, sir,' I said, telling an outright lie, but wanting to impress him.

Madame Bountiful snorted but Mr Mountbank chuckled.

'I'm glad to hear it! Well, I can't promise you a production with fifty fairies and four fine ponies at our own theatre here – we're not quite up to the lavish standards of the West End, but we shall do our very best to put on a good show.'

'And I shall do my very best to be *in* the show, even though I'm only the understudy,' I said.

'Aha! Well, we shall rely on you if anything untoward happens,' said Mr Mountbank.

Larissa was rolling her eyes affectedly at the conversation. Mr Mountbank looked in her direction and didn't look too impressed.

'Right, enough of my reminiscences. Let us look forward to our own production of *Cinderella*. Who can tell me the story?' he asked.

There was a little pause.

'I told the girls to read the story and said they must come fully prepared!' Madame Bountiful said quickly.

I put my hand up. '*I* know the story, sir!' I said.

'Of course she doesn't,' Larissa whispered. 'As if she'd have such a thing as a book in her house!'

'Cinderella was a girl just like me, with golden curls, and

she had a horrid old stepmother and two ugly big sisters,' I said, and gabbled on and on, embellishing Cedric's account, making much of the fairy godmother, and even miming putting on a ball gown and fitting my feet into glass slippers. When I got to the ball scene I stood up and pretended I was dancing with a handsome prince. I started making up their conversation:

'"Oh, you are the most beautiful girl I have ever seen!" said the handsome prince. "I especially love your gold curls!"'

Old Missus B couldn't contain herself any longer. 'For goodness' sake, child, stop this silly play-acting and making such a show of yourself!' she said.

'But Mr Mountbank said to tell the story, so I am,' I said.

'She's right, Madame Bountiful. And I must admit, I'm rather taken with her little performance. What's your name, little girl? I can't keep calling you number one.'

'I'm Tess, sir,' I said, and as I was standing up I bobbed him a curtsy to be extra polite.

'Then well done, little Tess,' said Mr Mountbank. 'Now, girls, our scripts still aren't ready yet, but you have heard most of the story from our little performer here. I want you to split up into fours, choose a corner for each team, assign yourselves parts, and act out the start of the story. I will give you ten

minutes and then I want to see how good you are at acting. Three of my fairies will have small speaking parts. I want to see who speaks up nicely and can act convincingly.'

Teams of four. And thirteen girls. Connor had taught me how to figure. There was going to be one girl left over. I was determined it wasn't going to me.

'How shall we split ourselves up, Mr Mountbank?' one of the girls asked.

'Any way you like. How about in your original numerical order?' he said.

I blessed him silently, even though it meant I was stuck with Larissa. Still I didn't mind the twins too much. If I tried hard we might even be able to make friends. They smiled at me cheerfully when I went to join them. But Larissa was scowling.

'Not you, stupid. Don't you understand? You're only the understudy. Go and watch. You're not supposed to take part. It's to choose who's the best of us fairies.' Larissa clearly thought it was already obvious.

'Look, Mr Mountbank *said*,' I argued. I looked over at him. He was watching us carefully. 'Please may I have a chance at acting, Mr Mountbank?' I asked in the sweetest, most polite

voice I could muster. 'Just in case I ever have to take over at any time.'

'Of course you may, number-one Tess,' he said, taking little Elsie on his pinstriped knee. 'You sit with me, little lass, and we'll watch the others. You may play with my watch chain if you like.'

Elsie smiled happily, not at all put out.

'You have such a cheek!' Larissa hissed at me.

Jenny and Penny fidgeted from one leg to the other, not quite sure whose side to take.

'Perhaps you two should play the sisters, seeing as you already *are* sisters,' I suggested.

'We want to be Cinderella,' they said in unison.

'Well, you can't be, because there are two of you,' Larissa said. 'It's obvious *I* should be Cinderella. I'm the most experienced because I've been in pantomime heaps of times.'

'We were in *Aladdin*,' said Jenny.

'And *Ali Baba and the Forty Thieves*,' said Penny.

'But I'm the one who knows the story, and Mr Mountbank said *I* should play Cinderella,' I said.

This wasn't strictly true and Larissa wasn't slow to point this out.

'Still, I should still play her because I'm the littlest and I have golden curls,' I said.

'I'm playing her, and that's that, street urchin,' said Larissa.

If I had really been a street urchin I'd have bopped her one on her pert little nose, but I had enough sense to realize that it wouldn't look good if I started a fight. Madame Bountiful would be furious and maybe Mr Mountbank would stop favouring me. So I heaved a big sigh.

'Very well. You be Cinderella, Larissa. And I'll be your mean stepmother who hates you and wants to punish you,' I said.

I entered into the spirit of the thing and berated Cinderella, threatening her with all kinds of punishments and making her scrub the floor with her bare hands. I said it in a mean, nasty voice – perhaps modelling myself on a certain Madame B. Jenny and Penny weren't very good at acting ugly sisters but when they wanted to mock Cinderella they each did a handstand and waggled their legs at her, which looked extremely comical.

Larissa was quite good at acting, I suppose. She managed to hang her head and look pathetic, and she even cried very prettily, dabbing her eyes with the back of her hands, but her

voice stayed very proud and confident, which didn't sound right at all. And Cedric had told me Cinderella had exceptionally small feet – but I noticed Larissa had unusually big clumpy feet (though I suppose she couldn't help that).

It seemed we'd only got started making up the play when Mr Mountbank tapped his cane on the floor for silence. He gently took his pocket watch from Elsie and consulted it.

'Ten minutes exactly!' he said. 'Right, girls, it's time to delight me.'

There was a little anxious muttering, everyone saying they hadn't had enough time to prepare properly.

'That's the point!' said Mr Mountbank. 'In our profession we have to learn to think on our feet. If we forget our lines we have to improvise. If someone heckles in the audience we have to carry on regardless. If an actor is taken ill an understudy has to replace them with no preparation.' He said the last with a little wink in my direction.

It was interesting watching each foursome perform. The first team he called for just stood there at first, chewing their lips and fidgeting, no one knowing what to say or do. I felt badly for them, but it meant our team could do much better. Then they acted a little and mumbled a few words, but they

were still very awkward. Larissa nudged Jenny and Penny, indicating that it looked like we were going to be easy winners. She even nudged me.

The second team were good though. Very good. Their Cinderella was almost too tragic, wailing and weeping, but the ugly sisters were funny and unfortunately the step-mother was extraordinary. She pulled comical faces and tottered about the stage with her behind stuck out, making everyone laugh. I couldn't help laughing too, but I felt worried. I thought she was as good as me in the part. Maybe even better.

Then it was our turn. I wondered about copying the last stepmother as she'd been so effective, but it would be obvious what I was doing. So I stuck to my own way of playing her, perhaps emphasizing her Madame Bountiful airs a little more. I spotted her watching me with her eagle eyes. I was scared she might see I was guying her and become furious, but mercifully she didn't seem to realize. Maybe Mr Mountbank did, because he spluttered into his silk handkerchief with a coughing fit – but he might have been laughing. He chuckled openly at Jenny and Penny's antics and I saw him nodding approvingly at Larissa's sadly pretty performance.

When we'd finished he gave us a clap and encouraged Madame Bountiful to do the same. She flapped her hands together as if they were two wet kippers.

'Well done, all of you. Now, I shall treat you like real actors and give you suggestions for how to improve your performance. You mustn't take it to heart. We have to learn to take criticism – even me!'

I thought it would be a silly noodle who dared to criticize Mr Mountbank, seeing it was his theatre and he was in charge of everything. Even fierce Madame Bountiful bowed down before him. He went on to tell the first team they really had to make more of an effort, and that saying anything at all, even nonsense, was better than standing stock still, speechless. He urged them to be bolder and to take risks, to throw themselves into the part and speak out clearly so they could be heard from the back of the auditorium. He was full of praise for the second team – especially the girl playing the stepmother. I drooped a little.

Then it was our turn for his criticism. Only there wasn't any!

'Well done, girls. You make a splendid team. I'm proud of you. I've clearly found my three speaking fairies. Twins, Jenny

and Penny? Or is it Penny and Jenny?' He looked from one to the other. They nodded both times and he laughed. 'You're little minxes, both of you. And very acrobatic. I shall make sure we work some of your tricks into the script. And we're old friends, aren't we, Larissa? You're a star born for the stage. You speak up well, you emote beautifully, while still looking demure and charming. You will be my lead fairy. Let us clap her, girls.'

There was muted clapping. The only girl who really wanted Larissa to win was Larissa herself. I forced myself to clap too, though it was a struggle.

'And well done too, Tess,' said Mr Mountbank. 'For a girl with no experience whatsoever you're a little wonder. I shall have great faith in you if you are called to the stage.'

It was praise that set my heart beating fast – but how I wished he'd called *me* a star.

Chapter Fifteen

I loved this whole strenuous new routine. I know Maggie and Connor were astonished. I'd always done my best to slide out of anything that meant hard work. I certainly hadn't tried to learn much at the Ragged School. But now I walked to the theatre, I sang, I danced, I acted, and it was wonderful.

I came a bit unstuck when the pantomime scripts were handed out after our first acting class. All the fairies got a copy, even though nine didn't have speaking parts.

'You girls must practically know the whole play by heart so that you understand the meaning of each scene,' said Madame Bountiful. She handed me a script too. I said thank you politely, though my heart started thumping.

'Why on earth have *you* got one? You're not even going to take part because you haven't *got* a part,' said Larissa, mean as ever.

'I see your point, Larissa, but it's important that even the understudies are familiar with the entire pantomime,' said Madame Bountiful.

'I think it's a bit point*less*,' Larissa muttered to the twins. 'I bet she can't even read properly.'

I ducked my head because I knew I was going bright red. She was right! Well, I could decipher short sentences here and there, and I knew the little, simple three-letter words, but couldn't manage any more. But I certainly wasn't going to admit it and be sneered at.

I went looking for Goody on the matinee day the next day. She came in at lunchtime so she could snack in peace and then apply her make-up and put on her nurse's outfit without having to rush. She loved having her own dressing room, just like the Mountbanks, though hers wasn't much bigger than a broom cupboard.

'Still, *I'm* not much bigger than a broom,' said Goody. She'd decorated it now, with a little red Japanese tea set, a silver kettle on a spirit stove, a tiny vase of fresh flowers, a fruit bowl

full of sugar plums, and a wooden doll with a smiley face.

'That's Smiler,' she said, making the doll bow to me. 'She's my lucky mascot. I daresay she'll bring you luck too, Tess.'

'Yes, but I'm only an understudy,' I said.

'Many of today's stars started off as understudies,' said Goody. 'And I've had a few peeps at you in the kiddies' rehearsal room. You're coming on a treat! You'll be all set to go if someone gets sick. The pantomime is always such a money spinner – that's why Mr Mountbank likes to give it a ten-week run. You'll be bouncing backwards and forwards onto that stage like a rubber ball, you'll see. So mind you learn exactly what to do – and why you're doing it. I can rattle off the whole of *Romeo and Juliet*. They don't need a prompter with me around,' Goody said proudly.

I clutched my script. I looked down at it one more time. The words blurred into each other meaninglessly, no matter how hard I stared. I felt a tear rolling down my cheek.

'Hey, what's this? Tears? Don't you cry, my duck. Tell Goody what's troubling you,' she said.

'I can't read properly!' I sobbed.

'Oh dear, there there!' Goody put her small plump arms round me in the kindest hug. 'Silly me, I should have realized.'

'If Larissa finds out she'll be so scathing.'

'She's got a poisonous tongue, that girl! I don't think you'll be the only fairy with a reading problem anyway. What about little Elsie? I'm willing to bet she can't read so much as *The cat sat on the mat.*'

'Yes, but she's only a baby. She's not expected to be able to read,' I sniffled.

'You're a baby too, my lamb,' said Goody.

'You know I'm older than I look,' I said.

'Well, it's looks that count. And who you know. You and me will have secret get-togethers over the next few weeks. I'll read aloud and you'll repeat what I say. We'll learn it together. We'll take it in turns being Cinder-blooming-ella if we fancy,' said Goody, cackling.

Dear Goody! I loved our snatched session together the following day. When we weren't going over the pantomime script, acting it out between us, we sang the songs together, and now I'd started to learn the dances, Goody helped too, skipping and twirling as nimbly as a true fairy.

'You really are like a fairy godmother to me,' I said.

When Maggie or Connor brought special cake or fruit home on Friday evening, I saved half of mine to give to

Goody the next day. She seemed quite overcome and had to blow her nose fiercely.

'What's the matter, Goody?' I asked anxiously. 'Don't you like lardy cake?'

'I love it, dearie,' she said, giving her nose another blow. 'But you shouldn't be giving me presents!'

'I want to. You've been like another ma to me,' I said earnestly.

That set her off again, and she had to blow her nose even more explosively.

'Well, if I'd ever been able to have a child, I'd wish she was a kiddie just like you, dear,' she replied.

'Can't you have babies then, Goody?' I asked as delicately as I could.

'Possibly. But I'd need a husband first, and I'm a bit fussy, see,' she said. 'I've had offers, mind you, but not from anyone tempting. Never trust a man. A shilling's your best friend. I'm best by myself: Little Goody Godber, the Pocket Venus!' She struck an attitude like the one on her poster. 'Right, let's get on with the play now, dearie. Shall we skip to my first scene with Cinderella? You can play her, and I'll be me, the fairy godmother, Gawd help me.'

'Who is playing Cinderella, Goody?' I asked.

'Miss Jemima Mountbank,' said Goody, crossing her eyes and sticking her tongue out of one side of her mouth.

'A Miss Mountbank? I didn't know there was one,' I said with interest.

'Daughter of the first Mrs Mountbank,' said Goody.

'Oh dear, did she die?'

'She didn't die, she was discarded,' said Goody, shaking her head. 'But the lord and master is still fond of Jemima. I daresay she's a sweet enough girl, but not an ounce of talent. She lisps and simpers enough to make you sick, but she'll make a pretty figure even in her rags, and she'll look a bit o' raspberry in her ball gown.'

'So who will play Prince Charming?' I frowned. 'Surely not Mr Mountbank – it wouldn't be proper.'

Goody went into peals of laughter. 'The idea! No, no, the prince will be played by Mrs Regina Mountbank – which will be a bit of a hoot because they can't stand each other.'

'But Prince Charming is a man!' I exclaimed. 'Mrs Mountbank is an older lady!'

'Better not say that out loud to anyone else!' Goody chuckled. 'Still, I have to admit she can look quite dashing in

a tasselled costume showing off her shapely legs. Pantomime's a strange performance. Wait till you see who plays the stepmother and her two ugly daughters, Chlorodyne and Pepsine. Three strapping men!'

I blinked in surprise, wondering if Goody was teasing me, but she seemed serious enough. 'Come now, let's do the fireside scene where I get to wave my magic wand – and then we'll do the scenes where you kids bob up as fairies or mice or dancers or bridesmaids.'

Four scenes. A fairy ballet at the beginning lasting ten whole minutes, then the mice turning into footmen scene, next the dance at the ball, and finally the wedding of Prince Charming and Cinderella. Though of course I wouldn't be in any of them, no matter how desperately I longed to perform.

I was so used to the routine that I felt lost on Sunday. I woke really early and couldn't snuggle down and go back to sleep. I crept downstairs and started doing the warm-up exercises in the living room. I even leaped on and off the sofa, flapping my arms as if I was flying.

'You'll bust the springs!' said Connor, coming into the room. He held out his arms. 'Here, I'll catch you, little fairy.'

'You might drop me,' I said.

'No I won't. Look at these muscles!' Connor said proudly, flexing his arms.

He'd always been strong but now all that hauling crates of china had broadened his shoulders and given him hard knots of muscles. I made a big jump and he caught hold of me easily and then twirled me round and round.

'You're doing ballet too!' I laughed.

We both collapsed on the sofa and stayed cuddled up together.

'Are you really enjoying this theatre lark, Tess?' Connor asked.

'It's the best thing ever,' I said.

'I do worry about you so. I hate it that you have to walk all that way to the theatre and back again. I'm going to work so hard at the market that one day I'll have enough to get my own stall, then another, then I'll own the whole market and we'll live in one of those big houses like your pal Cedric and we'll have a carriage. You'll be the leading lady at the theatre and will be driven there in style. How about that?'

'But you might have a lady friend by then and she'll want the carriage to herself,' I said. I combed Connor's hair back with my fingers, trying to make it go into a fancy style. 'You're very good-looking, Connor.'

'You're the only girl for me,' he said.

'You won't go off and leave us, like Pa?' I asked.

'Never. We're going to stay together. You, me, Maggie, Tommy and little Ada.'

'Well, maybe Tommy can go off and get himself a girlfriend,' I said. 'Only joking!'

'He's actually a little trooper down at the market. Good as gold, honestly. He's my little man there, ever so helpful, bless him,' said Connor.

'Do you think Pa would be proud of us?' I mumbled.

Connor hesitated. 'Maybe. How could he help not being proud of you, Tess?'

'So why did he run away from me?' I whispered into his neck.

'Search me. Perhaps he felt ashamed,' said Connor.

'Perhaps he just didn't care,' I said. 'Well, never mind, we don't care about him now, do we? My friend Goody says you should never trust a man. A shilling's your best friend.'

'I'd like to meet Goody some time to thank her for being so kind to you,' said Connor. 'Fancy you being friends with famous theatre folk! And our Maggie having her portrait painted by a proper lady artist. And little Ada too! She's coming on a treat now, isn't she, Tess?'

'She won't die, will she?'

'No! Not now she's got enough to eat,' said Connor.

'But Cedric's little sister died,' I said.

'Did she? Oh dear, how sad for them,' said Connor.

'Do you think if I picked some flowers and tied them in a pretty bunch and took it round to their back door they'd think I was being too forward?' I asked.

'I think they'd probably be very touched,' said Connor. 'Tell you what, let's go up on the common before the others wake and we'll pick a bunch of wild flowers.'

'Oh, let's!'

It was a joy to set off with my lovely brother. It was a beautiful day, quite cold, but the sun was already out and the dawn sky was misty blue, and Connor and I walked briskly hand in hand. I sang him the pantomime songs I was learning, la-la-la-ing when I forgot the words, and he sang along with me.

The common was twice as far away as the park, but we were so happy to spend time together that we flew along as if we had wings on our boots. I'd hoped to find primroses and cowslips, but it was the wrong time of year. Still, there were lilac-blue harebells and yellow hawkbit and purple Michaelmas daisies, and I managed to pick a really big bunch. I could hardly see over the top of them as we walked home.

Maggie and Tommy were up and dressed, and Ada was fidgeting and moaning in her drawer.

'I've already fed her a whole bottle full of milk but she won't settle. I think she's maybe teething,' said Maggie. She was busy making apple sauce to go with our pork chops. (We were eating like royalty nowadays.) 'You try dandling her, Connor; she likes you holding her.'

I spread my flowers out on the table and tried arranging them according to size.

'Oh, for goodness' sake, Tess, I'm going to be chopping up the veg on that table! Get those messy flowers off it! I don't know why you've picked them, because they're wilting already,' said Maggie.

'No they're not!' I said fiercely, though I could see some of the harebells really were beginning to droop.

'Perhaps you'd better take them to Cedric's house straight away,' said Connor.

'Oh yes, I want to go there! I want to see Cook!' said Tommy, jumping up and down.

'Shall I take them?' Connor asked Maggie.

'No, you stay and help here. I want you to mend the baby carriage – one of its wheels has gone wonky,' said Maggie.

So I arranged my flowers as carefully as I could, discarding a few that were obviously already dead, and tied them with twine. Connor handed Ada to me and she settled almost immediately, nuzzling into my neck.

'I think she's been missing me!' I said delightedly. 'She can come with me.'

'Is that tactful, as Cedric's mother has just lost her baby?' Connor said.

'She doesn't come down to the kitchen at the back. She always stays upstairs,' I said. 'And Cedric likes Ada. Maybe he'll find her a comfort.'

I couldn't carry Ada and the flowers, so I had to entrust my bunch to Tommy.

'Don't you dare squash them now,' I told him.

'I big boy now. I not squash,' said Tommy. To give him his due, he did trot along nicely beside me, telling me about the things he did down at the market. I told him about the pantomime but he lost interest quickly and talked over me.

I told Ada instead, murmuring against her fluffy head, promising her that I was going to be a proper star one day and hoped she'd be proud of her big sister. Ada gurgled as if in agreement, which made me even fonder of her.

When we got to Cedric's gate, I made Tommy hush and told him we had to be very quiet and respectful because everyone was so sad that their baby had died.

'Won't we get any jam tarts then?' he asked.

'No, we'll just hand in the flowers, say we're sorry, and then go away,' I said firmly.

Tommy looked very disappointed but trailed along beside me, letting the flowers droop.

'Hold them *up*, Tom!' I said. 'What am I going to do with you?'

'Put me in a sack and shake me!' he said.

It was what Ma always said to us when we were naughty. It made my eyes suddenly sting with tears, so I looked

suitably mournful when I knocked at the back door.

We waited. Even Tommy looked a bit anxious. Then Sarah-Jane opened it. She had a black band round her arm and seemed very serious – but when she saw it was us she smiled.

'Hello, you lot!' she said.

'Please tell Cook we're not taking liberties, but we're very sorry about the baby and we'd like to give you these,' I said, giving Tommy a little poke in the back.

He thrust the big bunch of flowers at her. 'We sorry,' he echoed, in a subdued murmur.

'Oh, bless you!' said Sarah-Jane, clasping the flowers as if they were the finest red roses. 'Come in, come in!'

Tommy stepped forward immediately but I grabbed him.

'No, we don't want to intrude,' I said quickly.

'You're not intruding at all, you're our little friends,' said Sarah-Jane. 'I'm so sorry I was a bit brisk last time. The poor missus was in a dreadful state and the baby . . . Oh dear, oh dear. But we're calmer now. Do come in and say hello to Cook and help me arrange these lovely flowers.'

So we trooped indoors after Sarah-Jane. Cook was busy at the stove, with the glorious smell of roasting meat already wafting round the kitchen.

'Look who's blown in with the wind,' said Sarah-Jane. 'And they've brought us these lovely flowers to say they're sorry about Cedric's poor little baby sister.'

'The little lambs!' said Cook, and she embraced us all. She had tears in her eyes as she took Ada in her arms. 'God giveth and He taketh away,' she murmured piously, but then she snapped back into her cheerful self. 'Sit yourselves down and I'll see what I can find in the way of elevenses.'

'Jam tarts?' Tommy asked eagerly.

'Not today, pet. I've been too busy preparing dinner to do any extra baking. But there's treacle tart for pud. Might you fancy a slice?'

'Oh, yes please!' said Tommy, and so did I, though we'd never had treacle tart before.

Cook took a beautiful big brown tart out of the larder and went to cut it.

'But you'll spoil it and there might not be enough for Cedric's family!' I said in a rush.

'Don't you worry, my dear. There's another finer tart with fancy pastry for them upstairs, though it will be a waste of my work because the missus won't eat and even the master hasn't much stomach for it at the moment. This one's for Sarah-Jane

and Clara, the lady's maid, and I daresay Alfred the policeman might be round for a slice and all. There's more than enough for you two to have your share – and I'll fill a little glass of custard for the blessed baby too.'

'You so kind,' said Tommy, giving her a hug. His arms couldn't reach very far round her but he did his best. 'I wish I your little boy!'

Treacle tart was delicious. I had a little spoonful of Ada's custard, pretending I was just checking to see if she'd like it, and that was marvellous too, wonderfully smooth and creamy. I rather wished Cook was our mother too, though of course no one could ever replace our dear Ma.

While Cook and Sarah-Jane were peeling vegetables they told us about the sad event. Cedric's mother had been taken very poorly and the baby had only lived a day.

'I saw her dressed up in her christening robes, lying so still and peaceful, a true little angel,' said Sarah-Jane. 'The missus was still bedridden and couldn't attend the funeral. We weren't sure what to do about little Cedric. It was thought best to leave him at home with his mama, but Cedric insisted he wanted to go to hold Papa's hand in case he was lonely. Oh dear, I'll start blubbing again if I don't watch out.

Come on now, you two. Stop scoffing and tell us about your own adventures.'

We launched into our exciting news. I boasted about being a pantomime fairy. Perhaps I didn't make it clear that I was only an understudy. Tommy boasted about his 'jobs' at the market, while Sarah-Jane ooohed and aaahed and Cook cut us another slice of treacle tart.

I forgot to keep spooning custard into Ada's open mouth and she started whimpering, which soon became a full-blooded roar. I stood up and rocked her in my arms, but now she'd started she didn't want to stop.

Then the door at the other end of the kitchen opened and a distraught lady in a long white nightgown came stumbling into the kitchen, her shawl trailing from one shoulder.

'Madam! Oh my goodness, let me help you back to bed!' Sarah-Jane gasped, rushing to her.

'A baby! I heard my baby crying!' the woman said, her whole face contorted with joy. She reached out eagerly to Ada.

'Now now, madam,' said Cook, her arms out too, but not actually touching the mistress. 'She's not your poor baby. She's gone to join the angels, remember?'

'No, she's here, look at her! Give her to me, little girl! She

wants me! Can't you see, she's crying for me,' she said, pulling at my arm.

I held Ada tight. 'I'm sorry, madam, but she's my sister. She's not your baby. You can hold her for a moment if you like though, but you can't take her away,' I said.

Cook and Sarah-Jane shook their heads, but the lady calmed slightly. She slumped in a kitchen chair, her nightgown awry, her feet bare. She looked so dishevelled She scared me, but I held Ada out all the same and handed her over, though I kept my arms outstretched, ready to snatch her back if necessary. The lady gave a deep sigh and cradled Ada carefully, murmuring to her. And weirdly, Ada stopped yelling, sniffled a little, and then settled, staring up at her as if she really was her mother.

Sarah-Jane gently straightened the lady's nightgown and wrapped the shawl round her. Ada sighed, closed her eyes and went to sleep. The lady carried on whispering to her, smiling, though there were tears streaming down her face.

Then Clara, the other maid, and Cedric came rushing into the kitchen.

'Oh, madam, there you are! You gave us such a fright

running away like that,' Clara gasped, flicking back the long white streamers on her fancy cap.

'Is that our baby, Mama?' Cedric whispered.

'She's our Ada,' I said. 'I'm so sorry I brought her. I didn't mean to upset your mama. I just came round to bring some flowers.'

'Yes, of course she's Ada,' said Cedric, sighing. 'She's too big to be my little sister. Mama, she's not our baby. Had you better give her back to Tess? She's my friend.'

'My baby,' said his mama. But then she shook her head so sadly. 'I wish she was my baby girl.'

'But Cedric here is your own dear boy, madam – and God willing, you'll have another little sister for him one day,' Cook said gently. 'Better give the baby back to her sister and let Clara take you up to bed. You're still not very well.'

The lady handed Ada back very reluctantly but kept her arms open and flexed, as if cradling an invisible child. She let herself be led away, sobbing. The kitchen was silent for a moment. I felt like crying too.

'I'm so sorry, Cedric. I didn't think your mama would know we were here. I promise I won't come back. Come along, Tommy.'

For once Tommy didn't argue or beg for another slice of treacle tart. We had a little hug with everyone and then went home.

Chapter Sixteen

I wasn't sure whether we'd done the right thing or not going to Cedric's house. I gave Ada extra cuddles for being such a good baby and helping to comfort Cedric's ma, and then happily ate my own Sunday roast. Midway through the afternoon Connor finished the repairs on the baby carriage so we went out to the park to christen it. Maggie had stitched and stuffed a new mattress out of more abandoned sheets and Ada made it plain that she appreciated it by gurgling all the way to the park and back.

We let Tommy feed the ducks with our own stale bread and found a discarded ball so we could have a game of catch. We'd never really had a proper family outing before. Pa always

wanted to go out by himself and told us to scarper if we followed him. Ma might have wanted to take us, but she was always too busy and tired out.

If only we'd learned how to earn our own money when Ma was alive then she could have left the chores and come to join us. To my amazement *I* was earning money now, even though we were still rehearsing and I was only an understudy. It was a meagre two shillings a week – but that added up to twenty-six penny buns. That might seem bad arithmetic, but if you order twelve at a time it's called a baker's dozen, and you get an extra bun for free.

Those buns could feed us for a week, though we'd be pretty hungry. Tommy earned a handful of pennies because folk at the market thought he was a bright little spark. Connor earned a lot more, sometimes as much as a sovereign, but he had to give old Bert at least half. Maggie earned the most from sitting on her backside and trying to look sad – which didn't take much of an effort! Ada had a tiny wage too – Miss Rosa insisted on giving her a sixpence every now and then because she was part of the portrait after all.

We treated ourselves to hokey-pokey ice cream in the park, which was such a treat. We were sitting down to dripping

on toast for our tea when there was a knock on our front door. We looked at each other. The only person who ever came knocking was the rent man, and Maggie had managed to pay him on Friday.

'Is it Pa?' I whispered.

'No, he'd just come barging in,' said Connor.

'It might be folks coming to complain about their sheets!' said Maggie.

'Or the nasty big boys,' said Tommy. 'They say they come and get me.'

'I'd like to see them try,' said Connor. 'You stay where you are and I'll go and see who it is.' He puffed himself up to look as fierce as possible and stamped to the door in his boots, making as much noise as possible.

'YES?' he said belligerently as he opened the door. Then he stammered, 'Oh, I'm so sorry, sir. Do come in – if you want to, that is.'

'Indeed I do want to,' said a very posh voice.

'Yes please,' said a small high voice.

'Please, come into our sitting room,' said Connor. 'I'll just be a moment,' he added, and put his head round our kitchen door.

'It's Cedric and his papa!' he mouthed at us. 'Come!' He beckoned urgently.

'Oh my Lord,' said Maggie, whipping off her apron and running her fingers through her hair.

'I like Cedric,' Tommy said happily, running into the living room, still taking bites of his dripping toast.

I stayed still. I clutched Ada. She was sitting on my lap, happily chewing a crust. I had a mouthful of toast in my mouth but I was so shocked I couldn't swallow it. Had the papa come to complain about my coming to his house with Ada and upsetting his poor wife? Maybe I'd be forbidden to ever go there again. He'd want Cedric's boots back too. I didn't need them for dancing now because I had my satin slippers, but I still wanted to have them a little longer because I loved them so.

'Tess! Come in the living room!' Connor called. 'Please sit down, sir. And you, Cedric.'

I walked into the sitting room holding Ada in front of me, like a shield. Cedric's papa, Mr Cedar, was a tall man, very upright and elegant in a beautifully cut black suit. He was sitting rather gingerly on the edge of our sofa, with Cedric by his side.

'Tess, it Cedric with his pa!' Tommy said unnecessarily, waving his arm around so that a little slurp of dripping flew into the air. It missed the papa's immaculate suit by a whisker.

'Tommy, watch that toast!' Maggie commanded.

'It's dripping toast and it's very tasty,' said Cedric. 'I had some last time I was here, when Maggie kindly washed my cream suit for me.'

'I believe you've been very kind to my son,' said the papa. He turned to me. 'And you must be the little girl who brought the flowers today?'

'Yes, that's Tess, my special friend – and that's her baby sister Ada,' said Cedric.

'I'm so sorry, sir,' I said. 'I was taking liberties, wasn't I?'

The papa put his head on one side. 'I beg your pardon?'

'Cook said I mustn't take liberties, when we first came,' I said.

'I'm afraid I don't quite understand, my dear,' he said.

'She mean we mustn't ask for jam tarts,' said Tommy. He tore a piece off his toast and offered it to Cedric. 'Like a bit?'

'Tommy! Cedric won't want your mangled piece! I'll make him a fresh slice,' said Maggie, horrified.

But Cedric had already taken it and put it in his mouth. 'Thank you very much,' he said politely.

'You certainly weren't taking liberties by bringing those lovely flowers to express your sympathy,' the papa said.

'They were just wild flowers off the common and they were drooping even though they were freshly picked. But I shouldn't have brought Ada. I promise I didn't mean your missus to hear her crying and get so upset,' I said, trembling.

'That's why I'm here, my dear. My wife is still suffering from our great loss, as you could see. But holding your little sister meant a great deal to her. She'd love to see the baby again.' He looked around, a little uncertain, then turned to Connor. 'I believe that in the current absence of your parents, you'd be the acting head of the household,' he said.

'Yes, I am,' Connor said proudly.

'Though I'm the eldest,' Maggie insisted.

'I wonder if both of you would mind if young Tess brought Ada round to my house as often as possible. It would be such a comfort to my wife when she's feeling the loss of our daughter so desperately,' he said.

'Oh my goodness,' said Maggie. 'Well, of course we're happy for our Tess and little Ada to help in any way we can.'

'And Tommy can come too, because he likes Cook's jam tarts!' said Cedric.

'Well, we'll come on a Sunday, but I'm afraid I can't come until very late the other days because I have a job now,' I said importantly.

'A job, little lady?' Cedric's papa asked, his head on one side again. I could tell he wasn't taking me seriously.

'Yes, Papa. Tess is going to be a pantomime star,' Cedric announced. 'She's a fairy in *Cinderella*!'

'And a little mouse and a ballroom dancer and a bridesmaid!' I said. It didn't seem necessary to point out that I might not get to perform any of these roles.

'Well, perhaps *you* might like to bring Ada round to our house on a regular basis?' Cedric's papa asked Maggie.

'I'd be delighted to, sir, but you see I have a job too,' said Maggie. 'I wonder if you've heard of the artist Miss Rosa Reynolds? She's painting my portrait and I get paid as her model.'

'And I have job too, at market!' Tommy announced.

'Now, I really doubt that, young man,' said Cedric's papa.

'Well, he does have a kind of job, helping me at the market,' said Connor. 'I sell china there.'

'He's got a marvellous patter. He sells heaps,' I said.

'My goodness me! What an enterprising family you are,' said Cedric's papa. 'Your mother and father must be so proud of you.'

There was a pause while we looked at each other.

'Our ma died,' I said.

'Oh my dear, I'm so sorry,' he said. 'And what about your father?'

'Pa's walked out on us,' Connor said bluntly.

'So . . . there's no one at all looking after you? But that's terrible. You're children!'

'Well, Maggie and I are practically adults,' said Connor with dignity. 'And we get by fine by ourselves.'

'I see you do. But perhaps you might need help in some way? I could go to the appropriate authorities?' Cedric's papa offered.

'How would that help?' Maggie asked curtly. 'We'd be put in the workhouse and we're not having that.'

'I can see that's not a good option,' Cedric's papa said awkwardly. 'And certainly I think you're managing splendidly. Perhaps you can simply bring the baby round whenever it's convenient. We will always be at home at the moment.'

'And you can play with me,' said Cedric. 'I've been so lonely.'

'I'm so sorry, son,' said his papa, drawing him onto his knee. 'It's been a very hard time for you too. I'm doing my very best to find you a suitable nurse.'

'But Sarah-Jane's so nice!' I burst out.

'She is indeed!' said Cedric's papa, twinkling. 'My wife and I are very grateful to her. And we're very grateful to you too, Tess, for befriending my son. Please do keep coming round when you can. I promise you you'll always be very welcome. It's very exciting news that you're going to be in this year's pantomime. I shall make sure that we have tickets for the opening night!'

That was a worrying announcement – but I couldn't bring myself to say that I'd actually be behind the scenes. I just smiled while Maggie saw them out and then we all flopped in the living room.

'Well, well, well!' said Connor. 'We certainly have some grand new friends!'

'Fancy practically begging us to bring Ada round to comfort his wife!' said Maggie. 'What do you think, Tess? She won't go completely barmy and try to make off with her?'

'Of course not! I wouldn't let her. She was very gentle with Ada. She's just sad,' I said. 'Remember when Ma was so upset when she lost the baby after Tommy was born?'

'I glad I not lost,' said Tommy. 'Can I have more dripping toast as Cedric ate some of mine?'

We had another slice and shared a big bottle of ginger beer, drinking a toast to our family.

We did our best to help. On matinee days we stopped rehearsals early so I sometimes collected Ada from Miss Rosa's and took her round to Cedric's house. Sarah-Jane would lead me up to the mistress's bedroom. She would lie propped on her beautiful embroidered pillows and hold our baby tight, crooning to her and rubbing her pale cheek on Ada's fluffy curls.

I'd be free to wander round the beautiful room, looking at the trinkets on her dressing table, sometimes even trying on an amber necklace or helping myself to a dab of cologne. She was so absorbed in loving Ada that she hardly noticed. If I became a famous dancer then maybe I'd have a bedroom like

this one day, with a pretty dressing table and a huge wardrobe full of beautiful silk dresses, a different one for every day of the month.

A couple of times Cedric's mama was well enough to be up and dressed, though lounging on her velvet chaise longue, but mostly she was in bed.

Cedric attended these visits too. His mama absent-mindedly patted his head or let him cuddle up beside her, but her eyes were always on Ada. He didn't seem to mind too much, perhaps because his papa always made such a fuss of him.

Sometimes we sat on the window seat together and I told him about the rehearsals. We still had to do the tedious little practice parts, singing 'do-re-mi', and bending our knees and wriggling our shoulders and rising up and down on our toes, but we sang the pantomime songs and performed our proper fairy ballet and mouse dance and the ballroom polka and bridesmaids parade, pointing our toes and holding our little bouquets. We were in pairs for the polka and the parade. I didn't have a partner, but I imagined one as hard as I could so I didn't feel too left out.

My skinny legs were developing real dancer's muscles in my calves, and I was always ravenously hungry now I was

taking so much exercise. When Clara came to settle Cedric's mama down for her rest I would gently prise Ada away and we'd go downstairs to Cook. She always had a special treat for me, gingerbread or iced biscuits or cream sponge or her special jam tarts – and she'd always give me a little bagful to take home.

She'd make Ada a special portion of creamy porridge and give her a bottle too. Ada would smack her lips appreciatively and chuckle when Cook held her up in the air and kissed her tummy.

'She's turning into a real little pumpkin,' said Sarah-Jane.

'As long as she doesn't turn into a golden coach like in the pantomime!' I said.

'So how do they manage that on the stage?' Cedric asked. 'The fairy godmother can't *really* work magic, can she?'

'Well, she has a magic wand,' I said. 'And when she shakes it there are all sorts of stars and sparkles – but that's just someone blowing them from the side of the stage. Then they dim the lights and someone else rushes in and takes the pumpkin away, and us mice scamper off stage and they push on a golden coach and the lights go up and then the audience is meant to gasp in wonder and clap. I do hope they do!'

'Hark at you, little Tess! You sound as if you've been on the stage since year dot!' said Cook.

'I really think it's my mission in life,' I said. Miss Moaning had always gone on about our missions, but perhaps I'd misunderstood, because Cook and Sarah-Jane burst out laughing.

I was deadly serious. Every day at the theatre made me love it more and more. The last two weeks before opening night we were allowed to rehearse on stage with the adult actors. It was a little alarming, because Mr Mountbank was playing Baron Blunderboar. He should really have been Baron Blunder*roar* because he bellowed all the time, whether he was acting or

directing. He'd grown his moustache in length and bushiness, and frequently twirled it, his eyes flashing.

He shouted at the cast if they dried – that meant they forgot their lines, or stood stock still like wax models, or marched off stage right when they should have gone left. He never shouted at Goody because she was always word-perfect and never once dropped her fairy wand, though she had to twirl it around a lot when she did her dance. He didn't shout at Cinderella either, because she was played by Miss Jemima Mountbank, his daughter by his first wife.

I would have shouted at her, because she didn't seem to have inherited a drop of the Mountbank family talent. She was as stiff as her own broomstick, and she sounded such a wet sap as she sighed and simpered her lines.

For once Larissa and I were in total agreement, whispering insulting remarks about her – but Mr Mountbank praised her royally, though he occasionally sighed to himself. His favourite phrase was, 'Well done, Jemima, my little fragrant flowerpot.' '*Hopelessly done, Jemima, my little stinky chamber pot!*' we whispered, having to stuff our fists in our mouths to stop ourselves shrieking with laughter.

It was perfectly fine for all us fairies to laugh at Mr Arthur

Stanford, who played Cinderella's wicked stepmother, and Mr Jack Juggins and Mr Knotty Knight, who were a scream as the quarrelling ugly sisters, Chlorodyne and Pepsine, because they were meant to be funny. They were so comical that I laughed until my stomach ached – and when I imitated their antics at home, I made Maggie and Connor and Tommy roar with laughter too, which was glorious.

Surprisingly, the best actor was Mrs Regina Mountbank, the second wife. She hadn't seemed bothered at our audition, barely paying attention and yawning when Mr Mountbank's attention was elsewhere. But as soon as she came striding on stage, slapping her thighs and striking an attitude, she became a perfect Prince Charming and even seemed believable when she declared her love for Cinderella, though off stage stepmother and stepdaughter clearly couldn't bear each other.

I trembled with excitement the first time the fairies were beckoned on stage to perform the opening ballet.

'Not you!' Larissa said to me, back to her old mean self. 'You're just the understudy. That means you have to sit and watch.'

'Quite right, Larissa,' said Madame Bountiful.

'Even so, I think we'll let little Miss Tess up on stage too,'

said Mr Mountbank, with a flamboyant twirl of his moustache. 'How else is the child to learn? It seems she's coming along in leaps and bounds already – literally!'

So I leaped and bounded my way through the ballet, though I had to stand back behind my fellow fairies. I was step perfect now, though I suppose I didn't quite have Larissa's style and grace – but I was better than half the others and couldn't help outshining little Elsie, who frequently forgot what she had to do. But it didn't really matter, because she was so much younger and smaller that she just looked cute.

She cried when she started off on the wrong foot for the third time and Madame Bountiful said she was a silly-billy – it was actually one of her milder comments, as even Madame Bountiful had a soft spot for Elsie. Mr Mountbank himself comforted her, and gave her a raspberry drop from his pocket, which gave me a pang. I'd really thought *I* was his favourite, and yet he'd never given *me* a raspberry drop.

'Let the child make a few blunders, Madame Bountiful,' he said, mopping Elsie's tears with his own silk handkerchief. 'It will only endear her to the audience. *However,*' he added, turning to the rest of us fairies. 'If any of *you* girls make a single mistake, I shall have your guts for garters!'

We didn't know if he was serious or not but decided not to test him out.

I loved dancing in the opening ballet. It gave me the joy I felt when I made up my own dances, but it was somehow better keeping to special steps and making a pattern as we performed. Goody danced with us as she was queen of all the fairies. I knew she could do comical dancing, but feared she might look comical in a proper ballet because she couldn't help being small and rather squat, but she performed with grace and dignity, and could even go up on her toes and twirl without a single wobble.

'How did you get to be so brilliant at ballet, Goody?' I asked her privately.

'It was all the training I had when I was just a tiny tot. Don't forget, I was Little Goody Godber, the Pocket Ballerina,' said Goody. 'And very popular too. Folk used to throw flower posies up on stage, and candy canes and sticks of barley sugar. I thought it great fun!'

'So you were a star when you were only five!' I said. 'Elsie's age!'

'That's me,' said Goody.

'And you knew, right from when you were tiny, you wanted to be on the stage?' I asked.

'Well, I come from a theatrical family, see. My ma and pa had a music hall act, two clowns and a lot of slapstick. They were quite famous for it, though never top billing. I had a sister who did an acrobatic act and a brother who juggled – it was in our blood. I came as a bit of a shock, being small. I think they'd hoped I'd join in the sibling act, but I've no spring in my little legs, and my arms are too short to juggle, so they trained me up as a dancer instead,' said Goody.

'And now you're a big star even though you're little,' I said, squeezing her hand.

'Bless you, duckie. I'm not a West End star, just a little woman in an outer London theatre, but it suits me fine. I reckon you're the one with the chance of being the really big star, little Tess. You've got that spark in you. I can see your name being top of the bill one day!' Goody said.

'I wish! But now I'm not even a proper performer, only the understudy,' I said.

'You wait!' Goody took hold of her wand and gave it a twirl. 'It's magic, ain't it?'

Chapter Seventeen

We were getting nearer and nearer Boxing Day, and the opening performance. I watched the sets being painted, the costumes being stitched.

The mice costumes were incredibly cute – grey, with big mouse ears and long pink tails. The ballroom dresses were amazing: flouncy silk with very full skirts. The bridesmaids' dresses were a glorious shade of pink, with rosebuds sewn round the neck and darker pink sashes with huge bows. And the fairy dresses were the best of all: white, with wonderful ballerina skirts and sparkly wings sewn onto the backs of the satin bodices.

'They're glorious!' I breathed, watching the two sewing ladies flash their needles.

'Yes they are!' said Larissa. 'But you're not getting any of the costumes, you do realize that, don't you?' she added, and shook her head at my seeming ignorance.

'But what if I have to go on stage if anyone's ill?' I said.

'You'll just have to wear their costume then,' said Larissa.

'But it might not fit! I'm smaller than the other fairies, apart from Elsie,' I said.

'Then you'll look stupid, won't you?' said Larissa.

But she was the one who was stupid, because wonderful Mr Mountbank sent *me* to be measured up by the sewing ladies and I had four costumes specially made for me!

'It's in case you have to go on,' said Mr Mountbank. 'I can't have you looking silly in an ill-fitting costume if you get your big chance.'

'Oh, Mr Mountbank, sir, you're the loveliest gentleman ever!' I said fervently, and I reached up and kissed his whiskery cheek.

He ruffled my curls affectionately, in the way Pa used to when he was in a very good mood. How I wished Mr Mountbank was my real pa, so that I could have been brought up in a theatrical family!

But I loved my own special small family most, and even

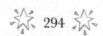

though I was so caught up in the show, I plotted and planned so I could give them each a special Christmas present. I made friends with the sewing ladies and they showed me how to stitch neatly. When they were making a leather jerkin for the Prince Charming costume, they gave me several scraps that I fashioned into two purses, one for Connor and another for Tommy, so they could store coins in them when they were at the market.

I used silk scraps from Cinderella's ball gown to make a little stitched heart for Maggie as a keepsake. I made another for Goody, and fashioned a little mouse out of the furry material for Ada to play with. I wondered if Cedric might like a purse or a heart or a mouse, but then had a better idea. I begged a square of bronze satin from the stepmother's gown and fashioned him a thumb-sized pair of boots to thank him for the long-term loan of his own boots.

I racked my brains to think of a present for Mr Mountbank. Goody suggested buying him a little comb for his moustache, but I worried that he might think it impertinent. I eventually used some of my rehearsal earnings to buy him a cigar from the tobacco shop I passed on my long way home. I asked the man behind the counter for the finest cigar he had, but nearly

fainted when he told me the price. I settled for one of the cheapest, but it still used up a lot of my savings. Still, I wouldn't have any money at all if it wasn't for Mr Mountbank, so I decided not to begrudge it.

The final dress rehearsal was on Christmas Eve. It was a very long day, and it was very painful for me because I wasn't really part of it. I couldn't tag behind the other fairies as I usually did. I had to sit quietly in the auditorium and watch with the two other understudies, a gentleman and a lady covering the adult parts. They didn't seem particularly interested in watching the show. The gentleman started yawning and fell fast asleep after half an hour. The lady had to nudge him sharply whenever he started yawning. She spent her time crocheting a soft grey shawl, trying to finish a Christmas present for her aging mother.

'I've got a spare crochet hook. Would you like me to teach you how to crochet so you can fashion a little square for your own mother, dearie?' she whispered.

I felt as if she'd stabbed me in the chest with the crochet hook.

'Thank you, but I haven't got a ma any more,' I murmured.

'Oh, you poor little mite,' she said, and patted my hand.

I sat still, imagining crocheting Ma the finest shawl in the world. Not in dreary old grey. I'd choose all the colours of the rainbow. If only she was here now. She'd love to see me dressed up in all my wonderful costumes. If I never got to go on stage, I'd perform the whole pantomime just for Ma, and she'd clap me and tell me I was her special girl.

The dress rehearsal didn't seem to be going very well. The fairy ballet right at the beginning was a bit of a disaster. Goody was brilliant as always, but the fairies jostled together and tripped over each other and poor little Elsie grew bewildered and burst into tears. One of the twins mistimed their acrobatic number and Jenny (or possibly Penny) landed awkwardly and hurt her leg.

Madame Bountiful came rushing on stage, absolutely furious, and soon it wasn't just Elsie who was crying, it was nearly everyone. I was almost glad I was only the understudy, sitting in the dark. I watched Jenny/Penny anxiously. She was limping badly. What if she was seriously injured? I'd have to go on in her place – and I knew that I didn't have a hope of managing their acrobatic routine, with flip-flaps and cartwheels and handstands. They even had hoists to lift them right up in the air at the end of the ballet so that it looked as if they were

really flying. It looked terrifying, though the twins had learned to perform their flying routine with style.

Mr Mountbank seemed less perturbed than Madame Bountiful. He went up on stage too and did his best to calm everyone down.

'We'll try the whole ballet one more time to give the girls a chance to get it right. What about you, little twin? Do you need to take a break?'

'I think I'll be fine, sir,' she said bravely, as her sister rubbed her leg for her and tied a makeshift bandage round her knee.

'That's the spirit, my dears. And let us all remember – a disastrous rehearsal always means a magnificent opening night!' he said.

They calmed down and tried one more attempt. It still wasn't perfect but at least they didn't bump into each other this time, and one of the other fairies steered Elsie into place. The injured twin still had a slight limp but it didn't stop her performing.

I watched Larissa intently, hoping she might have a fall this time. Not one to injure her terribly, of course – just enough to make sure she couldn't dance for a couple of days. But Larissa was the only fairy who danced impeccably both times, her head

held high, her arms in graceful arcs, her legs strong and supple so she didn't once waver. Mr Mountbank stood up and clapped her as she took a curtsy at the end.

I knew Gentle Jesus would want me to be pleased for her. I'm afraid I wasn't in the slightest.

Then at long last we got started on the proper pantomime itself, with Cinderella in her rags being bossed around by her stepmother and Chlorodyne and Pepsine, her wondrously ugly sisters. I hadn't seen Jack and Knotty in full make-up before. They looked incredible, with huge eyebrows, false noses and massively rouged cheeks and lips. Arthur was almost as outrageous as their mother in his bronze satin, with false bosoms, belly and behind giving him the funniest of figures. He still spoke in a booming baritone, but his two daughters spoke in squeaky falsettos as they tormented poor Cinderella.

She pouted and sniffed and put the back of her hand to her forehead in a pathetic way, but I still thought she was useless as an actress, though she looked pretty enough in a fetching short frock with just a couple of tiny rips – Maggie and I would have treasured it as a party dress. I waited for Mr Mountbank to give her copious notes, but he simply

muttered, 'Well done, my child,' though he couldn't help giving a small sigh as he said it.

Our tummies were rumbling by the time we got to the scene where Cinderella weeps by the fireplace and the fairy godmother appears down the chimney.

Mr Mountbank consulted his pocket watch and clapped his hands.

'Dear Lord, it's long past lunchtime. We will be here until midnight at this rate – rather fitting for this pantomime. We had better take a half hour break for refreshment, with the compliments of the house.'

Young Frank and two stagehands lumbered forward carrying enormous wicker picnic baskets and a veritable feast was set out on the stage for everyone – even the understudies! I ate pork pie and veal patties and cold sausages and a fruit tart with cream, washed down with a bottle of ginger beer all to myself.

When I had bolted everything down I shyly approached Mr Mountbank, who was sitting on the stage, dangling his legs and showing off his black patent boots with snow-white spats.

'Excuse me, sir,' I whispered timidly.

'Away with you, child!' said Madame Bountiful. 'Don't

you dare interrupt Mr Mountbank when he's having his meal!'

Mr Mountbank smiled at me. 'What is it, young Tess?'

'Please, sir, I've got a little Christmas present for you,' I said, and produced the cigar from the pocket of my frock, praying that it hadn't got too bent. I didn't have any proper wrapping paper so I'd hidden it in a handkerchief purloined from the clean washing pile at home.

Mr Mountbank unwrapped the hankie cautiously and seemed surprised by the cigar inside.

'I do hope it's a decent brand,' I said.

'It's an excellent brand, my dear!' he said, though I have no idea whether he really meant it. 'How very kind of you!'

'Perhaps she's simply trying to curry favour,' Madame Bountiful muttered.

I glared at her, glad that I hadn't tried to buy her a present too. Then I bobbed Mr Mountbank a curtsy and scuttled back to my place in the auditorium. I did a few steps of the mouse dance on the way to show him I could execute it beautifully, though I don't know whether he was watching or not.

Goody was watching and grinned. She had eaten so fast she had hiccups when her scene began, and had to keep

thumping herself on the chest and apologizing. She was so funny Mr Mountbank said he was in two minds whether to ask her to hiccup every time she played the scene.

They had to practise the pumpkin transformation again and again, trying to get it timed to perfection – and then something went wrong with the lighting and the stagehands scurried backwards and forwards trying to fix it. By the time we got to the ball scene everyone was exhausted, and the stagehand responsible for the chiming clock couldn't switch it off so it carried on long past midnight, which made everyone laugh hysterically.

We had a big cake and lemonade at five, and though the cast rattled through the rest of the pantomime, the big wedding scene at the end needed to be rehearsed four times before it was completely mastered. It was nearly nine o'clock when Mr Mountbank decided to call it a day.

'Go away and have a splendid Christmas tomorrow. Be back here at two on Boxing Day so we can have a quick run through again before the opening performance,' he said. 'A merry Christmas, everyone!'

All the fairies started hugging each other as they trooped off stage. I didn't get a hug, but then of course I was in the

auditorium. But Goody jumped down nimbly and came running over to me.

'Merry Christmas, ducks!' she said. 'My, what a blooming beggar of a day! I shall fall asleep as soon as my head hits the pillow and I daresay I'll kip through most of tomorrow too!'

'Will you be on your own for Christmas, Goody?' I asked. I hesitated. 'You could come to my house if you like. My sister's getting us a turkey because we're in the money at the moment, and there'll be plenty for everyone.'

'Oh, bless your heart, child!' said Goody, and her face crumpled as if she might be going to cry. But she smiled instead. 'It means a lot to me, your invite. But I'll have to decline. I have to look after my old pa – and you never know, I might get a flying visit from another old gentleman, him with the long white beard and the sack full of presents.'

That reminded me. I dug in my pocket and brought out Goody's present. I offered it to her shyly.

'A little heart!' she said. 'And you stitched it yourself? Oh, you dear sweet sausage!'

'Do you really like it?' I asked.

'It's the nicest present I've ever been given. Now, what can I find for you?' she said, delving into her reticule. She dug out

a large wrapped sweet. When I opened it up I saw it was a rosy apple made out of marzipan. 'You have a little munch on that on your long journey home. Shall I come a little way with you as it's so late at night?'

'Thank you so much, Goody, but you mustn't worry. I'm used to the dark,' I said, though when I went out of the theatre I felt a little pang as many of the fairies were met by proud, anxious parents. I couldn't imagine Pa ever bothering to walk me home when he had lived with us.

But I did have someone meeting me after all! There was our Connor in his cap and muffler, and an old blanket wrapped round his shoulders.

'Connor! Oh, Connor!' I cried.

'There you are at last! It ain't right keeping you this late when you're only a little kid,' he said, giving me a big hug. 'Here, let's wrap this blanket round you, Tess, seeing as you haven't got a proper coat.'

'I can't believe you've come all this way, after being at the market all day!' I said, hugging him back.

'I was worried when you didn't come home usual time. I thought someone might have made off with you,' he said gruffly, tying the ends of the blanket round my neck. 'So,

how was this endless rehearsal? You must be so tired!'

'I didn't do anything!' I said. 'I just sat and watched, hour after hour. Oh, Connor, I'd give anything to go on stage myself.'

'Well, you tell me the fairy girl you like the least and I'll lock her in a cupboard so you can go on stage in her place,' Connor joked.

'That's definitely Larissa! Oh, she's so sickening! How I wish she *would* get sick!' I said.

'That isn't exactly the true Christmas spirit, is it?' said Connor. 'Even though I started it. Let's sing a Christmas carol, eh?'

We'd only been taught hymns at the Ragged School, but there had been carol-singers at the market most of the day and Connor was now word perfect on 'God rest ye merry, gentlemen'. We marched home hand in hand letting nothing us dismay, finding comfort and joy in our own company.

Tommy and Ada were fast asleep when we got home, but Maggie was waiting up. She made us each a cup of cocoa and a slice of bread and jam, and then we went to bed while Connor pottered downstairs for a while. I hadn't eaten my marzipan apple and decided to keep it as long as possible. I wrapped it up and hid it with Cedric's boots. I wondered if he might want to

wear them on Christmas Day, and felt a little guilty, but it didn't stop me going fast asleep as soon as I curled up in bed.

Then it was Christmas morning and the bells were ringing in the church down the road. We woke up when it was still dark and scooped Ada out of her drawer and passed her around so we could give her a Christmas kiss. Tommy bounced out of bed, announcing he needed a Christmas wee – and then tripped.

'What are all these parcels?' he asked, as Maggie lit a candle.

'Hm, I wonder,' said Connor. 'Maybe Father Christmas came calling when we were fast asleep?'

There was great excitement as we tried to work out what they were, mostly by touch alone. By the time we'd trekked out to the backyard privy and dressed hastily it was getting light enough to read the names in block lettering on all five parcels. Mine was medium size and soft. I stuck my hand inside the wrapping paper and felt thick wool. I tore the paper away and saw a wonderful scarlet coat trimmed with white fur.

'Oh my!' I said. 'Oh my!' I was too dazed to say anything else.

'There now! I wonder how Father Christmas knew you were badly needing a warm coat?' said Connor.

He'd given Maggie a special winter outfit too, a long green jacket with a deeper green velvet trim, and a matching hat that made her look like a grown-up lady. Father Christmas was clever enough to guess that Tommy would be happy to wear my old tweed coat that didn't fit me any more. He'd brought him a hobby-horse instead with little bells on his reins, so Tommy christened him Jingle and rode him round the house. Ada obviously needed help opening her parcel, the biggest of them all. It was her own wooden cot on rockers, so we could soothe her to sleep.

I looked sideways at Connor. I'd seen him sawing up bits of wood recently but thought he'd just been working on fixing the baby carriage. I'd never suspected he could build such a wonderful cot.

Father Christmas hadn't given Connor a very exciting present at all – a second-hand pair of boots, stout enough, but still rather down at heel.

'Father Christmas hasn't been very fair to you, Connor!' I said indignantly.

'Perhaps he didn't have quite enough money left to spend on me,' said Connor. 'I don't mind, truly.'

'We made heaps and heaps and heaps of money at the market yesterday,' said Tommy. 'Old Bert gave Connor half, seeing as it was Christmas.'

I had a pretty shrewd guess where that money had gone, and gave Connor an extra hug – and his leather purse. He said it was the best gift he'd ever had. Tommy clamoured that he wanted one too and looked sheepish when I produced his own. Maggie liked her silk heart, and little Ada gripped her small furry mouse with her tiny fingers and gave his smooth velvet ears a good licking.

We had syrup on our porridge for a special breakfast. We drew golden initials with it on the creamy surface. Even Tommy managed it, spooning the biggest T ever so he could get more syrup. I spent the morning practising the pantomime even though I knew it was pointless. All twelve fairies didn't have the slightest sniffle and neither twin had had any limp at all by the end of the very long dress rehearsal.

Maggie was busy making our Christmas dinner. Tommy had taken Jingle for a canter up and down the street and Ada was lying on her back in her new cot trying to suck her toes – but Connor watched me all the time and even danced with me for the ballroom scene. He was my handsome prince and I was Cinderella. I felt I was a much better Cinderella than that sappy Jemima Mountbank. Her mama was going to attend the opening performance but she was to be seated at the other

side of the theatre so there was no contact with Mr Mountbank. We were looking forward to watching her to see if she would boo the second Mrs Mountbank playing Prince Charming.

When I'd swept my final curtsy at the end of my performance, Connor actually stood on the sofa and clapped and cheered so loudly I'm sure the whole street heard. It felt almost as good as a proper performance in front of hundreds of paying customers. Then Maggie called Connor to carve the turkey, glistening and gold from the oven. He'd never tried his hand at carving before – the only time we'd had turkey Pa had done it, and he was so sozzled from his Christmas drinking that he mangled it.

Connor did a splendid job, neat and efficient, making sure we all got a fair share of the white and dark meat, and Maggie served up roast potatoes and parsnips and Brussel sprouts like tiny cabbages, and we ate and ate and ate. Even Ada had chopped-up turkey and tiny portions of vegetables. She spat out her sprouts but ate the rest with relish.

Even though we were full to bursting we still had pudding – a wobbly raspberry jelly that shone ruby red, with a pink custard sauce. Maggie's face was bright pink too after her hard

work in the kitchen, and she blushed even brighter when we told her she was a magnificent cook.

'Almost as good as jam tart Cook,' Tommy murmured in Jingle's ear.

Connor and I washed the dishes afterwards as it didn't seem fair to leave them for Maggie, and then we sprawled in the living room, half asleep. Then there was a brisk knocking at the door.

'Oh Lord, who is it now?' Maggie groaned.

'It's Father Christmas come back with more presents!' said Tommy.

Maggie and Connor and I were looking at each other.

'It'll be Pa, won't it?' I said. 'Come to see if we're all right and to wish us a happy Christmas.'

Maggie darted up, seized Ma's old teapot, and hid it right at the back of a cupboard, with an old towel covering it. Although we'd splurged on Christmas it still jingled with hard-earned money and we knew that if Pa saw it he'd pocket it quick.

Connor's fists were clenched. 'Don't let on we've got jobs,' he warned. 'Maybe we'd be best off simply not answering?'

The knocker rapped again.

'But he's *Pa*,' I said, wavering. 'Maybe he's come to say he's really sorry and he's left that nasty woman and he wants to come back to us.'

'And maybe pigs can fly,' Maggie hissed, but she was in a dither too, not sure what to do.

There was a third knock.

Connor suddenly strode towards the door. 'I'm not scared of him. If he's drunk I'll send him on his way,' he said boldly and flung the door open, his chin jutting belligerently.

It wasn't Pa. It was Cedric's papa *again*, with a carriage outside our door and a footman clutching an enormous hamper. We stared in astonishment.

'A real horsey! Come see, Jingle!' said Tommy, charging out into the street with his hobby-horse.

'Merry Christmas! May I come in a moment?' Mr Cedar asked, looking rather nervously at Connor, who still had one fist raised.

'Yes – yes, of course, sir!' he said.

Mr Cedar came in and doffed his top hat to Maggie. She blushed again and bobbed an awkward curtsy. I did a much better one, a graceful sweep almost to the floor, which would even have impressed Madame Bountiful.

The footman came in too, struggling with the hamper, and laid it on our table.

'Can I offer you two gentlemen a cup of tea?' Maggie offered.

'If it's not too much trouble,' said Cedric's papa.

'Not for me, miss. I'll go and wait by the carriage,' said the footman hurriedly.

Maggie put the kettle on, and when she made the tea she told me to take a cup out to the footman even so. Connor and Mr Cedar were making uneasy conversation, both sitting on the sofa, so they had to turn their heads sideways to address each other.

'Where's Cedric?' I asked.

'Oh, he's with his mama,' said Cedric's papa. 'He's reading her a story, bless him. He's been a great comfort to her in her time of distress. And so have you, Tess. That's why I'm here, really. But first of all, please open the hamper. It's a few little gifts to show my deep gratitude.'

There were bottles of lime cordial and ginger beer, a bag of sugar plums, a bunch of purple grapes, a jar of preserved peaches, a large Christmas cake with thick icing, and a box of *two dozen* red and yellow and green jam tarts! Tommy whooped

at the sight of them and immediately started badgering to eat one.

'Quit it, Tommy. You've only just had a very big dinner,' Maggie said sharply. She was frowning at Mr Cedar. 'It's very kind of you, sir, but you've no need to give us all this food. We've managed to buy a lot of Christmas goodies for ourselves.'

'Yes, I can provide for my family now,' Connor said stiffly.

'I'm sure you're both right. You've been managing magnificently, I can see. But although you've shown great initiative in your unfortunate circumstances, I'm not sure your future is certain. Connor, you must be aware that the earnings of a market stallholder vary enormously according to the time of year. Maggie, I fear your payment for being an artist's muse is equally unreliable,' said Mr Cedar.

'But *I'm* going to be a pantomime star,' I insisted, although I knew that wasn't precisely true.

'I daresay you are, my dear. But in spite of your best efforts I feel you have to think of your future. The future of this little one in particular,' he said, looking fondly down at Ada. 'I believe she was practically starving to death a little while ago?'

'We did our best,' said Maggie defensively. 'We went without ourselves to give her milk.'

'I'm sure you did. But perhaps you might be interested in ensuring little Ada's comfort for ever?' Mr Cedar said, swallowing hard and looking at us intently.

We blinked at him.

'What exactly do you mean?' Maggie asked.

'I mean I would like to take her off your hands,' said Mr Cedar.

'Absolutely not!' Connor said fiercely.

'Please hear me out. My wife and I would like to adopt her and bring her up as if she were our own lost daughter. We will give her every luxury and make sure she's the happiest little girl ever. Mrs Cedar already loves her dearly. She's recovering well from her mental affliction and I am sure will be her old self very soon. I can see how much you all love your baby sister, but you must see she'd be happier with us. She's so little she will never know she comes from humble origins,' he said.

Connor flinched. 'We might be humble, sir, but I beg to differ. I think our sister will be happier with us, her own family.'

'Think very carefully now. Are you sure you want to condemn Ada to a life of penury, always fearful of ending up in the workhouse? What do *you* think, Tess? After all, you were the one who brought her into our household.'

 315

I went to Ada and picked her up, holding her close while she gently batted my cheeks with the toy mouse.

'I think we're as happy as Cedric,' I said. 'Maybe happier.'

'Well said, Tess!' said Maggie. 'I'm sorry, sir, but we're keeping our Ada and that's that. So you'd better tell your poor footman to cart your hamper back into the carriage.'

'Oh dear, I didn't mean to upset you so. I thought you'd be thrilled that Ada had a chance of bettering herself,' said Mr Cedar.

'Nothing could be better than being with her family,' said Connor. 'Perhaps you meant well, but can't you see it's insulting, thinking you could bribe us with these fancy goodies?'

'I'm sorry,' said Mr Cedar, standing up. 'Please keep the hamper, I beg you. It wasn't meant as a bribe, I promise. I am still very grateful to you, Tess, for cheering my wife – but perhaps it will be better if you don't come round to my house again.'

He bowed to us and then swept out.

'The nerve!' said Maggie.

'"Bettering herself"!' said Connor, grinding his teeth.

'No more jam tarts,' Tommy said mournfully.

'*Wait!*' I suddenly shouted.

'You're not going after him, Tess!' said Maggie.

'No, no, I've just got to give him something!' I said, desperately dashing upstairs.

The carriage had already started by the time I was out in the street, but I yelled for it to stop. Mr Cedar leaned out of the carriage window, clearly thinking I'd changed my mind.

'Please give this to Cedric for Christmas!' I gabbled, and thrust the little parcel of toy satin boots into his hand.

Chapter Eighteen

I woke up early with a churning stomach and couldn't settle back to sleep. I slipped out of bed but couldn't face breakfast, even though I knew I'd need as much energy as possible for the day ahead. Maggie and Connor had given me a special card, despite the fact that I wasn't going to be performing. It had a huge bouquet of roses on the front and inside they'd written *Good Luck, our Tess,* and they'd signed their names with lots of kisses. Tommy had scrawled a T on it too, with a wobbly kiss as well. Connor had even dipped one of Ada's tiny fingers in some runny egg yolk and put her own little yellow mark on the card.

I held the card to my chest, feeling a warm rush of love for my dear family. I danced along happily to the theatre, to

find everyone tense and anxious inside. I couldn't go in the big dressing room for all the fairies. Larissa's mother had insisted she had a little separate cubicle and I had to squat in there with them, both of them ordering me about.

'This button's coming loose on Larissa's ball gown, Tess. Sew it on at once while I put curling rags in her hair.'

'Just run down to the front of house and check that all the seats are sold out.'

'My face is so shiny! Go and ask that weird Goody person if she's got any pearl powder.'

I was happy to agree to the last request because it meant I could go and spend five minutes with Goody, who was her usual calm, funny self.

'Trust them to get in a flap-doodle!' she said scornfully. 'Still, better do as they ask, ducks, or they might complain to that Madame How's-Your-Father. Fancy a peppermint, my darling? Good for the old digestion. I don't want to risk another fit of the blooming hiccups. No windypops for me!' she said, thumping her chest.

'Don't you get nervous, Goody?' I asked.

'You're forgetting all those years I spent being a tiny child wonder. When you've been treading the boards as long as

I have, nothing can throw you. Unless they try it literally. I once had the misfortune to come up against a famous pantomime dame who thought it might be amusing to throw me up in the air. But I made sure I kicked him hard on my way down, so he didn't try that trick again,' Goody said, clapping her hands together dismissively.

'I do love you, Goody. Good luck tonight – though you won't need it,' I said.

There was a knock on her door and Mr Mountbank himself peeped in to wish her good luck himself. He was already in his Baron Blunderboar costume, with rather alarming ruddy greasepaint. He was smoking a cigar.

'Ah, little Tess! I'm enjoying your excellent cigar very much, my dear,' he said, smiling at me.

I don't know whether it *was* the cigar I'd given him or one of his own, but I was very pleased and smiled back at him.

'I'll be visiting all you little fairies soon – and I'll make sure I pop into Larissa's much-requested star dressing room!' he said, with a wink.

He was as good as his word. He came in and admired Larissa in her fairy costume and she twirled round on her toes

and preened. Mr Mountbank was now carrying a very large gold-coloured box.

'I'm giving one to all my leading ladies,' he said. 'Enjoy them, my dear. Maybe share them with your little understudy?'

Larissa fell on the box as soon as he'd left the cubicle. It contained the most wonderful-looking chocolates, some milk, some dark, some cream, some with nuts, some with icing, some with crystallized flowers!

'Oh my goodness!' I said admiringly.

'Well, you're not getting any!' said Larissa, and she grabbed *three* chocolates and stuffed them straight in her mouth. She chomped on them greedily, little drools of chocolate dribbling down her chin.

'Mind your make-up, darling!' said her mother, dabbing at her with a hankie.

My mouth was watering at the wonderful smell of chocolate. I'd hardly eaten anything all day.

'Mr Mountbank said you should share them with me,' I pointed out.

'As if I'm going to share them with an understudy!' said Larissa, helping herself to another couple.

'Please? Just one?' I begged, reaching out.

'No!' said Larissa, slapping at my hand.

'Now now, Tess, you mustn't upset Larissa. You don't understand – all stars get a little nervous before opening night,' said her mother.

I didn't say another word. But when young Frank knocked at the door, calling for Overtures and Beginners, I waited until Larissa was almost out the door before muttering, 'So I'll help myself while you're performing in the ballet.'

I was only teasing her, but she was in such a state she took me seriously. She turned round, seized the box, scooped up the rest of the top layer and crammed them all in her mouth, her cheeks bulging ludicrously.

'Larissa!' said her mother, shocked.

'She's not eating *my* chocolates!' said Larissa, chomping and swallowing frantically.

'Stop it, darling, you'll make yourself sick!'

But Larissa wouldn't stop, even though the chocolate was now all round her mouth like bizarre lip rouge.

'Quick, quick, you need to be warming up!' Madame Bountiful called frantically.

Larissa ran, her mother pursuing her with the hankie. I hurried after them, wanting to watch the ballet from the wings.

I saw Larissa join Jenny and Penny and the other nine fairies in their lovely white tutus, stretching and pointing their toes ready for the performance. Jenny and Penny were turning cartwheels for good measure. Jenny or Penny nudged against Larissa by accident.

'You kicked me!' she said indistinctly, her mouth still stoppered with chocolate.

'Sorry, sorry, sorry!' said one twin.

'Sorry, sorry, sorry!' said the other. But maybe they were getting fed up with Larissa too. 'I bet you wish you could turn cartwheels like us!' she added.

'Of course I can,' said Larissa and she demonstrated. She turned a perfect cartwheel and straightened up with a smirk – but then her expression changed.

'I feel bad!' she gasped. She clapped her hand over her mouth but then was violently, horribly, copiously sick, chocolate brown vomit spewing all over her white dress.

'Oh dear Lord!' her mother shrieked. 'Control yourself, Larissa!'

But Larissa continued exploding like a volcano. Madame Bountiful shrieked and went rushing off to find Mr Mountbank. He was in the wings in seconds. He took one

look at Larissa and clapped a hand to his forehead.

'Take that child back to the dressing room. Get young Frank to come running with a bucket and mop. Tell the orchestra to repeat the overture. And you –' he pointed at me – 'run like the wind, go to Wardrobe, change into your ballet dress and be back here within a minute. You're going on stage!'

'No!' Larissa's mother shrieked. 'She just needs a clean costume! The understudy's will do. You're fully recovered now, aren't you, Larissa?'

'Yes!' Larissa mumbled, but then vomited again, very nearly spattering Mr Mountbank's patent shoes.

He stepped back sharply, horrified. 'I utterly forbid that child to go on stage. She would ruin the entire show. Take her away this minute. Little Tess, MOVE! You're on!'

I moved lightning fast. I didn't even have time to be nervous. I had to do without a warm-up. As soon as I got back someone signalled the orchestra and they started our ballet music and someone else pushed me on stage. I threw back my head, lifted my arms, stood on my toes, and glided out, leading my troupe of fairies.

I was in such a daze that I wasn't totally sure of the steps, even though I'd known them by heart for weeks, but when I

went wrong a couple times it didn't really matter. I was the lead fairy and could put in extra fancy twirls without it looking strange. I still knew the exact moment when I halted, pointed upwards, and said my one line: 'But hark, our dear Fairy Queen approaches!'

Goody descended gracefully from the flies, smiling and waving her wand, sparkling in the limelight. I curtsied deeply to her. She added her own line – not in the script:

'Well danced, my little fairy star!' she said, and then she pirouetted on one of her tiny feet to rapturous applause. Goody sang her song about her godchild, little Ella, so poorly treated by her stepfamily, but she was determined to help her. We wished her well, she exited stage right, we performed a little fairy ring and danced around, and thank goodness my hands and feet did as they were told and I didn't miss a step.

I had a chance to look out into the dark auditorium. I could sense many, many faces, though I couldn't distinguish one from another. Then it was time to exit stage left, and many, many pairs of hands clapped enthusiastically. I felt I could soar right up to the flies without the help of any hoist and circle there triumphantly.

Mr Mountbank was there in the wings, nodding at me.

'Congratulations!' he murmured.

No one word had ever meant more to me. But I didn't have time to stand and bask in his praise. Madame Bountiful hissed that poor Larissa was still very poorly and I would be taking her place at least until the interval. I had to rush to find my mouse costume. It was hard work pulling off my ballet dress and stuffing my legs and arms into the furry suit, and the mouse hat with big ears didn't want to sit straight on my wild curls, but one of the sewing ladies clamped it down firmly.

I was back on stage again, squeaking with the other girls, my elbows at my side, my hands curled, my long tail bouncing along behind me. We skipped around Cinderella weeping prettily beside a big chimney place – and as she wailed, 'Ooh! Boo hoo! If only *I* could go to the ball with my sisters,' Goody came dancing right out of the fireplace, waving her wand, to yet more applause.

We had to crouch down and stay still so that we wouldn't distract from any of the speeches. I tried hard but I was so pumped up I had to give the whiskers on my mouse bonnet a tiny twirl – which actually got a laugh from the audience. Then there was the complicated transformation scene, where the

pumpkin was swapped for the golden coach in total darkness while we mice tore off our rodent heads, put on black coachmen hats with ribbons at the back, and red and gold cloaks.

I hadn't actually practised this, and I only had my cloak halfway on when the lights went up, but it didn't really matter – in fact it got another laugh.

'Don't ham it up too much, pet,' Goody warned as we came off stage together. 'I know the temptation, and the audience are loving it, but Mr Mountbank might not care for it.'

'I'll be as solemn as solemn can be from now on,' I promised her.

'Not sure about that! You're a performer to your fingertips!' said Goody, tickling me under the chin.

'Anyway, I'm not sure I'll be on the stage past the interval. Larissa will probably be well enough to take over by then,' I said, sighing.

'What did you *do* to her? Did you put a sickness spell on her, you little monkey?'

'Absolutely not. She ate nearly all her chocolates because she didn't want me to have any,' I insisted.

'Oh dear. Well, it's her own fault then,' said Goody. 'But lucky for you, eh?'

My luck lasted. Larissa had stopped vomiting by the interval, but her body was erupting in an even more disastrous way now, and she was stuck permanently in the theatre water closet.

'Poor Larissa,' I said to her mother, actually really meaning it – but she looked as if she wanted to spit at me.

So I went on again after the interval break, in my beautiful blue ball gown. We only had to circle round doing the polka, which was a simple *one, two, three, hop!* so I didn't have to worry about forgetting my steps. I had another line too: 'Look who's dancing with Prince Charming!' I delivered the line as loudly as I could over the orchestra music, and the folk on stage looked obediently at the spotlight of Miss Jemima Mountbank

partnered with her own stepmother, Mrs Regina Mountbank. Jemima looked wanly pretty in her white sparkly ball gown, but Regina looked more splendid in her blue silk knee-smalls, showing off her curvy hips and long legs. They both acted as if they'd fallen in love at first sight, but the moment they came off stage they both pulled faces, obviously detesting each other.

I wondered if Mr Mountbank had cast them deliberately for a warped joke. He was clearly enjoying his own part, strutting around the stage and enunciating his words in such an exaggerated fashion his moustache got covered in spit. I was careful to dance decorously with a ladylike little smile on my face whenever he looked in my direction.

Then time raced past to the wedding scene at the end, when I pinned little pink roses to the neck of my ballgown and clasped my rosy posy as we walked solemnly up the aisle after Cinderella while the organ in the orchestra pit boomed thrillingly. Mr Mountbank had discarded his Baron Blunderboar clothing and was dressed as a vicar now, asking if anyone had any objection to the marriage.

'We do! We do!' shouted Chlorodyne and Pepsine, flinging themselves around and beating their breasts.

329

'Pick me, Prince C, you're the he for me!' Chlorodyne begged.

'Pick me instead, with my mouth so red, I'll make the best wife for the rest of my life!' Pepsine proclaimed, kicking her sister out of the way.

'We love you too, can we marry you!' Jenny and Penny cried their line, cartwheeling up the aisle.

But Prince Charming insisted Cinderella in her glass slippers was his only true love, and Vicar Mountbank declared them man and wife and hoped they would live happily ever after. Goody waved her wand, producing more sparkles, and then the whole cast trooped off the stage. The audience clapped and cheered uproariously, and at a signal from Mr Mountbank I led my fellow fairies on stage. We all got a cheer, and then the others backed away while I stood between Jenny and Penny and we did our own curtsy.

'Hurray for Tess!' piped up a little voice from the front row.

It was dear Cedric, jumping up and down in his seat. Then right at the back there was a bellow from a voice used to commanding an entire market.

'Well done, our Tess!' Connor yelled, almost as loud as the organ.

I had had no idea that either of them had been there all evening watching me! I blew them both kisses – and then it was my turn to back away with the twins to the side of the stage while the rest of the cast took their bows. I was thrilled that the cheers for Goody were just as loud as those for Cinderella and her prince. She didn't bow or curtsy – she did a little dance instead, lifting her skirts and showing her spotted bloomers, which got another laugh.

I chuckled too, though she'd actually told me not to milk the audience for too many laughs. Dear Goody, she deserved all the applause she could get. We took many bows and then at last the red velvet curtains swished shut and it was all over!

Mr Mountbank actually picked me up and swung me round and round, my skirts flying.

'Well done, my dear! You saved the day!' he said.

'Can I go on stage again tomorrow too?' I dared ask.

'Mm, I think we have to let Larissa have her part back if she's feeling better. But I'm sure there will be countless occasions when you come to the rescue – and when I'm next in need of a little fairy you will definitely be my first choice!' he said.

Stick that in your pipe and smoke it, Larissa! I thought, but when I saw how pale and limp she was as her mother helped her home, I felt sorry for her too.

Cedric and his papa were waiting for me outside the stage door, offering me a lift home in their carriage. I was surprised Mr Cedar was being so gracious after we'd made it plain Ada was always going to be part of our family – but I politely declined.

'Thank you very much, but I'm already being taken home,' I said, spotting Connor in the distance, waving his cap at me.

Perhaps they'd have offered both of us a lift, but we didn't want to go back with them. We walked together, my Prince Charming Connor and me, swinging our hands and singing at the tops of our voices.

'You were so brilliant, Tess! It was such a shock when I saw you on stage! You were the wondrous star of the whole show. Do you know what? *We*'re going to live happily ever after too, like the pantomime.'

I just hoped Goody was nearby, ready to wave her magic wand.

Have you read them all?

LAUGH OUT LOUD
THE STORY OF TRACY BEAKER
I DARE YOU, TRACY BEAKER
STARRING TRACY BEAKER
MY MUM TRACY BEAKER
WE ARE THE BEAKER GIRLS
THE WORST THING ABOUT MY
SISTER
DOUBLE ACT
FOUR CHILDREN AND IT
THE BED AND BREAKFAST STAR

HISTORICAL HEROES
HETTY FEATHER
HETTY FEATHER'S CHRISTMAS
SAPPHIRE BATTERSEA
EMERALD STAR
DIAMOND
LITTLE STARS
CLOVER MOON
ROSE RIVERS
WAVE ME GOODBYE
OPAL PLUMSTEAD
QUEENIE
DANCING THE CHARLESTON
THE RUNAWAY GIRLS
THE OTHER EDIE TRIMMER

LIFE LESSONS
THE BUTTERFLY CLUB
THE SUITCASE KID
KATY
BAD GIRLS
LITTLE DARLINGS
CLEAN BREAK
RENT A BRIDESMAID
CANDYFLOSS

THE LOTTIE PROJECT
THE LONGEST WHALE SONG
COOKIE
JACKY DAYDREAM
PAWS & WHISKERS

FAMILY DRAMAS
THE ILLUSTRATED MUM
MY SISTER JODIE
DIAMOND GIRLS
DUSTBIN BABY
VICKY ANGEL
SECRETS
MIDNIGHT
LOLA ROSE
LILY ALONE
MY SECRET DIARY
THE PRIMROSE RAILWAY CHILDREN
PROJECT FAIRY

PLENTY OF MISCHIEF
SLEEPOVERS
THE WORRY WEBSITE
BEST FRIENDS
GLUBBSLYME
THE CAT MUMMY
LIZZIE ZIPMOUTH
THE MUM-MINDER
CLIFFHANGER
BURIED ALIVE!

FOR OLDER READERS
GIRLS IN LOVE
GIRLS UNDER PRESSURE
GIRLS OUT LATE
GIRLS IN TEARS
KISS
LOVE LESSONS
LOVE, FRANKIE
BABY LOVE

Curious about Jacqueline Wilson's fantastic historical novels?

If you want to read about the life of a Victorian foundling:

Hetty Feather is just a baby when her mother leaves her at the Foundling Hospital in 1876. When she starts her education at the Foundling Hospital she has the chance to find her real mother. Could she really be the wonderful Madame Adeline? Or will Hetty find the truth even more surprising . . . ?

If you want to read about a Victorian workhouse:

Lucy Locket lives with her father, the New Mother and the New Baby. Her beloved Nurse is replaced with a horrid governess, and she's desperate for someone to be kind to her.

Kitty Fisher is a performer who has always lived on the streets. Now that her one friend is gone, she's all alone.

When Lucy runs away from home, Kitty shows her how to survive and Lucy shows off her own skills. But the streets of London are dangerous, and the girls are under threat from thieves and – even worse – the workhouse!

If you want to read about life as

a Victorian nursery maid:

Charlie (DON'T call her Charlotte!) has a brand-new school project: she starts writing diary entries from the perspective of eleven-year-old Lottie, who has left school and has a job a nursery maid. Suddenly history comes to life . . .

If you want to read a twisty time travel adventure about Victorian London:

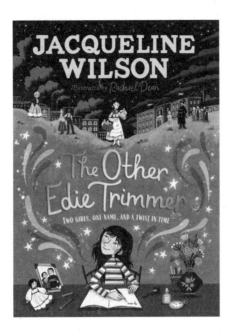

Edie is given a real Victorian notebook, and she's determined to write the best story ever. But when she starts writing, something strange happens . . .

Edie finds herself in Victorian London, and she soon realizes she's living the life of *another* Edie Trimmer – and is in danger of being sent to a real workhouse!

Will she ever be able to make it back to her family?

**If you want to read about life right before
the First World War:**

Fourteen-year-old Opal is sent to work at the Fairy Glen
sweet factory to support her family. She idolizes Mrs Roberts,
the factory's owner. The best thing about her? She's a
suffragette!

Mrs Roberts introduces Opal to the legendary Mrs
Pankhurst and her fellow Suffragettes. But the First World
War is about to begin, and will change Opal's life for ever . . .

**If you want to take a glamorous trip
back to the 1920s:**

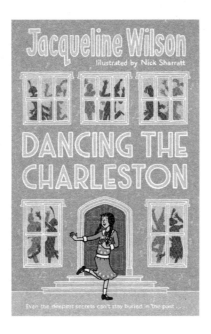

Mona lives with her dressmaker aunt in a cottage on the edge of the grand Somerset Estate. She wishes to have a life full of beautiful clothes and riches, but it seems unlikely.

When a new member of the family inherits Somerset Estate, Mona is propelled into a life of razzle-dazzle parties, new Bohemian friends and wonderful trips to London.

However, even with these changes Mona discovers that she can't dance away from her past.

If you want to know more about being an evacuee during the Second World War:

In September 1939, ten-year-old Shirley is sent away on a train. She doesn't know where she's going, or what's going to happen when she gets there. She finds herself in the countryside with two boys from the East End of London and the mysterious Mrs Waverley, where her life is changed for ever.

If you want to read about

a royal coronation:

It's 1953 and Elizabeth is set to be crowned Queen of England. Elsie Kettle can't wait to go and see the coronation in London, until she gets sick and is whisked away to hospital.

Before Elsie leaves the hospital, she has a very special visitor . . .